DECONSTRUCTING *Lila*

DECONSTRUCTING *Lila*

Shannon Leigh

Entangled Publishing, LLC
2614 South Timberline Road
Suite 109
Fort Collins, CO 80525

Visit our website at www.entangledpublishing.com.

Edited by Candace Havens
Cover design by Heather Howland
Interior design by Jeremy Howland

Print ISBN 978-1-62266-389-7
Ebook ISBN 978-1-62266-390-3

Manufactured in the United States of America

First Edition September 2014

10 9 8 7 6 5 4 3 2 1

This book is for my dad. Without your amazing strength and commitment to finding happiness in tragedy, I don't know that I would be the same person I am today. I am strong because of you. Thank you.

Chapter One

Lila Jean Gentry was about to initiate the most serious manhunt of her life. And her target, the man she thought about one hundred times a day, from the worn tips of his cowboy boots to the crown of his perfect head, didn't even know she was coming his way.

It was undercover love…

Lila fidgeted in the driver's seat. *Deep-cover romance?* She tried out the description, but it didn't fall from her tongue easily. *Secret seduction?* She groaned at the absurdity and gripped the wheel tighter as she steered into town. Since stealth, and apparently flowery prose, was not in her playbook, she was forced to rely on other assets such as her new cheekini panties from Victoria's Secret. And her intimate knowledge of her target's desires.

Just thinking about it all made Lila shift in the leather seat again. considering the current adventure with such longing produced tingly sensations she hoped would soon be satisfied.

But foremost she had to endure the gauntlet that was Hannington, Texas. First stop: the Grab & Get.

Lila cruised her Lexus under the red tin canopy of the Grab & Get. Her ex-hometown of Hannington, Texas, famous for its grand old bawdy days as a stop along the Chisholm Trail, had matured in the one hundred and fifty years since saloon owner John C. Henry sold whiskey out of a barrel beneath the old pecan tree on the corner. Matured so much that nowadays, instead of booze quenching the mouths of thirsty citizens, the ladies' auxiliary offered homemade lemonade and sugar cookies at the same spot, both as a reminder of days gone by and a deterrent against hellish excess.

Presently, the people of Hannington were pretty sin-free, though the summer temperatures might lead outsiders to assume differently—they didn't call Texas "hell's back forty" for nothin'.

Pulling her cream-colored Lexus alongside a high-octane pump, Lila pushed it into park and gazed through the grasshopper guts on her windshield to the people rushing in and out of the convenience store. Simple, hardworking middle-class folk, with three life priorities: family, politics, and high school football. And not necessarily in that order. Though Lila could guess from the last year's posters papering the Grab & Get's window, the Crusaders' contest for district champ ranked close to number one in the hearts and minds of locals.

The image brought back bittersweet memories of sweltering Friday nights in September beneath bright lights, cheering a certain quarterback as he danced across the end zone for a touchdown.

Lila smiled tightly at her passenger, a worn leather journal, dog-eared and scarred with age, cocooned safely in an acid-free box—her impetus for returning to Hannington after a ten-year hiatus. "Back to the land of football, Frito pie, and country music," she sang to herself. Three things she hadn't experienced since leaving. Three things, if the truth be told, she'd actually missed. More than a little bit.

Giddy and nervous now that she'd arrived, Lila hummed as she jerked the keys from the ignition and opened the driver's door to a blast of smothering, midday July air. The heat raced down her throat as she stood, sucking the breath from her lungs. She took a moment to let the scorched tissue in her lungs recover and fumbled with the gas pump.

Setting the pump lever to automatic, she marched across the steaming pavement, her heels sticking in the hot blacktop with each step.

She wanted to buy a diet soda and get off the main drag before someone recognized her; prolonging the inevitable showdown with folks in town suited her just fine, at least until she made contact with *him*. Although a decade stood between her and her past in Hannington, the people in the hardscrabble Central Texas town had long memories—some of them could remember the Civil War, though they weren't alive back then—and folks around these parts sure as heck never forgot a scandal. Especially when the gossip involved crazy Sarah Gentry's kid and the satisfaction of saying, "Like mother, like daughter."

Bypassing the staggering arrangement of Miller Lite (in the shape of the Alamo?), which if toppled could kill several small children and a few adults, Lila skirted the illegal eight-liners and their barrage of spinning sevens to pluck a soda from the cooler.

Cradling the icy bottle in the crook of her arm, she got in

line behind a pair of young cowboys in snug jeans, cinched belts, and scuffed boots. She ignored their appraising stares in bobbing heads and resisted the desire to stick her tongue out at them; she resisted it with every fiber of her being. She wasn't back in Hannington to cause a scene, or tuck tail and run like a disgraced cow dog. Either of which would earn a round of good gossip at the Dairy Queen. Hell no. She was here to fulfill a vow and change her life. After a few years of therapy, she wholeheartedly embraced her vulnerability (after too many years of denial) and intended to "dare greatly" as her therapist advised. To act upon all the bravery within herself to reclaim the love and adoration of her high school sweetheart. The flawed, courageous, sacrificing, kind, empathetic man she still loved, all these years later.

And she intended the vow to be for good this time. Forever.

The electronic display on the register flashed short affirmations in between lottery advertisements. One in particular caught Lila's attention: DON'T ALLOW THE ABSENCE OF GUARANTEES TO PREVENT YOU FROM LOVING WITH YOUR ENTIRE HEART.

She resolved to embrace that philosophy no matter what the future held. Embrace it like her life depended on it.

Finally, escaping out of the double doors, she focused on the familiar sight of her car and refused the impulse to look at people in the parking lot. Making eye contact was an invitation for conversation. A reason to pause and chitchat about the debilitating heat, the fund-raising drive of the Bell County Museum, or what brought her back to Hannington after ten years of I'll-be-back-when-hell-freezes-over.

"Lila Jean." The low, masculine drawl stopped her dead in her tracks like a gunshot in the quiet of night. Two more steps and she could touch the gold-plated door handle. Two more steps and she could escape in air-conditioning and pretend she hadn't heard the voice from her past. But that was something the woman she used to be would have done. Escape. Run. Hide. The woman she was today turned to confront the man on the opposite side of the gas pump.

Jake Winter.

Her heart squeezed painfully in her chest. Her breath locked and held in her throat. Her ears rang. Her vision blurred. Static buzzed in her brain.

She shook it all loose and focused on his sinfully beautiful green eyes. Always kind, always mischievous, and twinkling with thoughts of highly inappropriate behavior. His gaze pinned her between the pump and the window squeegee bucket.

"Wow. Gossip travels even faster than I remembered. Did they select you as my welcome party?"

Jake leaned against the bed of a beat-up red-and-white farm truck, dusty with grit and mud, his hands at rest in his pockets while gas chugged rhythmically through the fuel line.

"Lila, baby, you're already on Instagram. Consider yourself welcomed."

Lila felt slightly horrified, and somewhat honored, a reaction she would never admit to, even if pressed. "Who put me on Instagram?"

He laughed and Lila soaked the familiar sound in, resisting the urge to close her eyes and cherish the moment.

"Maybe Amy. She's the social media nut for Hannington." Jake jutted his chin toward the store and Lila followed his lead just in time to see a young redhead dropping into the passenger seat of a Ford Focus, phone in hand.

"I'm only getting gas. This here is a happy accident, but I can administer a proper welcome if you insist. And I can use tongue."

Lila rolled her eyes and took a deep breath, letting the first blush of sexual awareness warm her like the early morning sun. "Jeez. No. I'm good. This is excitement enough, thank you very much."

They smiled at each other and Lila thought the meeting wasn't as dramatic as she had imagined, about a million times in the last couple of months.

"So, are you here for a birth or a death?" Jake asked.

"Pardon?"

"I figure someone had to have either died or been born for you to come back to Hannington. Or are you just passing through?"

Lila thought about her response, one she'd practiced also a million times, and let her gaze wander over Jake. She took her time following the cut of hard muscle underneath his faded black T-shirt, down the not-so-subtle package behind his zipper, to his rock-hard denim-clad legs.

Traveling back up, she noted fine laugh lines framed his eyes, fanning upward to sweep his strong brows. Dusky stubble covered the perfection of his upper lip and strong chin.

He still took her breath away, even after all these years. Lila mentally filed away the confirmation that yes, she was still highly attracted to Jacob Winter. Time and two hundred miles of parched Texas landscape had not changed that.

"As a matter of fact"—her voice broke and she cleared her throat, buoying her confidence with the familiar chant: *dare greatly*—"I did come back to take care of some family business. Not exactly a death or a birth."

Jake's smile slipped and concern furrowed his brow. "Did Barbara give money to those sweepstakes people again?"

"What?"

"Nothing. Never mind."

"Jake—"

"It's nothing. You were saying, family business?"

He offered her a lazy smile and Lila fell into it, fully committed to the distraction. Memories of make-out sessions in the front seat of his 1970 Oldsmobile 442 sent shivers down her spine.

She dropped her soda and cursed him. "Stop that." The bottle hit the pavement with a dull thud, rolling to his feet.

Jake bent and picked it up. "Stop what, baby?" As his strong hand wrapped around the plastic neck, Lila remembered in a searing flash the feel of those hands pulling her in, circling the column of her neck, gliding lower.

"Trying to fluster me." She reached for the soft drink as he crossed the distance separating them, but Jake held it close, placing his second hand above the other, slowly rubbing the drops of condensation from the plastic with his thumb.

"Now you're flattering me. I don't know when I last flustered a woman."

"Please. I doubt ten years have changed your ability to win over a woman, even from a dead sleep. You always had game and from the looks of you, nothing has changed."

He offered the soda. "Better not open this for a while. It'll explode." His voice was low and suggestive. He'd forever been the king of the double entendre. *Damn him.*

It was crazy he'd been nothing more than a memory these

last ten years. Because now, Jake was solid. Alive. And every fantasy in one pair of snug jeans. She resisted the urge to shiver and curl her toes all at the same time.

Her high school love was all grown up.

"You don't look dressed for the pig wrestling at two o'clock, so I'm gonna guess this family business has you just passing through. Maybe pullin' a one-nighter."

She laughed and the release felt good. Right. "We both know twenty-four hours is all you really need to see everything around here."

"You just need the right tour guide. A lot has changed." She dragged her eyes away and scanned the parking lot. People chatted with their neighbors, talking about the start of school next month and yelling at kids to grab ice from the outside cooler for their weekend lake outing. Life went on. Nobody at the mini-mart seemed to notice hers had stopped, road blocked courtesy of this one man.

Meeting his level gaze, Lila smiled despite the tangle of bittersweet emotions strangling her heart. The cost of open vulnerability. "Has it changed?"

Jake nodded at the candy in her hand, an impulsive buy inside the Grab & Get. It squished between her fingers as the chocolate warmed in the heat.

"Yep. Looks like your diet has, too. Glad to see you're not so rigid about food anymore. You were always too skinny."

Another comment meant to distract her, but it brought to mind a conversation from years ago. Jake's hands had spanned her waist as he'd lifted her to retrieve a Frisbee lodged in the tree of her backyard. "God, you're tiny. Don't you ever eat?"

She'd dispelled his notion of starvation when they'd gone

to the Dairy Queen later the same day. Back then she'd eaten like every meal was her last. Especially when someone else footed the bill. With Granny working full time at the bank as a teller, and making do with minimum wage and two mouths to feed, things had been pretty tight in the Gentry household growing up. Every penny counted. And they typically weren't spent on fast food.

Lila patted her butt and thought about her racy panties. "No longer an issue. I assure you."

She felt her face flush as Jake appraised said tush. She took a calming breath. She was getting distracted. And sidetracked. No surprise there. He'd always led their conversations and she'd followed, basking in his intelligence and keen wit.

She'd follow him anywhere. Literally.

She changed the subject. "How've you been, Jake?"

"Not bad, all things considered with the economy." She searched his tanned, healthy face, noting the scar dissecting his left eyebrow. When had that happened? She looked closer, searching for clues to his life since she'd been gone.

While still inherently a sweet talker at heart, his gaze was harder, callused with experience. Gone were the exuberance and daydreams of the future, their midnight musings about having three kids, a dog named Max, and a place with a creek and a rambling old farmhouse. She'd wanted to wear a floral apron and bake fresh biscuits in a kitchen that smelled of coffee while the screen door banged behind three of Jake's children.

Of course, it had all been totally naive and unrealistic, considering her background. But for a while, she'd dreamed.

She said the only thing she could trust herself to say. "You look good. Really good."

Jake stared, his expression closing down. "You mean cancer free."

And there it was.

Used to, she'd check her watch to see how long it'd taken them to reach this ugly point in the conversation, but she was all about doing things differently now. Embracing the feelings of inadequacy to set them free. To diffuse the inner voice that told her repeatedly: you're not good enough.

So Lila switched gears. She wasn't going to let Jake build another wall around himself, so high she couldn't scale it with the highest ladder. No, ma'am. She'd learned how to get what she wanted back in Dallas, and Jake was about to find out she had all new strategies.

"It's been nice catching up, Jake. Tell your folks I said hello. If you want to get together tomorrow for pig wrestling or whatever, I'll be at Granny's." And then she turned her back on Jake Winter and walked to her waiting car.

Throwing her purchase into the passenger seat, Lila wondered what he would do next. Her body tingled in anticipation.

Suddenly, he was there, trapping her in the open vee of her car door, his chest pressing deliciously close. Her body hummed in response. She curled her fingers into fists to keep from reaching for him.

"How long are you staying?" He propped a tanned forearm on the roof and leaned in farther. A muscle in his jaw clenched.

"However long it takes," she admitted.

"For what?" He crowded her. The therapist she'd spent dozens of hours with had warned her defensiveness could be the result of her sudden appearance. Of her extended stay.

Which meant Jake felt vulnerable.

Which meant he still cared.

Stage one of the manhunt: complete. Jake still cared about her.

She smiled and resisted the urge to stroke his cheek and kiss his lips. "That's for me to know and you to find out, baby."

Jake backed up, sweetly confused and properly flustered. "Are we playing a game, Lila?"

The fact that he asked the question meant she had a fighting chance. This wasn't a football game he could predict and plan play-by-play.

He simply had to live it. Which was the source of all their problems.

Shrugging her shoulders, she winked and slid into the driver's seat.

Jake quietly returned the gas nozzle to the pump for her, gave a farewell nod, and strolled to his truck. Metal hinges creaked with age and use as he opened the door. Turning the key, he fired up the vintage Chevy and fiddled with the AC.

Lila grinned with her success at no one in particular and left the shaded canopy of the Grab & Get.

Chapter Two

Jake watched in his rearview mirror as Lila smiled. And then the weight from ten years of resignation hit him like a hammer. He'd fought the urge to reach out and drag her into his arms. To feel her pressed up against his chest. He wanted to know if she still smelled like summer sun and flower gardens.

And because he was tired today from a late-night planning session with a new client, he did stupid-ass things, like stand in the middle of the Grab & Get lot on the hottest day of the goddamn summer and ogle old exes, as if he were ready to drive back to his place and jump in bed.

Very bad idea, thinking of the two of them together in bed. One thing they were always good at, even up to the very end, was sex. And lots of it. At various times of the night and day. In exciting, body-bending positions. Hands down, his favorites were the sessions at 2:00 a.m. and 4:00 a.m.

Lila had always been intuitively sexual and sensual. Her willingness to experiment and trust him in and out of bed was one of the things he loved most about her.

Jesus. Love. Loved?

He pushed away thoughts of feelings and focused on the here and now.

He needed some physical activity all right, just not that kind of physical. At least not with Lila. A bone-draining run along the back roads of nearby Indian Gap should work. But that wasn't in his schedule.

He was so screwed.

But Lila wasn't. She'd done the right thing back then, calling off their relationship. Pride filled his heart.

Look how far she'd gone in Dallas with her business. She never would have done the same here in Hannington. As a cotton-farming town that went belly-up during the Depression and didn't recover, the same opportunities just weren't available. Hell, they'd never been available unless you were into farming or raising cattle, or joined the military at nearby Fort Hood.

One thing he knew for sure. Lila Jean had grown up. Her blue eyes reflected the clarity of the sky overhead with a peace he'd not witnessed before. And that sexy tumble of blond hair? It was shorter than he remembered, but skimmed her bare shoulders to softly kiss her tan skin. She looked mature, her pose saying what her face didn't: that she'd learned a thing or two about the world and how to work it to her advantage.

No doubt about it. She'd done the right thing when she'd left him. So what was she doing back in town now, wasting time with him at the convenience store?

"Who was that?" John Casler, Jake's closest friend and project foreman, passed a Gatorade in through the open window and climbed into the passenger seat of the cab.

Jake shrugged and adjusted the rearview mirror to cover his discomfort. "Someone I used to know."

"You want to get to know her again?"

Breaking the seal on his bottle, Jake swallowed a third of the contents. The truth was, it would be better, safer, for both of them if he didn't get to know her again. Especially in a carnal way. Once he went down that road, it was hard, *ha ha*, to turn back.

He wiped his mouth on the back of his hand and looked directly at Casler. "Nope."

Casler watched him with quiet intensity. They had worked together for almost seven years, and Casler knew him better than anybody. Knew that his one-word answers meant he wanted this discussion over. In the past.

"Old girlfriend, *mi amigo*?"

Christ. He wasn't going to let it go.

Jake switched the AC higher, though the ancient system did little to cool the cab in hundred-degree heat.

"You could say that." And so much more. Like how he had once counted every tiny freckle on her entire body. Right before he kissed them all. And that at one time he loved nothing more in the world than running his fingers down her naked back to the dip in her spine near her ass.

Pulling out of the convenience store lot, they headed a few blocks down Main Street to the Dairy Queen to grab lunch for his crew.

Jake attempted to ignore Casler's questioning stare. Little good it did him.

"So what's her name? I might want to ask her out."

Jake's hand gripped the steering wheel, the leather squeak-
ing softly under the strain. Casler was only screwing with him.

"You don't want to ask her out. She's married."

"*Mierda.*"

Casler always cursed in Spanish.

"Why were you hanging out with her then?"

"Because I'm her husband."

Lila peered at her grandmother's redbrick bungalow with
green-and-white-striped awnings, and contemplated how
many times she'd played on the big side porch, busying herself
with books and journaling, waiting for her family to come
home. It felt like thousands. And here she sat, once again
stalling, though this time Lila played the part of returning
family.

Though carefully orchestrated over months of therapy
and dozens of phone calls with her Granny, Lila's return to
the town of her birth was bittersweet at best.

The melted candy bar, now re-formed under the blow of
the air conditioner, whispered to her as it slipped across the
lap of her silk skirt and fell between the seats. Her hand dived
in, but it was too late. The chocolate was gone, drowning in
the under-the-seat darkness, requiring a flashlight and body
contortions to retrieve.

Probably for the best. She'd advanced beyond the days of
fixing boy troubles and family drama with chocolate.

She gripped the wheel between shaking hands and breathed.
Many years had passed since she'd lived in the house. Memories

of her past life resided there. Memories of her mother, who ran out when Lila was five, pictures of her dead father, whom she didn't remember, and reminders of the naive girl she'd been at eighteen when she'd married Jake.

She looked at her reflection in the rearview mirror, affecting a stern, disappointing expression. "Quit whining and get your rear in there!" Her angry voice echoed in the empty car, her mouth dry despite the soda.

Jerking the door open, she slid out of her seat and strode inside. Her heels sank in the thick, cushy carpet and a blast of cold air hit her face, cooling her heated cheeks. Her grandmother's favorite rose potpourri assailed her senses.

She listened, but didn't hear the familiar sounds of TV drifting from the den. "Granny?"

No response.

Had she missed her? Maybe she'd gone out to the grocery.

Dropping her purse and the box containing the journal on the mahogany console table near the door, she followed the trail of oriental runners back to her grandmother's bedroom.

Stopping just outside the door, she watched in shocked surprise as a nurse fussed over Granny. Barbara Gentry, age seventy-two, lay propped up in bed, a casted arm heavy on her chest.

"Lila Jean, is that you hovering out there in the hall?" Granny's no-nonsense voice called to her.

She made her feet move across the carpet to stand at the edge of the bed, like she had so many times as a child. Never mean, Granny was nevertheless stern, demanding manners and politeness.

"What happened, Granny? Are you all right?" She wiped

a trickle of moisture from her eye and attempted a smile. Her grandmother looked tiny and frail amid the white linens and plaster cast, her silver hair in disarray.

"I'm fine. It's not the end of the world." Shooing the nurse away, she patted the rumpled chenille comforter with her good hand. "Stop that crying and come down here where I can see you better."

Lila hitched a hip onto the iron bed, taking her grand-mother's hand. She admired the ever-present jeweled ring on her finger, the birthstones of her father, Granny, and herself. She loved the ring. It reminded her of the closeness and traditions of family.

The tears started again. What kind of granddaughter was she that her own grandmother was injured and Lila didn't know?

"Lila, it's not your fault your crazy Granny slipped outside while trying to talk on her cell phone and feed the cats at the same time. I should have been watching for that rascal Nate. He trips me every time!"

Lila laughed in spite of herself. The image of her grand-mother surrounded by cats, hands full of food with her ear pressed firmly to the phone, was very real.

"See now, it's not too bad. It's a broken arm, nothing more. I'm sure it will annoy my bowling team more than it will bother me." She fussed with the covers, throwing the neatly tucked afghan off the bed.

"When did this happen? And why didn't you call me? I should have been here. Sooner."

"Day before yesterday. It's not that bad and I can still take care of myself. I just can't bowl. The Bombshells will have to replace me this season."

"Granny, I wish you would've called—"

Her concern fell in the wake of Granny's shrewd change of subject. "This doesn't affect us or our plan one bit. Just my ability to whip Howard's hind end if he stands in our way. But we'll deal with that as we need to. You, missy, need to get it in gear, however, and save Miss Pru's old house from the wrecking ball."

While Granny liked to let on that "the plan" was a conspiracy the two women shared, Lila knew the effort was in itself simply a trigger to bring her back to Hannington. Back to the beginning. And back to her true self.

"Ever since that idiot mayor of ours got it into his head to tear it down, it has been nothing but a fight. The Bombshells haven't been real successful at making the case, what with all the town hall records from that time mysteriously disappearing."

Granny waved her good hand in disdain. "A fire, my ass. Looks suspicious if you ask me. Anyway, you're here now and old Howard is about to get his butt handed to him."

Lila sat back on the bed, confused. "Why didn't you use the journal? With that and the building, you could probably get in with the Texas Historical Commission."

Granny pushed back on her pillows, sitting as straight as she could manage with one good hand. "I don't know anything about a journal."

Lila hopped from the bed and padded back down the hall to recover Miss Pru's book from the entry table.

She returned to the bedside and laid it in Granny's lap. "This showed up last week. A brief note said: 'This is part of your past. Thought it could be part of your future.' I assumed it was from you. More ammunition in our war to save Miss Pru's place."

Granny stopped flipping through the book to give her a scolding look. "Lila Jean. I would never be so cryptic. Nor anonymous."

"If you didn't send it, then who did?"

Granny snorted. "Let's look at this inscription." She held her breath as Granny carefully laid the front cover open. Seconds ticked by in silence.

Finally, Granny looked up. "Oh, dear. It seems we have quite the mystery here, don't we?"

From the Journal of Prudence MacIntosh

Lesson Number One —

For women, resolution can be a powerful weapon. Once you make a decision, remain true. Do not change your mind or give in to persuasive arguments. Your man will come to respect you for it and so will you.

Chapter Three

"I'm reading a prostitute's manual on how to have a great sex life." Lila looked over the spine of the book in her hands to Mark Shrine, her in-house architect.

"Excuse me?" He swung the door all the way open and glided into her office, interested in her out-of-the-ordinary reply to "what's up?"

Mark took the overstuffed leather chair across from her desk. He snuggled into the cushy cocoon, eager for an interesting story like a kid before bedtime. When she'd hired the man six years ago to redesign historic downtown buildings for her, she had no idea he was so...so inclined to drama. But they'd made an immediate connection and become fast friends and he offered a sympathetic ear when she needed one. Which, these days, seemed to be more often than not.

And with the chain of events currently unraveling, she was in need of a good sounding board to make sure she wasn't straight-up bananas.

"So, what's the story?" He sipped a diet soda and crossed his legs.

"Someone—my grandmother most likely—sent me this old journal. It dates back to the 1870s! And, are you ready for this?"

Mark nodded.

"It's from Hannington."

"That little pissant town you're from?"

Lila smiled. "According to my grandmother, it's not so pissant anymore. Lots of folks are buying up ranch property with their oil and gas money and building weekend homes."

"Okay. Yeah. Interesting. But let's get back to the relevant part. A prostitute's guide to a great sex life? Why would anyone send it to you? You don't have a sex life!"

"Ha ha." True, she didn't.

"So what's the deal with the book? Is it one of those personal accounts of 'life on the streets,' 'a look inside the bordellos of old'?"

Mark loved stories. With him, any event could seem dark, mysterious, and tawdry. It was one of the reasons she enjoyed his company so much. The man made her laugh with his genuineness and exuberance.

"From what I can tell, the author wrote it for publication, but this is the writer's working copy. There are journal entries throughout, in between the passages meant to be published."

"Intriguing."

Lila bit her lip. "Mark, do you believe in fate?"

"You mean like *Kismet*?" He threw his head back and stared at the black iron piping running along the ceiling. "God, that was a great movie."

"Seriously, do you think every one person has a special somebody out there?"

His head snapped up and he met her gaze. "Oh, this is more like *An Affair to Remember*." Setting his can on the glass side table, he sat up straight in the chair. "What are you saying, Lila? That you found a special somebody?"

Suddenly nervous now that she was on the precipice of revealing her little secret, she stared at the book, waffling. Although her therapist encouraged her to deal with her emotions. Examine them. Revel in them. Feel the vulnerability. And then let them go.

Damn them. They were the culprits behind her panic attacks, these persistent emotions. And Lila was more than ready to let the little suckers go free.

"Unresolved issues," the therapist said. "A fear of abandonment," the therapist said.

Lila had shrugged at the time. They were her issues and she'd worn them like armor for years. But now, finally, motivated by age, maturity, and the lessons in this journal, she was ready to let it all go. To gamble. To pick up the pieces of her abandoned marriage and fully love the man she could no longer live without.

She refused to end up like her mother.

"Oh, no. You don't ask me a question like that and then go and clam up. What gives? Do you have a man or not?"

"I used to."

Mark slapped the arm of the chair. "Oh shit. Here we go. I'll grab the beer. Do you need a burger with it? A nice dose of booze and grease will ease the pain."

Lila laughed and waved away his concern. "I'm good.

Though a burger from the Love Shack would set my crap straight right now."

Mark joined her laughter and grabbed his soda can again, tossing back the last of his aspartame-filled goodness. "So who was this guy? And why are we talking past tense? Did he die?"

Lila's mood sobered quickly.

She pushed away from her desk and walked to the windows overlooking downtown Dallas, in an attempt to escape her melancholy feelings.

Her father had left her. Then her mother. And then him. Her high school sweetheart, *her husband*. He'd pushed her so far away from his love, Lila had been forced to leave, retreating to Dallas.

"What happened?" Mark broke the silence and came up next to her, nudging her shoulder with his own.

She looked into his concerned hazel eyes, but saw another pair of eyes, smoky jade and swirling with dark emotion. Emotion she could never experience, share, or relieve him of.

He'd been so shattered. So lost. And believing his sacrifice was true and right, he'd forced her away, pushing her to seize opportunity and life without him.

Shaking the memory loose, she focused on Mark. "You never answered my question about fate. Do you believe in it?"

"I don't know, Lila. I like to think everybody has a soul mate out there, but in truth, I haven't seen it happen for too many people. There is a lot of settling for close. And almost."

"What if I were to tell you this book"—she held it up between them so the gilded pages shone in the overhead lighting—"was a sign?"

He studied her face, his cynicism evident. "Of what?"

"It's time I went home. Dealt with my past. And kicked its ass."

Mark liked it when she talked tough. It was their inside joke, because Lila was anything but an ass-kicker.

"Lila, what the hell are you talking about?"

"By itself, I might be able to shrug it off. But I like to think of it as a sign. An arrow pointing me home. And then last week, I got a phone call from an attorney regarding some money due to my mother."

"Your mother? You mean your grandmother?"

"No, my biological mother." *How to make this particular story short and not so depressing?* She loathed discussing this particular pain. It made her feel weak. "After my dad died overseas, she kind of…well, she kind of went off the deep end and took off out West somewhere. I haven't seen her since I was five."

Mark rubbed his forehead. "Damn, Lila. I didn't know all this."

Realizing this was probably way more than he wanted to hear, she stepped away from the window, trying to establish some distance between the bombshell she'd dropped and herself.

A similar behavior executed by her mother over and over again. A behavior Lila was desperate not to repeat. So she turned back to Mark and grabbed for his hand. He squeezed it reassuringly. "What did the lawyer want?"

Lila cleared her throat. "Somebody on my dad's side left my parents money. The attorney needed to know if my mother was still at her current address. In California. In Los Angeles to be exact."

Mark's heavily lashed eyes widened. "This dude knows where your mother is?"

"He at least knew her last known address, which is more than I ever had."

"Whoa."

"Exactly." Lila leaned against the bookcase for support. "And then this week, this journal shows up in the mail." Flipping her leather satchel open, she pulled the book into the light once more. "Look at the inscription on the inside cover."

Mark opened the cover and read the faded ink on the first page. She'd read it so many times today she could repeat it, verbatim.

"To my daughter: Lila Gentry. Follow the path to happiness, little one. I will be there to guide you, all the days of your life. Your mother, Prudence MacIntosh."

She saw the confusion in his face and helped him muddle through it. "Lila Gentry was my great-grandmother on my father's side. Miss Pru, it seems, was my great-great-grandmother."

"Son of a biscuit."

"Exactly."

"Excuse me, ladies, but I've finished up here and I gotta get to Mrs. Motheral's down the street before she up and climbs the refrigerator again looking for her cigs."

Lila smiled at the home health care nurse. The old iron bed frame groaned and then settled back into place as she got up. "I want to talk to the nurse to see if she has any special restrictions for you."

"As long as I can get a double cheeseburger from the DQ, she can restrict whatever she likes."

Lila didn't need to see her grandmother's frown. Her challenging, I'll-put-up-a-fight tone said everything.

The nurse stood patiently by the upright piano in the front parlor, her lips twitching over the sheet music selections on display.

"You sure got your hands full, Miss Gentry." Her eyes turned up to Lila's and her mouth widened into a broad smile.

She liked the nurse immediately. "What's the diagnosis?"

"She'll heal, but it will take longer considering her age and all. The hard part is going to be keeping her from moving around too much while the bones in her shoulder knit back together."

Yes, keeping Granny from bowling and gardening would be next to impossible. "Is there anything special I need to do?"

"No. Just keep her entertained."

"Easier said than done." Barbara Gentry did not like movies, video games, books, or idle conversation. She lived for bowling, long walks, dominoes, and gossip.

"You'll think of something." The nurse patted Lila's arm. "I'll drop by each morning for the next couple of days until you get settled. Just to check in on y'all, and see how things are going."

Lila nodded. How hard could it be to care for her granny?

Reaching into the depths of her bag, the nurse rooted around. "I gotta get organized one of these days." She retrieved a card at last, handing it to her. "Just call me if you need anything."

The name on the card said "Steve Ann Richards."

She must have read the look of confusion in Lila's eyes.

She smiled a smile that said she'd heard the question a million times before. "My parents were counting on a boy, you know, and when they didn't get one, they went ahead and kept the name, adding Ann to soften it."

"Oh."

The phone rang and her grandmother's voice carried down the hall. "No, Judith, I'm fine. Lila's here now, so I don't need you to rush over with a pot of chili. Save it for Charley. Lord knows the man needs it worse than I do."

Steve Ann smiled. "She sure is proud of you. You're all she's talked about the last couple of days." Steve Ann looked down the hall to Granny's room and then back to Lila. "I don't want to alarm you or get in the middle of your family business, but your grandmother has also been talking about passin' along all of her motherly wisdom before she commits to her final rest. She said there's no one else to do it, what with her daughter—your mother, I reckon—outta the picture."

Lila tried to swallow over the growing ball of panic in her throat, but choked instead. And then suffered more horror over embarrassing herself so.

"Hey, hey. It don't mean nothing." Steve Ann rubbed her arm briskly. "It's typical for ladies her age. That's what I wanted to tell you. Don't get upset when she starts talking about teaching you everything she knows before she passes on to the Lord. It's normal. Now that you're here, she'll be able to rest better and she'll ease up on the talk."

"But, is she, I mean, ready to, you know…"

"She isn't anywhere close to giving up that bowling ball for the harp."

"Thanks," Lila murmured, trying not to think of her future

without Granny. Nope. She wasn't going there.

She watched from the door as Steve Ann's extended cab truck pulled away from the curb. Shutting out the late-afternoon heat, and the grief that came with the notion of losing her Granny, she closed the front door and padded back to her grandmother's room.

"Good grief, Judith, it's not the end of the world. I'll be back on the bowling team as soon as the cast comes off. Shirley Maple can fill in for me until then."

The Bowling Bombshells were no longer blond, young, or single, but they could still bowl better than anyone in Bell County. They'd managed to defend their undefeated title in the women's league since 1943. And they played every week in Temple, never missing a league night, with the exception of the end of World War II in September 1945.

Lila caught her grandmother's attention with a wave. "Can I get you some tea?" she whispered. Granny nodded, shooing Lila on with her good hand, the phone tucked securely under her chin.

Out of earshot in the kitchen, Lila found the tea bags and searched her grandmother's Depression-era pitcher collection until she found the polka-dotted one used for iced tea. Buoyed by the familiar chatter drifting down the hall from her Granny's bedroom, she considered her plan for the coming day, making a mental note of one errand she needed to complete pronto. She prayed she wouldn't run into Jake Winter again. Unexpected run-ins were not in her plan. Carefully orchestrated and rehearsed encounters were.

But what the hell. Miss Pru said life was full of the unplanned. And that was the only thing you could plan on.

Lesson Number Two —

The best way to get a man to sing your praises is to be subtle. Go about your business, the everyday chores necessary to keeping and pleasing a man, but do not speak of them. Let him discover your abilities and he will be thankful. Even boastful where you are not.

Chapter Four

Jake crossed over into the aged, tiled foyer of the Dairy Queen, the dinging bell overhead announcing his entrance amid the sticky scent of yesterday's Blizzards and hamburgers. He nodded at several familiar faces occupying the bright yellow booths in the dining area.

Stepping up to the counter, he reviewed the overhead menu out of habit. His eyes fell on the section titled "Treats" and his thoughts went immediately to Lila, full of determination, kindness, and beauty, a package wrapped up in a hot body that kept him up at night.

His wife. Home again after all this time. He couldn't stop thinking about the high heels she was wearing, the ones that evoked endless images of her naked, and him doing things to her body that would make her beg. Not that he would get the opportunity anytime soon to see her naked. No way. Sex without strings wasn't in Lila's vocabulary. And sex with commitment wasn't in his at the moment, so he might as well stop punishing himself by thinking of her in bed.

"Jake, are you wantin' to order something, or are you just enjoying the view?"

His gaze fell to Mary Beth waiting at the register. She'd worked behind the dull brown counter for as many years as he could remember, her DQ uniform consistently and unavoidably gaping open where it fit too snugly across her ample chest. Anna Nicole Smith discovered in a Texas Dairy Queen, she was not. But nice as the day was long, that was Mary Beth.

"Give me ten Hungr-Busters with cheese, fries, and a gallon of tea."

"You want any Dilly Bars with that? We knocked the freezer burn off just last night." Mary Beth's lips twitched.

"No, thanks."

"How 'bout your usual salad with grilled chicken, then?"

"Yeah." Jake rubbed a hand across his face.

An excited whisper from the dining area caught his attention, though he didn't acknowledge it—that simply fueled the fire.

"I saw her, y'all! With her big hair and fake boobs. She gave Jake a good once-over and peeled out of the Grab & Get."

"Are you sure it was Lila, Janie? Your Lasik's not quite healed and the other day, you thought Howard was Jesus Christ crossing the courthouse square."

"Shut up! The sun was in my eyes. Which are fine now, thank you very much." Janie paused for a deep breath. "Of course it was her. I know what Lila Gentry looks like and I don't care how long she's been gone. Once a trailer park brat, always a trailer park brat!"

Threasa shushed her sister. But Jake had heard all he needed to hear. Word of Lila's arrival had gotten out.

Super. Now all he needed was Casler to come out of the toilet and incite further talk by jawing up Lila's physical attributes. Hell, they could have their own Hollywood love triangle, Texas-style, and a reality TV show to go with it: *Bell County Wives.*

Mary Beth handed him his change and narrowed her penciled eyebrows as she surveyed the dining room. "Your order will be right up. And while you're waiting, you mind taking Janie's refill out there?"

Jake watched as Mary Beth disappeared around the back of the soda machine with an empty coffee cup, returning seconds later to hand it to him.

"Do I want to know what's in this?"

"No."

He raised the cup in salute.

"Thanks," and strolled to an empty booth across from the Thompson sisters. Janie's unfocused blue eyes followed him the entire way, but Threasa avoided meeting his smile. They were as opposite as two sisters could be: Janie, a bored, mean-spirited woman with big money, big hips, and an even bigger mouth, while Threasa resembled a fresh-faced magazine model quietly abiding beneath a straw Resistol cowboy hat.

"Afternoon, ladies."

"Howdy yourself, Jake. How's business?" Janie offered a wide smile full of teeth, though moments ago she had maligned his wife's perfect breasts. And he knew deep down, she didn't see the hypocrisy.

"Can't complain. Natural gas money keeps business rolling

my way. And speaking of, how's Howard getting along with his wells out east? Heard he had some trouble."

Janie's lips hardened. Howard Armstrong was a moron. How he had managed to accumulate any money or become mayor was a mystery to Jake. Though now that Howard had it, he couldn't stop blowing it on bad land deals, questionable business ventures, and overmanagement.

"It's all fine. He's moving a couple of wells. Salt water ruined two sites, but we should be drilling again in a week or two."

Threasa sighed. "Tell your husband to hire a geologist, Janie. For pity's sake."

Jake recognized Casler's heavy tread on the tile behind him. And sighed. At six foot six, the carpenter was built like a boxer, lean, mean, and tough as hammered nails. If there was something Casler enjoyed more than bustin' Jake's balls, it was giving Janie Armstrong hell.

"Howard doesn't need people knowing how much the wells produce," Janie chastised her sister.

Jake glanced at Threasa, anticipating how she would respond to the opening. But she had eyes only for Casler, following his movements all the way from the front counter to where he stood now, towering over their booth. Casler threw Threasa a distracted smile and zeroed in on her older sister with a look that said, *Did I step in shit?*

Which she returned because John Casler was a card-carrying member of the blue-collar majority. Worse than that, the poor son of a bitch was half Native American and half Mexican.

But Threasa Thompson didn't seem to mind. Who would

have guessed?

"Jake," Janie continued, oblivious to the pending confrontation, "Threasa and I were just reminiscing and I was telling her I saw Lila Gentry at the gas station. Do you know anything about that?"

Jake was still watching Threasa and Casler, the latter of whom remained clueless of his admirer. "Now that you mention it, I think I did see her. She must have been the hot blonde in the Lexus."

Casler whistled long and low. "*Totalmente caliente.*" His eyes swept Janie's strapless summer dress and gold heels. "And that's without effort."

Janie's cheeks reddened, though Jake seriously doubted she understood the Spanish. "Is she staying this time, Jake? Or are we still too small-town for her?"

Jake grew suddenly tired of Janie's bitterness. Of all the pettiness and jealousy. Lila could have ended up like that. Married to an unhappy, cancer-ridden, self-medicating, numb drinker with no prospects of a happily ever after.

They'd dodged one mean bitch of a bullet when he had the good sense during a selfless moment to realize he was doing a bang-up job knocking all of the optimism and adventure out of his young wife. What legacy was he going to leave? Only grim reality and resignation.

Screw that.

So he'd set her free. And dammit all if she wasn't back.

Huh.

"It's not so much about the town as it is her asshole husband," Jake offered.

Casler slapped him on the back. "Don't be so hard on

yourself, man. If I were gay, I'd take you. Though I would have to sleep on the left side of the bed."

Out of the corner of his eye, Jake saw Mary Beth set his order on the counter. He pushed Janie's tainted coffee to the side, unwilling to contribute further to the woman's bad mood, and stood, stretching his legs. "Ladies." He sauntered to the front and grabbed his lunch, a chuckling Casler in his wake as they headed out to the truck.

"That damn woman is so spoiled, salt couldn't save her."

Jake's response was cut off as he spotted Lila across the street at the post office. He'd never seen another woman move with the unconscious grace she possessed. It wasn't artifice. It was her. Pure and simple. From the way her hips rolled, to the prim set of her shoulders that highlighted her perfect breasts.

"Take the truck. I'll catch up with you." Jake tossed the keys to a surprised Casler and set the Dairy Queen bags on the hood before jogging across the street.

By the time he made it, she'd disappeared inside the building. He wandered around to her car and leaned against the rear fender, settling in for a wait.

Passersby looked at him with curiosity and waved tentatively. He rarely stood still for more than five minutes and to be standing there, doing nothing, threw people for a loop.

Minutes later Lila came back out, glowing with happiness and confidence. She smiled at people as they passed her on their way inside.

The years spent apart melted away in a searing rush and his chest constricted. He wanted to grab her up in his arms and nuzzle the side of her neck, a welcome-back kiss to let her know he'd missed her for the three minutes she'd been in the post office. A gesture he'd initiated a hundred times during their short marriage.

The fresh pain of that loss grabbed him by the throat and squeezed.

Lila's stride broke midway across the small parking lot as she spotted him. Happy slipped off her face and hid behind an emotional wall.

Ah, Lila. Did I do that to you? Make you so guarded? If he were another man, he'd punch himself in the face for damaging Lila so.

"Jake," she said, coming to a stop near the trunk of her car. He got an eyeful of creamy skin beneath the deep vee of her blouse.

"We need to talk," he said.

She glanced around the lot as people came and went, clearly uncomfortable.

"Haven't you had enough of parking lots already? I've finished my business researching the origins of a mystery package and need to get back to Granny." She frowned.

"Nah. Nice and public." It was hot enough to keep the conversation short, and he really had only one point to make. "I can appreciate that you're home to see Barbara and old friends, but I don't want there to be any misunderstanding between us, Lila. In my mind we're divorced. Maybe not legally, but where it matters."

Did he sound sincere? Because he couldn't believe the shit he'd just said. He'd become a pretty good liar over the years, masking his grief and pain. Covering up the weakness. Praying for a cure from cancer, only to be disappointed time and time again, did that.

Her features were closed to him and he couldn't tell if she was upset over his declaration, or annoyed about standing in the heat.

He ran a hand over the back of his neck, the muscles there tense and aching. He wanted to hold her. He wanted a second chance at living again. He wanted a lot he couldn't have. "If we can be friends and move on with our separate lives, I'd welcome it. It's been years since I had anyone to watch late-night TV with." *Shit. Stop. Talking. Idiot. Everything was coming out all wrong.*

Lila smiled. "I did move on. And that road brought me right back here. I say moving on is overrated. How about moving forward?"

"Look, I want to keep things simple. Uncomplicated. That's all I'm saying." Except for the part where he really, really wanted to see her naked.

Lila leaned in and stabbed his chest with an index finger. The touch sent a line of fire all the way down his stomach to the front of his pants, tightening his balls.

"Jake. Sweetie." Her blue eyes shone with sharp-edged emotion. "I know you're not stupid. You may want uncomplicated, but when has life ever served up that particular dish? I for one have never had it easy. It's always messy, in-your-face complex. I gotta deal with it. So I suggest you learn to handle it, too. Because I'm not going anywhere."

Jake held his breath until her hand dropped away. He let it out in a long push as she stepped to the driver's-side door and climbed inside.

It dawned on him she planned to boil his blood and then leave him stranded in the post office parking lot. Despite better judgment—not that he had ever possessed such a thing—he shrugged and figured *what the hell?*

And before she could back the Lexus out, Jake eased open the passenger door and slid in next to her, smiling when she turned shocked eyes on him.

Maybe he would get out of this with some semblance of self-dignity. "You're right. Life is complicated. Now, take me to my office."

Lesson Number Three —

Do not wait for quiet, private moments to show your man you love him; those times are too seldom. Show him in the middle of the dusty town street, in the barn while feeding the livestock, or, heaven help me, on the way to Church. Reach out and lay your hand on his arm, get his attention, and look deeply into his eyes. He will do the rest.

Chapter Five

Lila didn't know whether to be irritated with Jake's demand or excited by the prospect of having him all alone for five minutes.

She chose to be excited. Cautiously excited. She sneaked a glance from beneath lowered lashes before backing the car out of the lot. He consumed the entire passenger compartment with his tall frame and muscular legs, and spilled over onto the console that divided the seats. She could feel the heat from his arm where it rested next to hers.

She took a deep breath. "Um. Tell me about Reverie. How's the home-building business recovering out here?"

Jake tapped his index finger on the gearshift mounted on the console between them, a habit she remembered from way back. He considered the question. "Tough. Natural gas money has all but dried up. There are a few folks building, but nothing like it was a few years ago."

Lila nodded. "Are you surviving it okay?" Times had been

difficult in construction, but Jake's fairness and integrity had earned him a reputation, taking his business through the hard times—or so Granny had told her.

"As good as can be expected. I set money aside. I can maintain my core crew, including Casler. Things are picking up again and we have a big project now, out on the west side of town."

"I see." Lord. She sounded like an idiot. Really? Making small talk? How long could she keep this up before diving headfirst into a topic she desperately wanted to discuss? Like, how were his labs? What did the doctors say? Was he seeing anyone? And would he have dinner with her?

But what did she do instead? Smile. And nod.

"Well. That's awesome."

Jake turned and looked at her, a smile turning up the corners of his mouth. "Awesome?"

Lila's cheeks reddened under his scrutiny. "What? I can't say awesome?"

"Absolutely. Just didn't think you were the type to use trendy language. It's interesting."

She couldn't keep her own smile under wraps. "Interesting how?"

He stopped tapping the gearshift. She knew this behavior, too. Jake was reflecting.

"I guess you've changed. Grown up. For some reason, I never considered what you'd be like and sound like at thirty. It's interesting."

"And not sexy?" Lila slapped a hand over her mouth and laughed.

Jake's composure held, but then what did she expect?

The only outward sign that her comment had an impact was a slight widening of his nostrils.

"Did I just say that?" she asked. "Sorry."

"No. Don't be sorry. Age definitely agrees with you. I'm sure you get a lot of men hitting on you."

Lila thought of Mark, and how he had to frequently inform her as to when men were actually hitting on her. "I don't know. I'm a bit dense when it comes to the bar scene and dating."

His brows lifted in question.

"I don't date really. Too busy with work."

"Interesting."

"Stop saying that word!"

"What?" He threw up his hands. "Fine. It's not interesting. But curious. Why the hell aren't you dating? You should be having a crazy good time right now. Age agrees with you. You're fucking hot."

Lord help her. He thought she was not just hot, but *fucking hot.* Lila swallowed and nearly choked at the sudden dryness in her mouth.

She considered a dozen different responses to this admission and settled on honesty.

"I am having a crazy good time. I'm home. With Granny and about to jump-start a new life. And a new project. I couldn't be more excited."

"Hmmmm." Jake opened the passenger door as she parked outside his building. Heat washed in, covering them both.

She knew the hint of a project would have him wondering for a while.

"You gonna tell me about this project?"

Lila smiled and this time didn't attempt to dull the wattage of her smile. "Of course. There are no secrets between us."

He grunted and crawled out of the car. "Have a good one, babe."

Lila held on tight to the endearment for a moment and then backed away from Jake's office and headed for Granny's.

Catching up on all of Granny's usual errands was taking Lila more time than she would have imagined! She couldn't figure out how one little old grandma could be so busy with the local ladies' auxiliary, Bible study, fund-raising for veterans, bowling, potluck dinners, Friday night cards, and animal rescue.

She hadn't even made it to Miss Pru's, for crying out loud!

"Lila, here's a list. The people at the IGA will help you find it all. Just ask for help at the check-cashing counter."

Lila took the grocery list from Granny's outstretched hand, examining the slanted script. She didn't bother reminding her grandmother she'd been grocery shopping on her own for some time now.

"What are the chicken livers for?"

"Nate. He won't eat anything but chicken livers. Be sure to get the freshest. He won't eat 'em if they're over a week old."

Nate. The cat. *Good grief, when did the woman start feeding the cats chicken livers?*

"And while you're down there, you can check out Miss Pru's place. Judith said that turd Howard put a demolition notice on the building yesterday."

The doorbell chimed and Lila almost sighed aloud in relief. "That'll be Steve Ann. I'll let her in and then I'm off to the store. And to conduct recon!" She smoothed the shawl across Granny's shoulders and rubbed her good arm. "It shouldn't take too long." How long could it take to buy chicken livers and eyeball a building?

Steve Ann blew into the house, all hustle and bustle, her arms empty for a change. "Good morning, Lila. How's Mrs. Gentry this morning?"

"She's doing okay, but I think she's worried about her hair." Granny had demanded a hand mirror to investigate the status of her short white curls. The do reminded her of the style sported by the former governor of Texas, Ann Richards: high, tight, and white.

The nurse patted her own ash-colored coiffure. "Give Mary Jo a call over at the Curl 'n Swirl. She might be able to fit her into the schedule on short notice."

"Thanks, I'll do that." She danced a half circle with Steve Ann, laughing as they rearranged themselves in the tiny entry.

"Granny has a grocery list for me, so I'd better get going." The intense heat of midmorning blasted her in the face as she stepped out onto the carpet of turf-like grass on the porch.

Steve Ann lingered at the glass door, a frown marring her pleasant face. "Hon, is that what you're wearing to the IGA?"

Lila looked down at her short silk skirt and matching blouse. She'd chosen it specifically for its neutral color and breezy fabric. "Is there something wrong with it?"

The nurse pursed her lips, her hands planted on generous hips. "Well, not particularly, unless you want to make Janie

Armstrong green with envy. Otherwise, it's a little much for the grocery."

"Oh." Lila's shoulders drooped and she slipped back inside. As she squeezed past Steve Ann, she managed to mumble, "Thanks. It's been a while."

"No problem, hon. We'll get you…ah, reassimilated in no time."

"Right."

Dressed once again, this time in denim shorts, sandals, and a white T-shirt, Lila plunged into the heat, crumpled shopping list in hand. The walk to the town square flew by as she reacquainted herself with once-familiar landmarks.

The Bell County Courthouse dominated the square with its Renaissance Revival style and bold, boxy lines. Lila took in the restored dome and clock tower, missing from the grand white structure since the 1930s. It made the building seem complete finally, and she suddenly realized how lacking it had truly been all those years she was growing up.

On the east side of the square stood the Book Nook, directly next door to Melinda's Kitchen, both new businesses she didn't know. On the west side, the Farmer's Bank—been there for years—and on the north side, the Curl 'n Swirl, an old favorite with the retired set.

A large white sign on the south-facing building caught her eye. Stepping across the street and into the shade of the veranda, she read the sign on Mr. Goodwin's General Store.

DEMOLITION NOTICE. Typical verbiage. Blah, blah, blah. Except no public hearing or committee meeting. No information on who filed the application for demolition. And certainly no notice regarding the historic status of the building.

Miss Pru's.

This was the place. And it appeared her Granny was right. Someone had it in for the building and they were willing to violate city policy and procedure to get rid of the thing.

She stepped off the sidewalk and backed into the street for a full view. The four bay windows of the upper story were boarded over. The four windows flanking the bay, two on each side, were open, but the leaded glass had seen better days. Paint flaked away from the masonry brick, and the rigid aluminum canopy, bisecting the smaller overhead transom windows from the large store windows, sagged with weather damage in several places.

Nothing that couldn't be salvaged and restored. Though that opinion was based on a cursory exterior inspection. She had no idea what the interior was like.

Lila remembered the storefront from her childhood. Mr. Goodwin, a kind old widower, had sold candy, sodas, and good memories to the children of Hannington. She'd savored many a Coke float inside those four walls while mooning over a certain football player.

Now the city wanted to demolish it. She couldn't let that happen. Not when she knew it once belonged to her family and might be housing yet more secrets of Prudence MacIntosh.

If she could buy it before the thirty days were up.

She climbed the concrete sidewalk again and peered at the notice taped to the inside of the window. Posted June 19. Twenty-nine days ago. Before she ever made into Hannington.

Lila's blood pressure escalated and her skin went tight all over. This was total BS. According to Granny, the notice just went up. And they were claiming the waiting period was expiring?

The fate of the building would be decided today, but not by some out-of-touch city bureaucrat. It was local. And it was personal.

She spun around, facing the knobby limestone facade of the county courthouse. Marching across the street, she dodged the few cars crawling down Main during the early afternoon and pushed through the heavy oak doors of the courthouse. Lila skidded across the waxed marble floor of the entry in her haste, nearly losing her footing in the thin strappy sandals she'd chosen in place of her more sophisticated summer heels.

"Ma'am, you take care now. Enough people've fallen there who wasn't paying attention."

Standing straight again on two firmly planted feet, she caught the concerned gaze of an elderly black man on a high-backed stool. The shine on top of his bald head rivaled the sheen on the marble under her feet. He sat behind a low-slung security desk, which was nothing more than a folding table with some change trays laid out for personal items.

She hurried over to the table, her sandals slapping the floor and sending an echo up into the dome-shaped vestibule. "I need to track down the owner of the Goodwin building across the street. Where can I find deed records?"

He smiled, causing the wrinkles in his weathered face to sink deeper. "Oh, yeah. That Goodwin building been up for sale forever. You want to register a complaint with the city about the owner?"

"Why on earth would I want to do that?"

"Many people don't like that building. Don't matter if it was a candy store at some point." He placed heavy emphasis on the word candy, like it was an idea worthy of scorn. "People figure time's come to tear the thing down once and for all. Put something decent up in its place." He grunted, folding his arms over the rounded belly straining against the sky-blue cotton of his uniform.

Wait a minute. She put her satchel on the table, leaning in closer to the man, one hand on her hip. She felt the hurried beat of her heart beneath her cotton top.

"Why don't the people in Hannington like it?"

He pushed his glasses up the bridge of his nose with a gnarled index finger. "Young lady, you ain't from around here, are you?"

She shook her head, letting the man believe she was an out-of-towner.

"Well, lemme just say that it had an indecent beginning. Lots of illegal activities, if you know what I mean. Some old gal ran, uh, an escort service out of there back before the turn of the century."

Despite her need to get to the records room, Lila had to ask. She had to know: "What happened to the woman? And her business?"

He unfolded his arms, placing his hands flat on the table in front of him. Glancing toward the open doors of the vital statistics room in an obvious effort to be discreet, he licked his lips and met her eyes.

Oh, yes. He had a story to share.

"After operating there for some years, and it's my understanding the mayor condoned her business and her gals, a new sheriff was elected and she got run out of town shortly thereafter.

"She didn't go peacefully. Oh, no. Way my daddy used to

tell it, she got run out at the end of a double-barreled shotgun with the town hot on her heels. She had a man here in town, a regular customer who liked her, but he wadn't here to help her."

Lila listened, dying to know the outcome of what surely were Miss Pru's last days in the town of Hannington.

"What happened then?"

The old man shifted his body back onto the stool, the springs in the seat creaking with his weight. "Nothing really. Most of her girls were already gone by then. The rest got run out with her. Boardinghouse tried to make a go of it for a while, but no one could stand sleeping in the place. Said funny things happened there. Noises and creepy things."

Lila picked her bag up off the table after he had a peek in the open zipper, and secured it across her shoulder.

Could his story be true? "What was the woman's name? Does anyone know?"

He scratched the glowing bald spot on his head, his eyes screwed closed until the whites disappeared. "Something Irish. MacIntosh or MacIntush. Something like that."

He knew her name. Was it possible Miss Pru fled town like he claimed? Drawing back from the table, she looked around the empty vestibule. She had to buy that building. Now.

"Deeds?" she asked in a whisper.

"Basement, room 35."

From Miss Pru's journal concerning politics and bribery:

I am not anything special.

The mayor took the liberty of reminding me of this today, as he sat in my parlor.

On the surface he seems harmless enough. Of average height and build, he has rugged features lined from years squinting across hot Texas hillsides. A hardworking, decent man, one would assume.

But a puritanical fire burns in his eyes, lighting him from within. The fire burned bright today. I knew to guard my words and actions closely.

One of the newer girls carefully rubbed his shoulders, trying in her own way to diffuse the tension in the air.

I may not have the fire of the righteous, but when backed into a corner by a lawman such as he, one who regularly pretends to be against the very evil he promotes, yes, even takes money from those he objects to, I do well defending my own.

I am aware my place is not the only fancy house operating on this end of Hell's Half Acre, as the mayor was so kind to remind me. Houses like mine are allowed to operate as a necessary evil to control men's baser urges and keep the community safe.

There are other hurdy-gurdy girls, and one or two madams paying the mayor for the privilege, but I can admit none possess the presence of mind to treat customers with the genuine respect or courtesy as I do.

I digress. Back to the mayor.

"There's an election in the fall, Prudence."

"But your term is not expired yet, Mayor. Surely you are not announcing an early retirement?" This I

also knew. Politics in a small town could mean death to a woman in my business. It paid to be aware.

He chuckled, for the moment indulgent in what he assumed was my ignorance.

"Not by a long shot. But a new sheriff will be elected and you might not have it as easy as you have under the old."

I had been following the town's call for a new man to clean up the streets of the Acre. Rounding up girls and saloonkeepers would solve the problem for a few hours, but the sheriff could not keep them in jail forever. And once they were let go, back down to the Acre they would come.

Surely the townspeople knew as I did, the lawmen bent on ridding the area of vice were the very same corrupt men allowing the practice to continue. And making a nice profit in the process!

No. It took something more than arrests to clean up the Acre. It would take something the townsfolk did not want to do. It would take getting their hands dirty and working to reform the people they wanted to incarcerate.

But the new sheriff would not be elected for months; we all had until the fall. Time enough to determine a course of action when the new man was elected.

"What would you suggest, Mr. Mayor? That we leave the Acre? Run like rats to infest another town?"

He did not want us to leave any more than I did. He simply wanted more money.

"Now, dammit all, Prudence. That's not what I'm

suggesting. Leave it to a woman to jump the gun and start puttin' words in my mouth. I mean for us to come to a new agreement with the sheriff. We got a system here and we want to keep it."

Neither his greed nor his plans for further corruption shocked me. He had been the mayor for all the years I had lived in Hannington, and I imagined he would be here years after I was gone.

It was not a comforting thought. "All right. What do you suggest?"

What he said next did shock me.

"Word is, you've got the ear of that rich cattleman, Pierce. I figure we can use that to our advantage."

No. Not Luke. A lump lodged in my throat and it was difficult forming the objection when all I wanted to do was rail at the mayor.

"Mr. Pierce has come into the saloon once or twice, but we are nothing more than acquaintances — "

"Now you're being modest, Prudence. That ain't like ya. I heard you and Pierce was cozy, you've even been out to his ranch."

Dear Lord. I knew nothing good could come of my association with Luke Pierce. I knew at some point I would bring the man grief. I just did not know it would be in the form of the mayor.

I bit the words out, hurrying to have the wretched man gone from my parlor. "Just tell me what you want."

"Hold up there, girl. We don't want to get ahead of ourselves. You just keep being cozy with Pierce and I'll let you know when the time's right."

"Or what?" I had to know if this was his idea of an ultimatum or simply torture. The man was known for both.

"Now, Prudence, don't start getting yourself upset. We got a few months before the election. Sit tight."

He stood, disentangling himself from the arms of my girl. "I'll be back later to finish this." He slapped her cheek playfully and smiled, revealing the charisma that continued to get him elected term after term.

"Behave yourself, Prudence. And stick close to Pierce. He's our ticket to winning over the new sheriff."

He let himself out through the front door, and as I watched him disappear from view, the thought occurred to me I was in real trouble.

For the first time, thoughts of the well-being of a man took precedence over myself and my girls. I was growing very fond of Luke Pierce. Very fond.

Lesson Number Four —

Stand up for yourself. Do not let folk railroad you or make you feel bad. Have pride in who you are and what you do, and the people trying to bring you down to their level will admire you. So will your man.

Chapter Six

Jake glanced up from his spreadsheet in time to sce Casler slam the door on the tiny construction site trailer. The force rocked the mobile rectangle on wheels, and he felt a sway under his feet.

"You plan on staying pissed all day?" he asked Casler. Ever since the run in with Lila, the carpenter had been irritable.

Casler threw his tool belt on the couch adjacent to Jake's desk and rooted around in the mini-fridge. Finding nothing but bottled water and Gatorade, he settled on the water.

"I might." He ripped the plastic cap off, throwing it behind his back where it landed in the sink.

"You want to take it easy? The maid's not due back for another couple of years."

He purposely ignored Jake and plopped down on the sagging couch, where he sat for several minutes, stewing. Jake let him simmer and went back to his budget.

Finally: "You wanna give me this sofa? I'll pay you five

dollars for it."

"You wanna tell me what has you in such a foul mood? I've had to soothe hurt feelings all afternoon because of you, and I'm about damn tired of playing everyone's mama."

Casler had been sharp with the guys. Not overly harsh, but enough to keep them on their toes.

"I can't believe you kept the little woman hidden from me all these years. Kinda shocks the system to find out your best friend is actually a married wingman."

Jake uncrossed his arms, throwing his pen on the desk. He stretched back in his chair, lacing his fingers behind his head. So that was it. Casler felt bad for talking about his wife.

A lot of people would never know it looking at him, but Casler was fierce when it came to treating women with courtesy and respect. And he obviously thought he'd disrespected Jake's wife.

"Probably never. And don't worry, man, you didn't disrespect me. Or my wife."

Casler frowned in response to the revelation and smoothed his long hair, which he kept tied back.

He didn't want to talk about it, but he owed Casler some kind of explanation. They'd been friends too long. "We've been over for a long time. Over before I met you. So there's nothing to bring up. She hasn't been back here for a while. Her family typically goes out to Dallas to visit her."

"Right." Casler slouched farther down on the couch, stretching his legs out until they almost reached the opposite door. "Just try to keep me informed of the really important shit. You know, like any hot wives I shouldn't hit on, or a stack of bricks getting ready to crush my melon."

Jake still sat with his hands folded behind his head, impatience flaring his nostrils. Now he was getting pissed. He hated explaining himself. "What is it you want to know? You want the dirt on who left who?"

Casler slapped his thigh and leaned forward. "Hell, no. That's your business. I just hated making an ass out of myself by talking about your wife the way I did."

"You're always an ass. This wasn't a special occasion."

"Cool. So what's the story?" He took a pull off the water bottle, settled back again, and crossed his ankles.

"I thought you said it was my business."

"It is, but I thought I'd hit you up while you were feeling all fragile and shit."

Jake lowered his hands and sat up straight at his desk. "Since we're feeling so *chummy*, why don't you tell me about Threasa Thompson?"

Casler blinked, confused. "What can I tell you? Nice girl, but her sister's a bitch."

Jake leaned his elbows on the desk blotter and tipped forward in his chair. "Have you ever looked at Threasa?"

"Sure. I looked at her today in the Dairy Queen."

Jake shook his head.

"What?"

"What was she wearing?"

Casler threw his empty plastic bottle in the sink alongside its cap. "Clothes. A hat. I don't know."

"That's right, John. You don't know. When was the last time you went out with a nice woman? And not the ones you pick up over at Ferrill's Lounge."

"Is there such a thing? A nice woman?"

"Stop changing the subject. Dating. When did you date last?"

Casler pushed himself up off the couch, clearly uncomfortable with the direction change in the conversation.

"Christ, Jake. Men our age don't date." He paced to the sink, grabbing his bottle up and crushing it flat. "You don't date," he said, pointing at him. "And why the hell are you asking me about Threasa Thompson?"

"I'm wondering if you take any time to appreciate all the beauty you have in front of you. Like Threasa, for example. The woman is hot. She's built like a runway model. Miles of leg."

"You been checking her out?" Casler said, incredulous.

"I'm not dead."

"Yeah, me neither."

Jake pushed back from his desk and stood, his budget forgotten. "So, are you going to ask her out?"

Casler jerked his tool belt off the couch and slung it around his hips. "Hell, no."

Jake pushed past him, headed for the door and the freedom of the open site. With his hand on the handle, he turned and looked straight into Casler's eyes. Just because he'd thrown away an opportunity for a happily ever after like a stupid bastard didn't mean Casler had to, too. And now that Lila was home, regret and second-guessing hounded him like starved mosquitoes with the scent of blood.

"You're a dumbass. Maybe she's better off pining for you."

"Excuse me?" Lila raised her voice, trying to get the attention of the records clerk behind the four-foot wall of institutional filing cabinets.

The sign on the outer door indicated the office closed in five minutes, and Lila needed to get the property owner's name today. *Right now.*

The sweater-clad woman, quietly filing, didn't respond.

Was she deaf? Or was Lila being ignored? Figures, the first time to dress down in shorts and a T-shirt, and her corporate kick-ass clothes might have gotten her the attention she desperately needed.

Trying a second time, Lila raised her voice even louder. "Excuse me, ma'am."

"Hey now! What's happening over here?"

A man in his early fifties with a large belly only slightly larger than his belt buckle stepped into the basement office waving a filing folder full of papers.

Maybe he could get the woman's attention. He looked like he knew his way around. "I need help finding a deed before the office closes. I've been trying to get someone to wait on me, but so far I haven't had any luck."

"Well, come on back here then, and let's talk to Carol." He led the way around the formidable row of cabinets until he stood in the clerk's line of sight.

The woman looked up, her gaze slowly focusing on the two in front of her. She appeared unconcerned with the strangers in her domain.

"Carol, this young lady needs some help!" he shouted. Lila wasn't sure if he shouted for Carol's benefit, or if it was because he was the shouting type. He looked like the shouting type, in a "TV minister wearing shiny cowboy boots" sort of way.

Carol reached up behind her ear and adjusted her hearing aid.

This seemed to frustrate Lila's savior. He slapped the filing folder full of paper against his jean-clad thigh. "Miss Carol!" he began in a voice strong enough to be heard in the back rows of the biggest cavernous church in the city. "It's not five yet. You're not supposed to shut down until"—he stopped in mid-sentence, pointing dramatically at the large steel wall clock hanging over the doorway—"the clock says five o'clock."

The pronouncement didn't seem to rattle Miss Carol one bit. She ignored the man and turned to Lila. "What'cha need, missy?"

Apparently, the man wasn't satisfied with Carol's customer service, because he dug his heels in—all two inches of them— and glowered at the both of them.

"I need to find a deed on the old general store next door. I would like to—"

"Carrie Goodwin owns that building. Or she did. The city condemned it and we're tearing it down tomorrow."

Lila looked from Carol to the evangelical cowboy. He'd said "we" are tearing it down.

She had a bad feeling about the situation.

"What do you mean 'we' are tearing it down?"

Carol suddenly perked up. Whether it was the clock striking five or the possibility there was about to be a yelling match, Lila didn't know, but the woman came to life, her eyes wide-open and focused.

"You're not from around here, are you?" Her lack of

townie status had already been established with the guard in the foyer. She didn't feel like repeating the process again.

"Look, I need to stop the demolition on that building. Who do I talk to to make that happen?"

Carol's face lit up and she practically clapped her hands like a schoolkid on the verge of summer vacation.

"Well, that would be me," Cowboy said. "But I can tell you right now that building is coming down. No one is saving it." He delivered the news with folded arms and narrowed brown eyes.

Who the hell did this guy think he was, the town dictator?

"I want to buy it." She met his frosty gaze, mirroring his posture. Though she didn't look the part currently, Lila used her best don't-mess-with-me-Dallas-bitch voice. "Now."

He didn't bat an eyelash. "You can't."

"What do you mean I can't? The sign says I have until tomorrow."

"Unfortunately, the courthouse is closed for the day." He nodded arrogantly at Carol and then looked pointedly at the open door.

Lila didn't move a muscle.

"You'll have to come back in the morning."

Lila wouldn't leave until the matter was settled in her favor. She'd camp out here all night if she had to. Miss Pru's was not going to lose one tiny, scarred old brick on her watch.

"No. I'm here now. And since you seem to be the man making decisions around here, you can just tell me why you're blocking the sale of that building to a willing buyer."

People passing by the records room stopped to listen. Lila could make out a gathering crowd of three or four excited, animated faces hovering in the entryway.

Either Mr. Preacher-in-Boots didn't care or he liked the attention. Probably the latter, the show-off. Either way, it pissed Lila off. She just wanted to find the owner of Miss Pru's and buy the damn thing. Not confront good ole boys at the county courthouse during what should be Miller Time.

"Sweetie, I don't have to explain anything to you. You're not one of my constituents."

One of his constituents? Who was this guy? "Pretty sure of yourself. Mind telling me your name so I'll know who to vote against when you come up for reelection?"

"This here's Mayor Armstrong." Carol chose that moment to slip into the conversation, delivering Lila the unexpected blow.

The mayor? Man, she knew how to pick 'em.

"I'll remember that when I slip behind the curtain to cast my vote."

He puffed his chest out and arched a brow, holding his ground like an overfed dog that has no idea he's too fat to fight.

"So that's it?" she asked him after several seconds. "You're going to tear down a building despite the fact that I'm willing to buy it, fix it up, and return it to the town's tax base?"

"You must be a genius, miss, because you've finally got the point. Now, if there's nothin' else I can clarify for you, I've got a city council meeting in an hour."

And he turned and strutted in the direction of council chambers.

"What an ass," Lila murmured under her breath. Carol couldn't hear her anyway.

"We call him Mayor Assface," Carol said, trying to swallow her laughter at Lila's surprise.

Lila felt a smile coming on even though she was mad enough to bring down the courthouse. "How did he get elected?" she asked Carol.

"His father was the mayor for twenty-five years and when he retired, he passed the torch to Howard. Folks around here don't like too much change, so they figured one Armstrong was as good as another."

Carol did a good job of keeping the sarcasm to a minimum, but Lila got the impression she'd never voted for Howard Armstrong.

"So what do I do now, Carol? Do I have any recourse here?" Lila was too far out of her comfort zone here in Hannington. Back in Dallas, she knew who to call at city hall, and what attorneys to hire to get things done. She ate little men like Howard Armstrong for breakfast. But that was there, and she was here. Time to call in backup.

Carol pushed her heavy tortoiseshell-rim glasses higher up her nose and looked up and down the counter to make sure she wasn't overheard.

"If a person were to circumvent the mayor through a real estate attorney, it might get the process started back up. There are other parties involved in the disposition of the property and he can't make the final decision until everyone has been notified and responded."

The smile she fought earlier turned into a full-blown grin. "I bet you can recommend an attorney for me, right?"

Miss Carol winked and retrieved a business card from her desk.

"Carol, you're a sweetheart. And severely underpaid, I'm sure. If you ever want another job, come talk to me please. I could use someone like you on my side here in Hannington."

"You're a Gentry, right?"

Uh-oh. Lila felt her joy skidding to a halt. "Barbara is my grandmother. I'm Lila."

"That's what I thought. I just wanted to know your name so that when I come looking for that job, I know who to ask for."

Carol closed the drawer on the cabinet. "If you go now," she said, checking her watch, "you'll be able to catch Rose Garner leaving her office. She has to pick up her kids at the day care in a few."

Rose Garner. Her old friend.

This was going to be fun.

Lesson Number Five —

A smile and a polite thank-you are two of the best weapons in your personal arsenal. A kiss is not half bad neither.

Chapter Seven

"Goodness, Lila! I'm so sorry I took so long. I had to drop the kids at home and then get gas."

Rose Garner's brunette curls bobbed around her head as she dug in her giant leather satchel for the keys to the Goodwin building. Lila had known the petite mother of two since Rose had squished mashed potatoes in her hair over a boy in the sixth grade. Fortunately their disagreements had progressed to more civilized terms and the two still kept in touch through emails and late-night phone calls during *The Tonight Show Starring Jimmy Fallon*.

"No problem. I'm just dying here in the heat. It's not like it's a hundred and ten degrees or anything." She gave Rose a wink.

Finally seizing her keys, she juggled the massive puzzle until she found the right one. Lila tapped her chipped nails on the doorframe, considering a French manicure for herself. Granny's garden was taking a toll on her hands.

While Rose muttered to herself about ancient locks and oversize keys, Lila peeked impatiently through the dirty front window, ignoring a string of escalating curses when the door wouldn't budge.

"I don't understand all this sudden interest in the Goodwin building. It sits here empty for years, and all of a sudden, when the city is set to demolish it, I've got people comin' out of the woodwork to check it out."

Lila gave her a sideways glance while wiping the glass for a better view. She almost laughed out loud at Rose trying to strong-arm a 125-year-old door in her lime-colored capris, sleeveless ribbed sweater, and matching lime ballet flats. She'd wager the door would whip Rose if she didn't want to get inside Miss Pru's so bad.

"Are you serious? Who else is interested besides me? And why are they 'in the know,' when I've gotten nothing but crap from the mayor?" she asked Rose.

"A few people have called over the last week as the deadline got closer. After taking a look at the amount of work this place needs, I guess they decided against it because I haven't heard back from them. Looks like you're the only sucker dumb enough to truly consider signing the bottom line."

The key slid into the lock at last and Rose put a shoulder against the door, pushing it open. Stepping ahead of Lila, she found the switch, and the sudden glare of lights silenced both of them.

It was a disaster. Not just dusty and unkempt, but wires hanging out of the walls, floor tiles peeling back up to reveal the dirty crawl space beneath, and ceiling tins missing or battered with water damage.

Lila stepped carefully around the busted-up remains of a low candy counter and inched closer to the stairs ascending to the second floor.

No way was she chancing it. They would probably give way beneath the extra weight she'd gained succumbing to bread pudding and potato salad over the last few days.

Glass crunched underfoot as Rose stepped farther into the store. "After Goodwin's closed up, kids used to break in through the back door and hang out in here, telling ghost stories, drinking. You know, typical teenage boredom.

"The Goodwins' kids didn't want the place, so it sat here, open to vandalism and neglect until the city acquired it two years ago through condemnation. They've since wised up and decided it was too costly. The plan is to demolish it, making room for a rec center."

Lila tried to ignore the glaring faults, and instead focused on the simple but beautiful Victorian design. The walls were solid brick, and underneath the grit, she detected a warm patina. The ceiling tins were original and with a lot of work and cleaning, could be eye-catching again—in a good way.

A massive oak bar stretched the length of one side of the room. Intricate woodwork full of ivy and elaborate flourishes scrolled across the top of the bar and ran down the sides to the cabinets below. Sturdy pillars graced each side, framing the shattered mirror spanning the twelve feet between.

The bar could be saved, only because it would take an F5 Texas twister to do it damage. She could have the mirror replaced easy enough and, well...the rest would take hard work and skilled contractors. She'd seen worse in Dallas. She could handle one little old candy store.

"I want it." She turned to Rose, who cleaned dust off her ballet flats with a wet wipe. Her head shot up at the Lila's confident tone.

"You do? You haven't even seen upstairs!" Her eyes were wide with surprise. "Don't pull my chain. I'm already going out on a limb by opposing Howard on this."

"Yes. Definitely. I want it. Do you have the paperwork with you?"

Rose glanced away, avoiding eye contact. She swallowed and licked her lips, and then swallowed again. "I guess now would be a good time to tell you the only contractor who can do work on the building is Reverie Construction."

Lila's breath left her chest in a giant whoosh. "What?"

"When the city condemned the building, the contract for demolition was awarded to Jake. But it's been stalled for months and months. Reverie Construction has a lien on the property. The buyer will have to negotiate with Jake first. It's that or nothing, Lila."

Jake. She had to go through her husband if she wanted the building. If they worked together daily, it would provide an opportunity for them to renew the relationship, learn to trust each other again. He would be forced to look at her, talk to her, stand side by side without running the other direction.

Would he do it?

She simply had to convince him.

"It's mine. Don't you dare sell it to one of those other in-terested buyers, or let the mayor send a demolition crew down here. I'll talk to Jake and get this whole thing straightened out."

Rose escaped to the front door with Lila close on her heels. Once outside, she pulled a manila folder and a pen from her briefcase. "Let's get your signature before you wake up and change your mind."

Lila's head spun with the reality of taking on the neglected building as she watched Rose drive away. She didn't have her regular crew of restoration specialists with her in Hannington. They were on other jobs back in Dallas. She'd have to improvise.

Contemplating her options, she rushed over to the IGA to get Granny's supplies before it closed for the evening.

Soda machines greeted shoppers outside the double doors of the grocery, acting as sentry for random bicycles stacked against their dented exteriors.

Lila bypassed a group of overall-clad farmers deep in conversation near the machines. She caught the final volley to what must have been a heated political debate. "I don't give a rat's ass what school Sheriff Williamson hails from, the man can't continue to act like Clint Eastwood on a mission and hope for reelection."

The doors swung closed behind her and the smell of cabbages and fresh meat besieged her senses. Founded by immigrant cattlemen in the 1850s, Hannington stuck to old-world traditions, which meant fresh greens at every meal and the choicest cuts of meat.

Grabbing a handbasket from the carryall stand, she headed to Produce.

"Mrs. Winter?"

Lila heard a deep, masculine voice coming up behind her in the aisle.

"Mrs. Winter?" The voice, more insistent and closer now, stopped directly behind her.

She turned, realizing *she* was Mrs. Winter. Nobody had called her by that name in, how long? Ten years?

Lila looked up into the deepest brown eyes she'd ever seen. He had a tan face with sharp, high cheekbones marking his Native American ancestry. His straight black hair was pulled severely back into a ponytail and dropped behind the width of his shoulders. Shoulders that blocked the entire aisle and anyone attempting to get by. The man was a wall, a human barricade.

"Ah, I think that's me."

He held his hand out. She stared at it for a minute before accepting the shake. His fingers swallowed hers and she felt the unmistakable rasp of work-roughened calluses against her own palm.

"Good to meet you. I'm John Casler."

"Nice to meet you, Mr. Casler." Actually, she didn't know what to think. Who was this man calling her by her married name?

"You can leave off the mister. Call me Casler. Or Takoda."

She didn't think she would be calling him anything, anytime soon. Those brown eyes bore down on her, seeming to search out her truths where she kept them buried, making her uncomfortable.

"Is there something I can help you with, Mr. Casler?" She said, putting emphasis on the "mister."

"Yeah. I just needed to meet Jake's wife in person. I didn't think I would get invited over for a family dinner, so..." He shrugged his shoulders.

Was he Jake's self-appointed bodyguard?

Like the man needed one against his own wife. Oh, hell. Was that it? Was Casler here to keep her away from Jake?

"I wanted to find out what has him in such a pi—ah, awful mood lately," he added finally.

Oh. *Oh.* So Jake was not so indifferent to her presence, then. Lila smiled.

"Well then, as a friend to Jake, Mr. Casler, would you be so kind as to relay a message?"

His eyes flashed suddenly, reminding her of a dark storm building behind a mountain range.

"Casler," he said.

It became a staring contest and she honestly didn't know if she was up to winning. But before she had to back down ungracefully, *Casler* relented.

"Sure, what's the message?"

"I bought the old Goodwin's General Store and we need to talk about his involvement."

"You trying to rope Jake into something he doesn't want to be part of?"

"Casler." She spoke patiently, keeping her voice even and calm. She didn't want to draw attention to herself in the IGA. "I'm not sure what you think is going on, but my presence here is not meant to hurt Jake. Although I appreciate the bulldog routine you've got going. It's his contract, and I just want to talk to him about the project."

He laughed outright, a sharp bark that sent her back a

step into the shelves of cereal.

"I believe you," he said. "It's not the intentions that worry me. It's the damage I'm planning for. When you leave again."

Now she was *irritated*. "Look, we're obviously on the same side. Jake's side. But why don't we leave the decisions to the people involved in this relationship? Like Jake and me?"

He had her backed up against the shelves and unless she wanted to scale him like the wall he was, he would have to back off. "Do you need a command to make you heel? I'd like to get by."

He finally stepped back, waving her forward. His eyes never left her face, but he didn't say a word as she passed.

When she got to the end of the aisle, Lila turned to find him still watching her with wariness. "And the name's Gentry. Lila Gentry, Mr. Casler."

She quickly finished her rounds, her blood still boiling. She hoped she didn't miss anything on Granny's list. If she did, it would have to wait until tomorrow.

She tried not to think of John Casler and whether or not he still lurked somewhere in the store. It seemed that more than one person in the world wanted to protect Jake Winter.

As if the man needed protection. Old fears tried to worm their way into her head. She forced them back, refusing to give in to former insecurities. The litany of old statements echoed in her head, nevertheless.

Jake could do so much better than Lila Gentry. What'd she do to get him to marry her, blackmail him? She's after his family's money and his good name.

She'd heard them all that summer she and Jake married. And they'd hurt to the core. It wasn't until therapy years later that she really understood just how much they'd eaten away at her confidence and sense of self-worth. Shame, the therapist had labeled it. Excruciating vulnerability.

The young woman behind the checkout glanced down at her battered bag of bagels. "This don't look so good. You want me to call for another?"

"No, I battered it, I'll take it," she said, discouraging further attention. She didn't want any more excitement today.

The cashier shrugged and passed the bag across the scanner.

Lila wrote a check for the total and handed it over, anxious to put distance between herself and Casler.

The cashier's pregnant belly swelled above the counter and the woman placed a protective hand over the mound as she leaned forward across the low counter to examine the check. Lila felt a slight pinch in her chest. She would not be jealous of this poor pregnant woman, working for minimum wage, in the tiny town of Hannington!

So why did she choose that moment to touch her own flat stomach?

"This is an out-of-town check."

She looked blankly at the woman, hoping to encourage an explanation for the obvious statement. "It is," she said finally, realizing the conversation was going nowhere.

"I can't accept out-of-town checks. I'll have to get the manager." She pushed back from the counter before Lila could stop her, grabbing the store intercom microphone roughly by the neck. "Check approval on two!"

Lila smiled apologetically at the man in line behind her. And she spotted John Casler standing two people back.

He shifted his bread and beer to the other arm and smiled slowly, letting her know she'd won. For the moment.

She scanned the faces around him, noting the barely veiled looks of scorn and wariness the other shoppers cast his way. Casler pretended not to notice and kept smiling at her. And only at her. But Lila knew he sensed their disapproval. She could tell by his slightly flaring nostrils and rigid posture.

Looked like she and the man had more in common than a friendship with Jake. He apparently knew a little bit about being an outcast, too.

Facing forward again, she saw the manager lumber out of the customer service booth, making his way to the register. He wore a faded green apron, smeared with dirty streaks of red, which Lila hoped were not bloodstains.

He stood next to the cashier examining the highly suspicious document on the counter. Lila's check.

The manager's head shot up suddenly, his brown eyes pinning her across the checkout counter. *Oh, hell, here it comes.*

"Are you Barbara Gentry's granddaughter?"

"I am."

"I didn't recognize you. It's been a while."

Ten years. "It has."

A moment of silence reigned as Lila committed a sin against good Texas manners: she didn't small-talk. Guilt and doubt threatened to choke her, she wanted to be gracious and polite, but she simply wasn't ready.

Not with Casler standing there, watching her from the back of the line. She needed more time to regain her balance, her poise, and her backbone. She was at the mercy of Hannington, under a giant microscope with the entire town picking her apart. Sweat trickled down her back.

She threw off the mantle of doubts and plastered a smile on her face. "I'm visiting Granny and helping her out while she has a broken arm"—she read the name on his manager tag—"Randy. It's good to see you again. How's your family?"

He proceeded to tell her about his mother, the town librarian Lila remembered as mean and rail-thin, while he took down the vitals off her license.

"This check is good." He passed it back to the cashier who rang it in. "I heard you're gonna buy that ole candy store across the street."

Good grief, news traveled fast in this town.

"Yes." She smiled at Randy, hoping he'd get a clue from her one-word answer.

"Lotta interestin' history turning up lately. I heard the ole gal that once ran a whorehouse there married a big rancher around here. Pierce. Big cattleman back in the day. Course, mosta the ranch has been divvied up, but it useta be a big place, way back when."

Pru mentioned Pierce in her journal, but Lila didn't remember reading anything about the two marrying.

Could this guy be right?

"That's interesting. I'd like to research the history of the building and its former owners. Do you know where can I get more information about this rancher?" She hoped he wouldn't say the library, and if so, she hoped his mother wasn't still the librarian.

Randy rubbed his jaw, thinking. "I'd go talk to Threasa Thompson. She owns a small ranch outside of town. From what I hear, part of her place used to belong to this Pierce guy."

Threasa Thompson. Lila remembered her vaguely from high school: a tall, thin, quiet girl who missed a lot of school to help her grandfather with his ranch. The same ranch?

The checker wadded the receipt, dropped it in one of the bags, and pushed them across the counter to Lila. It was time to go.

"I'll do that. Thanks so much for your help, Randy." She smiled at the manager and lifted her bags off the counter.

She felt a pair of hot brown eyes follow her outside. When she was across the parking lot and in the square, she breathed easier.

Luke Pierce. She whispered the name as she walked.

Had he really married Prudence? A rich cattle baron and a prostitute? Not outside the realm of possibility, but never in her family history had she run across anything so interesting.

It appeared her job in Hannington had taken on a new twist. Win back estranged husband. Make the town like her again. And find out what happened to one Prudence MacIntosh *and* one Luke Pierce.

Lesson Number Six —

All people are scared on the inside. Bluff your way to confidence. Eventually, you will become confident, and men like women who know what they want. Trust me.

Chapter Eight

The handles of the plastic grocery bags dug painfully into Lila's palms. Her sandals slapped against the asphalt, her feet feeling heavier with each step. It was going to be a long walk back to her grandmother's in the late-evening heat. To distract herself, she thought about the early entry she'd read that morning in Pru's journal.

> *The man had hair like a woman.*
>
> *That was what I had been hearing for the last couple of months. But today, I saw for myself.*
>
> *"Where can a paying man get a decent drink 'round here?"*
>
> *Luke Pierce pushed through the swinging doors of the Two Nellies saloon and stood at the entrance, his arms draped over the tops of the curved shutters. I thought an eclipse was in progress until I turned and saw him standing there, blocking the sunlight. He surveyed the card tables and serving girls with a quick,*

calculating eye.

The man must have been six foot and a half, if not taller. His hair was indeed long. It hung loose and free around his shoulders, an enviable chestnut color. He had just come from the bathhouse down the street. No one could appear that fresh and cool in this heat.

A tiny pang of jealousy lodged in my heart upon seeing him. To enjoy the freedom of wearing your hair down, not confined beneath a cap or nailed to the scalp with pins, must be heavenly.

I may be a woman of questionable virtue, but I wore my hair up during the day as any self-respecting woman did.

There was some commotion among the smaller, shiftier variety in the saloon with Luke's arrival. I assumed they were nervous, and rightly so. It was rumored Luke Pierce was a master card player and an unrivaled marksman. He did not lose when he played, or if he did, nobody ever lived to tell about it.

"You come to the right place, sugar." The hurdy-gurdy girl known as Little Sally extricated herself from the arms of a local and sauntered in his direction, her two-bit smile as wide as it could get without revealing her missing front tooth.

The harlot. When she was not turning tricks, she was unconscious in the opium shack on the edge of town. She refused help of any kind with her addiction, content to languish in a hazy stupor.

Luke ignored her, giving her a wide berth as he strode up to the counter. Each footstep pounded against the pine boards of the pockmarked floor, jarring through the soles of my satin-heeled slippers.

Lord, he was a huge bear of a man, complete with a brown wool suit. It stretched across his body, straining at the seams to cover his endowed frame. The suit makers surely grinned with glee when Luke paid them a visit; all the material required to cover the man them a visit; all the material required to cover the man boggled the mind.

I was behind the bar, pouring the usual rotgut into clean glasses, when his eyes fell on me. They were light brown, a rich whiskey color. The expensive kind, not the watered-down swill we served here.

He smiled, and the ends of his heavy mustache lifted, easing the look of criminal intent on his lined face.

If I did not know better, I would have said he was working with Bill Cody out of Wyoming. He had that dangerous, unpredictable showmanship air about him.

But Luke Pierce was a cattleman, a baron to rival all Texas cattle barons. I heard tell his herd stretched farther than the eye could see, and as I discovered upon arrival in town, the naked eye could see for miles.

He was not handsome in the refined, upper-class sense, although his clothes were as rich as any gentleman's. It was his devil-may-care attitude that lit him from inside.

I have to admit I was most curious about Luke Pierce.

"And who are you?" His voice was belly deep and sounded ill-used. A cigar smoker, maybe. Or perhaps all the smoky-backroom high-stakes poker games men *of his station liked to play had worn his voice.*

I looked down the bar to see Thomas Blevins, the owner of the booze house, give me a nod. I knew the routine without him telling me. Rich customer. Give 'em whatever he wanted.

That was usually my motto too, but I was more discriminating with my customers than Blevins. I did not play cute with every cowboy who walked through the door.

Luke was still waiting for my answer when I turned back. "Prudence," I said at last, knowing where this conversation would lead, but curious despite myself.

It elicited a giant knee-slapping laugh from the bear of a man.

A prostitute named Prudence was often a source of hilarity around here.

The flecks of yellow in his eyes sparked with amusement. "Prudence! You're the best-looking thing I've seen all day. Come and have a drink with me."

He slapped a large bill on the bar and shoved it in my direction.

Yup. Just as I expected. Why should this man be any different from the others? I was a working gal, and payment was expected.

But something about this good-natured, long-haired, jovial man dressed in a wool suit struck me. Struck me as right, in spite of the money on the bar. I felt comfortable with his eyes on me. Comfortable in his presence.

Safe.

Why hadn't she taken the car? *Because Jake had implied she'd gained weight.* Lila hated to admit her rear might be a tad larger than when he last saw it. Though it might be bigger, she comforted herself with the thought it was all muscle. She'd worked hard over the last couple of years to keep herself in shape.

But did he care? Oh, he'd been looking. She'd caught his eyes dropping to check her out. Whether he acted on the interest was a whole other story.

Lila huffed along, juggling bags from hand to hand, hoping the weight would shift and let the blood circulate. It didn't.

Stopping on the sidewalk under the shade of a large pecan tree, she set her burden down, allowing her reddened palms to rest. A hot breeze lifted the blond tendrils of hair around her face.

From behind her she heard a truck slow and roll to a stop. Afraid to turn, Lila stared at the rough bark of the giant tree. It could be anyone, perhaps the owner of the house beyond the pecan? But she had a tickle of giddiness in her belly that it was neither. The tickle that meant Jake was near.

"Hope you don't have ice cream in those bags." Jake's lazy tone drifted across on the breeze.

Her heart beat painfully and her belly tightened. Would she ever outgrow this physical reaction? Lila turned to face her husband. He relaxed behind the wheel of his truck, an arm propped against the outside of his door. His hair looked wind-blown, pushed back from his face in disarray. If she squinted, the truck disappeared and she could imagine him in her bed, his hair messy and his skin hot from an afternoon of lovemaking.

His gaze took her in.

The bottom of her stomach fell and a rush of desire went straight south.

"You don't, do you?"

Grappling with a flood of emotions that screamed *Please hold me,* she'd forgotten the question. "Don't what?"

"Have ice cream? It's going to melt in this heat." His brows rose in question, seemingly unaware of her discomfort.

"No. But I've got chicken livers that need to be refrigerated."

He looked down at her purchases but didn't ask. "You want a ride back to Barbara's?"

The question was simple. Did she want a ride? She practically jumped up and down right there on the sidewalk considering the prospect. Being cloistered in the cab of a truck with Jake Winter brought back memories. They'd steamed up many a cab window after they were first married.

But that was then, before their spilt. She'd have to work extra hard to get him to overlook their past, and this might be the opportunity to get close. To lay a soft hand on his thigh. To brush her shoulder against his. To stare at his mouth when he spoke and lick her lips.

Yeah, it might be fighting dirty, but she had to take 'em as they came. Anything to convince him they deserved a second chance.

He eased from behind the wheel and stepped around the hood of his truck to stare at her. His eyes fell to her sandals and traveled back up again, lingering on her chest in a familiar, possessive gesture.

He had attitude, and it broadcast loud and clear in the

way he moved. Like a man confident in his skin. In everything he did, conscious or not. She knew from experience most of it was unconscious, although he could ratchet it up for more effect when he wanted.

Lila felt a trickle of sweat slide between her breasts. Yes, this was exactly what she wanted. What she needed. Now if the man would simply kiss her!

"You sure you don't have anything sweet to eat?" His tone implied teasing, but her temper ignited. She was hot, turned on by a man who claimed they had nothing in common anymore—if they had nothing in common, why was the front of his jeans tight and why was her breathing shallow and labored? And all while standing on a public sidewalk with half the town driving by.

She had to think hard to form a coherent sentence. "No, nothing sweet. I've got to watch my weight, you know."

His head lifted, meeting her gaze. He smiled again and shook his head. "Well, let's get Nate his livers."

Lila climbed into the truck after the bags were settled on the cab seat squarely between them. He did it intentionally. It couldn't have been clearer that he wanted her to stay on her side of the truck than if he'd said the words out loud.

"How do you know the livers are for the cat?" She asked in an offhand manner, but the idea that Jake knew more about Granny's life than she did stung.

He pulled the truck away from the curb and turned on a shower of icy air. "Whenever Mom butchers chickens, she saves a few livers for Barbara and I take them over to her."

"Oh." She stared straight ahead through the front window, feigning interest in the passing scenery, but the heat curling off his body had her stomach in knots. God. He smelled good. It reminded her of early Sunday mornings, naked, under cool cotton sheets.

She curled her hands into fists to keep them off him. She wanted those Sunday mornings back. She wanted to stroke her feet over his, feel the rasp of his hairy shins as he wrapped his legs around hers, the comfort and security in his whole body embrace.

Jake cleared his throat. "What's the diagnosis on Barbara, anyway? She due to live another thirty years?" There was a standing joke about Barbara Gentry in town. People predicted she'd outlive most of the Bombshells, as well as most of the town.

"She'll be fine as long as she slows down and allows that shoulder to heal."

She saw him glance over at her from the corner of her eye. "You up for that?"

She turned to face him, her emotions controlled. "What?"

He resumed his watch over the road ahead, his expression no longer lazy. "You've never been able to handle sickbeds or the people in them."

Her heart wounded at the accusation in his words, her gaze snapped back to the front. What he brought up occurred years ago, when she was a young, newly married woman barely out of high school. She hadn't known how to cope then. Why couldn't he give her a break? Give them a break?

"Jake, I was eighteen at the time. I was scared. My husband was in the hospital." They had no idea at the time that his weight loss and lack of appetite were preliminary symptoms of something worse. Much worse.

Her explanation met silence. She peeked across the seat; his profile was hard and uncompromising in the glare of the afternoon sun.

"I didn't mean to run out on you that night, but I was scared witless, terrified you were going to die on me."

"So instead of letting me help you, you fled."

Her body rocked with the steel under his words. "How could you help me? You were the one in the hospital bed."

"We could have talked. You should have told me what you were feeling."

She hadn't. Not at first, too wrapped up in what he was feeling. What he was enduring.

After that night, the accusations came with increasing severity over the next year. She couldn't handle commitment, he said. Couldn't handle the day-to-day uncertainties life dished out. She was married to a man with Hodgkin's disease, who might not live to old age. They had no business being married, he'd said.

No business being married. God, it had almost killed her when he said that. For years afterward, she sometimes wished it had been her with the diagnosis. If it had been the other way around and she'd been the one to get sick, they might have made it. As a couple.

After Jake came home from the hospital, he closed up, shut himself off from her. He wouldn't allow her to comfort him, or even accompany him to the doctor's office. With her background chock full of insecurities and low self-esteem, she'd bought into his objections, fell prey to her shame, thinking he knew what was right for the both of them.

Bottom line, he didn't want her anymore. Couldn't afford

the attachment, he claimed. And after a year of living as strangers, Lila left.

Not to return for ten long years.

Jake turned his truck into the drive of the white bungalow at 534 Priddy Drive. Granny sat in a lounge chair on the front porch drinking iced tea. Steve Ann reclined in an adjacent chaise longue, flipping through a magazine.

She'd get it now. No way would Granny let this one alone. Coming home with Jake in tow was fodder for the gossip mill. She hadn't exactly told her grandmother yet she wanted to patch things up with Jake. Though the sharp old matron wouldn't miss a beat.

"There's the old lady now. I'd better say hello." He opened the driver's door despite Lila's negative hiss.

He grabbed the bags, savoring the silent challenge with a quirk of his lips he threw her way. He eased from the truck and slammed the door in her face. "Barbara, my girl, how the hell are you?"

She could hear his voice clearly, full of easy Texas charm. He bent low, kissing Granny on the cheek.

Why couldn't he do that to Lila?

Granny wrapped her good arm around Jake, rubbing his back like a familiar child. "Fine now that you're here."

Lila watched from inside the truck. The cool air dissipated in the encroaching heat.

Jake stood and disappeared in the house with the grocery bags, Granny close behind.

She couldn't sit in here and watch the reunion like an idiot! Grumbling, she jumped from the truck and grabbed her pocketbook, throwing the strap across her shoulder. In her haste, the fastener on the leather wallet sprung loose, spilling the contents of her financial life onto the driveway.

Bending to retrieve flyaway business cards, she didn't see Jake's shadow fall across her for several seconds.

She saw his scuffed leather work boots first. They stood directly on top of a postcard advertising free panties with a purchase. She followed the crease of his faded jeans up to the vee of his thighs. The familiar bulge made her face flush. Made her fingers itch to touch. Her eyes flew the rest of the way to his face.

"I'm appreciating the view as well." He wiggled his eyebrows in the direction of the gaping neckline of her cotton T-shirt, taking advantage of her position.

If she really thought he meant what he said, she'd stay down there forever. Let him look all he wanted. But she knew he was only teasing.

"Can I collect my things?" She pointed an index finger to some business cards beneath the toe of his boot.

He squatted until his face came level with hers.

Lila could smell him. Clean, strong, and so totally male. He moved his boot, and before she could react, he scooped the card up, holding it out for inspection.

"Victoria's Secret?" He read the title. "Shop there often?"

What should she say? Yes? In the hope he would come swooping into Dallas and carry her off to bed? Three straight days in bed might satisfy her initial lust. Maybe.

Not that it was likely to happen.

"And if I do?" she queried, almost out of breath.

"You must be making some guy's night. That's for sure." He handed her the card and stood, looking off across the street.

No, no guy had shared a night with her in a very long time. The only person who'd seen her silkies lately was Fiona, her Maine coon cat.

Lila stood, confused—and dammit, irritated—by his sudden distance.

"Y'all gonna stand out here all night, or are you gonna come inside for some iced tea?" Steve Ann's voice broke the mood and Lila looked to the nurse on the porch.

"Mrs. Gentry wants you to fix dinner, Lila. And Mr. Winter, she wants you to stay."

Lila strode to the front door, anger making her brave. She added an exaggerated swing to her hips, rolling those muscles she'd worked so hard for. She claimed her glass from Steve Ann's outstretched hand and took a long, deliberate drink, licking any trace of moisture from her lips.

"Uh-huh, that must be some damn fine iced tea Mrs. Gentry got in her kitchen." The nurse's comment was low enough to reach Lila's ears only and she cast a sideways glance at Steve Ann. In that second they exchanged an intimate assessment of the situation.

"Okay. I'm getting my things." The woman knew how to take a hint.

She hoped Jake took note.

The door to his truck wrenched open.

Looking across the drive, she saw Jake slide behind the wheel. Disappointment soured in her mouth and spiraled down her belly until she thought she might yell. Anything to stop him from leaving.

"Tell Barbara I can't stay for dinner." He nodded his head

and turned the key in the ignition, filling the drive with the purr of the engine. Lila watched him pull away and point the truck south, back into town. As much as she wanted to drag herself away and step inside the cool foyer of her grandmother's house like his brush-off didn't matter, she couldn't.

And she didn't even get around to asking him about Miss Pru's!

Lesson Number Seven —

Men love a nearly naked woman. They also love admiring a woman dressed in risqué clothing. Wearing the latter will ensure you get to the first, quickest.

Chapter Nine

Jake barely saw the road ahead. His gaze turned inward, to the cowardly way he'd left his wife standing on her grandmother's front porch. She'd looked exactly like she had when he'd returned from his first bout of chemotherapy. Full of hope and love. And unbelievably beautiful in a short denim skirt and peach tank top. Her sun-kissed skin glowed like gold and every time he got near, he couldn't help but run a palm over her shoulder, down her back, or up under her skirt.

And then he went and ruined it.

He reminded her of the remission that day, the uncertain state of his health, and the possibility the cancer would return in the future to claim him.

He made his uncertainty a certainty. Sacrificing their love to keep her safe. Undamaged. And emotionally whole.

And he didn't just remind her of it once. He'd done it over days and months, until the time had stretched into a year, and finally Lila couldn't handle it anymore. Her willingness, ah,

Christ, her open sexuality hadn't been enough to douse his pain. His worry. Of someday leaving her alone.

So he'd pushed her. And she left. He'd all but packed her bags and made her do it.

"Son of a bitch." The memory of her crestfallen features burned the back of his eyes.

Why'd she have to come home? Just when he'd stopped thinking of her every minute of every day, she'd walked back into his life, resurrecting painful memories. Physical needs. Making him agonizingly aware of what he'd given up, then and now. And goddammit, did he want it all back with a fury he didn't expect.

Her behavior indicated a coyness, a more mature sexual awareness he didn't remember in his young wife. The thought it might be due to the tutelage of another man replayed endlessly in his head, pissing him off.

Lila in the arms of another man. He evoked the image, punishing himself. Lila's mouth open in ecstasy, her legs wrapped around another man's waist, and her fingers gripping his neck in passion.

He slammed on the brakes and threw the truck into park alongside an empty patch of asphalt. He jerked open the door and jumped out of the cab, his fists clenched, ready to battle an unseen enemy. He strode off the blacktop of the county road, kicking up dust behind him.

He had to regain control. He wasn't going to survive her visit if he got worked up each time she shook her hips in his direction.

"Jake! What the hell are you doing?"

Turning, he saw Otis Wells hanging out the driver's-side

window of his pickup. A perplexed look twisted his work-worn features.

Just what he needed. A lecture from the man who was the closest thing to a father Lila had in Hannington. Old Otis didn't look like father material with his gruff appearance and whiplike tongue, but when Michael Gentry didn't return from an overseas military tour to care for his baby daughter, Otis stepped in to fill his shoes. He played the part with all of his heart, bursting with pride over Lila's successes back in Dallas. And Jake had heard about each and every one over the years.

Like the time Lila landed her first big project with the City of Dallas to renovate a pair of historic buildings as offices for administrative staff, and then when the Dallas League of Women Business Professionals named her entrepreneur of the year. And he couldn't forget the time she made the cover of *D Magazine*. Otis left copies lying all over the construction site, and in his car. Hell, they were all over the town.

Jake kept his own copies locked away in a bedroom drawer. But he never told Otis. And he sure as hell wouldn't tell Lila.

Exhaling his frustration, he strode around the hood of his truck and crossed the yellow dividing line to Otis.

"I thought I saw a brown recluse in my truck."

Otis's slightly bulging eyes widened at the mention of the deadly fiddleback spider common to Central Texas.

"Crap! Did you kill it?" Otis inspected him, looking for visible signs of a bite.

"No. I didn't find it. Must have been seeing things."

Otis didn't have any reason to believe Jake made it up, but the puzzled look on his face said volumes. He needed to head Otis off before he started asking questions Jake didn't want to answer. "What are you doing out here? It's kinda late, isn't it? Anything going on at the job site I need to know about?"

"Yeah," Otis said, raising his arms in frustration, "Jenna Hillcrest came to check on the progress this evening and started ranting about the lighting. Said it wasn't recessed enough to create the mood she wanted. Casler about choked her. She's got all the work stopped and demanding you come take a look at the screwup yourself."

More women. Not what he wanted at the moment. "I'll get in touch with her and smooth things out."

"Damn straight," Otis said, nodding his head sharply. "We can't get nothin' done until you deal with her."

The bald head ducked back into the cab and Jake didn't hear another word from Otis as he punched the gas and flew down the road.

Following the dust trail, Jake headed back to town, ignoring the persistent voice in the back of his mind urging him to accept what Lila so obviously offered.

To let her push him back on the bed, unzip his pants, and climb on top sans panties, and slide down until he rested fully inside her.

God. How many times had they done that? Too many to count, though not enough to last him a lifetime.

But to do so again was to open himself up to the pain of unpredictability. Cancer patients couldn't count on grandchildren or retirement. If the chemo hadn't made him sterile, what guarantee did he have he'd live long enough to see his kids graduate?

Lila lifted the deviled egg platter with her free hand and carried it and a bowl of baked beans to the dining room buffet. When Granny said the Bombshells were coming over for a visit, Lila had been excited and started cooking immediately. She couldn't remember the last time she'd seen her grandmother's old friends. In a way, the ladies were like additional grannies, always looking out for her and offering advice.

Sometimes bad advice, but she still appreciated it.

Surveying the sideboard now loaded with pickled okra, fresh tomatoes, fried chicken, and coleslaw, she worried maybe she'd made too much food. Could a group of grandmothers eat so much?

She rearranged dishes, making room for the new additions. Behind her, dominoes slapped against the hardwood of the dining table with an unexpected aggressiveness.

"Lila, how's the interior design job?" said Agnes Mitchell, a sweet purple-haired lady who regularly rolled a game of 270 and insisted Lila was an interior designer. As one of her granny's oldest friends, she didn't have the heart to correct the woman every time she asked about "the job," so she let it go, along with Mildred Hughes's suggestion she wear more cherry-red lipstick and tight halter tops.

"Really well. I contracted for the renovations—"

"Lila, have you seen Jake since you've been in town?" Mildred's eyes, framed by sky-blue shadow, gleamed with mischief over the top of her wadded Kleenex, which she kept perpetually up her nose.

The other Bombshells sat straighter in their chairs, alert to any tidbit of gossip.

Lila gritted her teeth and kept smiling.

"Oh, good grief, yes! She's seen him. He was here yesterday dropping Lila off from the IGA. He brought in Nate's cat livers and said he'd fix the toilet in the guest bath tomorrow." Granny spoke up, grabbing the attention of the domino gang with infinite finesse.

"He'll be here tomorrow to fix the toilet?" Lila repeated. He hadn't mentioned anything to her about the work.

Granny leaned over the table, holding her dominoes like an old pro: three in the left hand, two in the right. Her mouth turned down in sudden concern.

"Honey, do you need to see Doc Smigel about a hearing aid?" The ladies swiveled their heads in unison, gazing at Lila with barely contained curiosity. "I told you yesterday we needed to have someone look at the commode."

Lila tried to act like she didn't care, but the thought of him in the house sent her blood racing. Was he finding ways to see her? She didn't want to hope, but what else should she think? That he really had time to fix the toilet?

"Hon, you should wear something tight and clingy when he comes over tomorrow." Mildred switched out the older yellow tissue for a fresh pink number.

She frowned. "I'm sorry?"

"You know, wear something that dips low in the front and cuddles the rear in the back. Men are suckers for a tight rear, and you got one, my dear."

Seduce Jake here? In her granny's house?

Her heart pounded and her mouth dropped open. She looked from Mildred to Granny, disbelief paralyzing her vocal cords.

"Lila's got plenty of ass-huggin' outfits." Granny patted Mildred's arm and laid a double-six domino on the table, bringing her score up another thirty points.

"Granny!" Lila's voice croaked.

Barbara Gentry's cornflower-blue eyes met hers, all innocence.

"We're all women here. Don't act like such a prude, Lila. If you want Jake back, you're going to have to fight for him. And that means pulling out all the stops. Use what God put in your arsenal. Knock his eyes out."

Dropping into the empty side chair, Lila attempted to gather her tattered dignity. "Who said I was trying to win Jake back?"

"Oh, sweetie," Alta Meyers said in a let-me-comfort-you voice. Her red nails clicked together as she shuffled the pile of bones for the next round. "You may be able to fool those ding-dongs in Dallas, but we've been around a while. There's nothing finer by your side or in your bed than a good man. And you're missing both."

"Amen." A chorus rang around the table.

Was it so obvious, then? Did everyone except Jake know why she'd returned to Hannington?

Lila grabbed two deviled eggs off the sideboard and gobbled them down before the inner hound reminded her of the size of her rear, which Mildred thought was so tight. Compared to ladies in their seventies, it was indeed tight.

So why didn't he want her back?

Before she could ponder the wise decision of seeking advice on her love life from Granny's bowling team, she blurted out, "So why does he act like he's not interested, then?"

Agnes excused herself from the table, making her way

to the open bathroom door down the hall. Her words floated behind her.

"He's been a bachelor since you moved to Dallas. You can't expect a man to give up freedom so easily. He has to be convinced."

Granny frowned over Mildred's first play. They were partners, but the other woman continued to lay down dominoes that didn't score.

"I think what Agnes is trying to say is that Jake needs to be persuaded. Your reappearance reminds him of a lot of things, not just your marriage." Granny lifted her scorekeeping pencil and scratched delicately at the scalp beneath the fresh hairdo. Not a hair moved beneath the helmet of hair spray. Mary Jo the stylist was good, almost worth her weight in gold.

"But he's been well, no sign of the cancer. Not since I left."

"That's what I mean. Not since you were here. Those are painful memories for both of you. He might need more time cozying up to the idea, is all," Granny said.

"Oh."

"Good sex makes a man forget almost anything!" Agnes's voice echoed off the pink tile in the bath and out the open door.

Lila chose to ignore the last comment for a variety of reasons. Standing, she seized another deviled egg off the platter and headed toward the back door. "Thanks for the advice. Ladies. I'll let you get back to your game."

Mildred waved the shredded pink tissue at her. "Anytime."

"Maybe you should call the little lady back, Jake. She said she wants to talk about the Goodwin building."

Jake looked up from the blueline machine where he ran copies of his blueprints.

"Let me worry about it. And stop harassing her in the grocery store, for God's sake."

He'd heard about Lila's run-in with Casler, not from her, but from the store's manager, Randy. The man had all but run across the street when he'd seen Jake to tell him the story.

He didn't like Casler playing the heavy when the guy was actually nothing but a puppy dog. And besides, he certainly didn't need a go-between for him and Lila.

"It would be a bitch of a job, no doubt, but would pay through the ass."

"Stop sweet-talkin' me. You might convince me to take it," he told Casler as he lined up the blue chalk–coated line, setting the machine for his copies.

"Well, sounds like she's gonna do the job whether you help her or not. I just figured there might be something in it for me."

He wasn't fooling Jake for a minute with all his blustering. Casler couldn't care less about the money. It was the challenge he enjoyed. And if it meant he could give the city council the finger while doing it, Casler was all for it.

"She can't do the first thing until I release the lien on the building."

So why hadn't he? And why had he been avoiding her calls? For the same reason he lied to Casler now. He still had it bad for little Lila Gentry.

He looked up from his blueprints to find Casler's attention

drawn outside through the plate glass window. He followed his gaze to Threasa Thompson heading in their direction.

The woman was all grace and understated beauty with long, long legs and willowy arms. She had her hair back in a ponytail and a baseball cap pulled down low over her eyes.

Jake looked at Casler. Casler kept watching Threasa. Jake cleared his throat. Casler didn't notice.

He shook his head and returned to his blueprints. "You're a dumbass if you don't ask her out," he told him over his shoulder.

"Shit," Casler said under his breath. Jake heard the bell on the front door ding as it opened and he saw Threasa walk in. She didn't notice them at first, but headed for the counter where she talked to Bob, the owner of the copy shop.

"What's she doing here?" Casler whispered.

Jake looked at him. "Go ask her."

Casler stood there, his feet rooted to the floor. Just as Jake reached to push his shoulder, Threasa turned and saw them.

A blush crept up her face and spread across her checks, giving her pale complexion a glow. She smiled and waved, and headed in their direction.

"Hi, Threasa. How are things at the ranch?" Stupid ice-breaker, but Casler needed some help with his mouth shut like his lips were glued together.

"Going okay at the moment. Just needed to get some copies of these specs. I need some work done in one of the barns."

"Well, you know we'd help you out and cut you a friend price," he told her.

Threasa glanced at Casler, but still he said nothing.

"It would have to be a real friendly price for me to be able to afford Reverie Construction," she said, laughing.

"I could do it during my down hours," Casler interjected, surprising them both. Jake had been hoping he'd chime in. He hadn't thought the man so dense he couldn't take the hints Jake had laid out for him.

The statement caught Threasa off guard and she gaped at him while the silence stretched out among the three of them.

Jake considered returning his attention to his blueprints to give the two of them some semblance of privacy. He hadn't seen a more awkward couple since his days in high school.

"Well, ah, John, that's a real nice offer," she said, flustered and looking anywhere but at Casler. "Let me think about it and I'll let you know."

"Whatever. Just thought I'd offer. I got plenty to keep me busy."

He pushed past her, and Jake watched him walk out the front door and head in the opposite direction of their work truck.

Casler did not take rejection well.

"Oh, I hope I didn't offend him, Jake," Threasa said, clearly upset over the idea she had. "I just meant I wasn't sure if I could afford it. I need to check with the bank to see if they'll extend my line of credit."

"Don't worry about him, Threasa. His bark is way worse than his bite. He'll warm up to it and see the light."

Threasa gave him a puzzled look and said good-bye, leaving Jake to consider his own words.

Yeah. Talk about seeing the light. That described his relationship with Lila and what he needed to do to convince her to give up this idea of converting the Goodwin building and making a move back to Hannington.

Lesson Number Eight —

Sometimes, taking charge in the relationship will get you what you want. Even if it does not, your man will notice the effort.

Chapter Ten

Lila watched Steve Ann drive away with Granny strapped into the passenger seat. With the toilet broken and Granny off to the doctor, she was left behind to meet Jake. Alone. In the house where they'd first made love as teenagers. In her old room, on the very bed she'd slept in since coming back.

Did she smell a setup? Lord, she loved her Granny. The woman played matchmaker, guardian angel, and endangered landmark protector all at once.

The anticipation of being alone with Jake broke her out in a sweat.

Glancing down at the fire ant mound at the edge of the curb, the Bombshells' advice from yesterday rang in her ears. *Seduce him.*

Racing back inside, she jerked open her closet and examined the neatly hung rows of shorts, skirts, blouses, and pantsuits. *What to wear?* She wanted to look sexy and experienced. Jake had already seen the young, green girl she'd been in high school.

She stood frozen, realizing for the first time none of her clothes were appropriate for catching a man. It simply wasn't the image she portrayed back in Dallas. Educated, chic, and experienced, yes. But sexy, available, and ready for an afternoon romp? No.

Pulling out the dresser drawers, she prayed for something better. The only thing remotely sexy was a pair of thigh-highs. She wasn't quite ready to meet Jake at her Granny's front door in nothing but thigh-highs.

Oh, but definitely later. If they got to later.

Besides, what if he looked her over and said, "No thanks?"

Throwing the terrible thought from her mind, she scurried out of her skirt and camisole. She had fairly nice legs, tan from the hot Texas sun. She needed something showing leg, arousing, but practical in the heat.

Granny said she'd boxed some of her old clothes up and put them on the top shelf in the closet. She had no idea what it might contain, but surely she'd find something. Hell, better yet, a T-shirt a couple sizes too small would be perfect. She'd even be stylish. That and no bra.

She struggled with the box, spilling the contents onto the bed. Sure enough, several pairs of old Levi cutoffs and some faded T-shirts tumbled out.

The doorbell rang.

Lila glanced at her bedside clock. It had to be him. She grabbed the first pair of shorts on top of the pile and wriggled into them, covering her pink lace thong.

They still buttoned. *Thank God*. Her rear wasn't that big.

Giving her reflection a cursory glance in the mirror over

the dresser, she unhooked her bra and tossed it into the closet.

Which T-shirt? Did it matter?

The doorbell sounded a second time.

She pulled a faded blue one from the pile and shoved the rest of the mess onto the floor on the other side of the bed where it wouldn't be seen.

Just in case. In case they needed the bed.

Stopping in front of the mirror, she tousled her hair, put some shine on her lips, and added a smile. And vowed to keep the talking to a minimum. They needed sex to break the ice. Talking could come later.

She rushed to the front door, kicking off her sandals as she reached for the knob. Jake had already backtracked to his truck when she came out onto the porch. "Hey, sorry about that. I was out back and didn't hear the bell."

He turned at the sound of her voice and his stride broke. His eyes narrowed as he took her in. Lila's chest swelled with the intensity of his gaze and she thrust her breasts forward with a subtle arch of her back.

"Where's Barbara?" His voice tightened. She noticed the growing bulge in his jeans. She felt her own response to his appraisal slide deliciously between her thighs.

"Doctor's appointment in Temple. Steve Ann took her."

He said nothing, but returned to his truck, grabbing the toolbox from the back. He climbed the porch and avoided her gaze. She noticed his white-knuckle grip on the handle.

Her control slipped. Brushing her off wouldn't be an option this time. She stepped in front of his advancing body and was almost singed by the heat rolling off him. He stopped short of colliding with her chest.

Dammit. "Glad to see you, too." She smiled, hoping to ease the tension and add some play to this experience. "Come in and I'll fix some iced tea."

His eyes shone like hard emeralds and she felt them pierce her here and there. Tension edged the corners of his full mouth. He swiped a hand through his dark hair, pushing it back from his forehead.

At least she got a reaction out of him. Not to mention how her body bent and bowed to get closer to his.

"I have to be back at the job site. I don't have time for tea."

He reached behind her for the handle to the glass door and Lila stepped into him as she turned, her breast and hardened nipple grazing his inner elbow.

A current of electric awareness shot through her. A lovely zing she hadn't felt in forever.

Jake's sharp intake of breath indicated he didn't feel as immune as he seemed. The tiny clue bolstered her resolve and she followed him into the house.

Jake stormed into the bathroom, slamming his toolbox on the countertop.

What the hell did she think she was doing? If she had any idea what he wanted to do with her body right now, she'd run the other way.

He'd been relieved when no one answered the door, providing him the perfect excuse to send a workman out later to fix the commode. But then she'd stepped out onto the porch looking like the old Lila. Her golden hair, loose and hanging in disarray around her shoulders. The rounded form of her breasts, outlined under the thin cotton of her shirt, and her tan thighs made his hands itch. He ached to open those thighs and lose himself between their soft, satiny skin. To drive into her until he had no sense of self, but only a sense of them. Together.

She glided in the bathroom behind him, bringing her soft scent into the tiny room, filling his nostrils with the remembered smell.

Much more of this and he would toss all of his resolutions he'd fought to make and sustain right out the window.

He concentrated on the contents of his toolbox to no effect. He'd forgotten what he needed to fix a toilet.

"You sure you don't want anything to drink?" Her voice, husky and very close to his ear, kicked his blood pressure up a notch. He caught her gaze in the mirror over the sink as she stood next to him.

"Maybe I will have some tea." *Anything to get her out of there.* He wanted to hold her and press her back against the tile wall, devour the warm scented skin of her neck, and slide off her shorts. And then he would fill her. Slowly. An inch at a time.

"Sure." She disappeared down the hall and he breathed in relief, assessing his reflection. His fists were clenched against the sink, the knuckles white with strain.

He needed to get a hold of himself. Rekindling a relationship with his wife, even a sexual one, was not to their benefit. It would simply make things messy, more complicated, and highly dangerous. He didn't need to go through another breakup with her.

And they would.

Hunched over the tank, he saw her out of the corner of his eye when she sauntered in, holding two icy glasses. Setting his on the counter, she claimed a seat on the edge of the tub, her back resting against the shower wall. From his viewpoint, he saw way too much leg for his comfort. Her clinging denim shorts ended right below the juncture of her thighs. He had an overwhelming urge to slip a hand inside her shorts, against the mound of hot flesh there, dipping his finger inside to test the heat. To feel the silky slide of wetness and know she was ready for him.

He turned his head away until he stared at white porcelain. "Don't you have things to do? I don't need a supervisor." His voice sounded gruff even to his own ears.

"Nope. I thought I'd keep you company. Talk to you about this little project I want to do."

He concentrated on the mechanics of the tank, ignoring the sultry invitation in her voice. "The Goodwins' old place. Yeah, I heard about it. Bad idea." He meant to end the conversation. If he could stop her from talking, it would make his job a helluva lot easier. Then he could make his getaway.

"Bad idea? You don't even know what I want to do." The tiniest bit of irritation trickled into her tone.

That was his Lila, hackles raised, ready to do battle, to fight an injustice. "It's not like Dallas. There aren't ready buyers willing to lay down a few hundred grand to restore some old commercial building and set up shop," he told her.

She didn't respond. He didn't need to turn and see the quiet anger brimming just under the skin. He felt it. And Christ almighty if it didn't turn him on more.

"Does it have to be this way between us? Why can't we talk to each other like normal people?" A hand glided up his back to his shoulder, making the muscles in his stomach clench with the effort to ignore the pleasure.

Her touch scorched him. Control slipped fast. He had to move out of her reach, before he turned and buried himself in her neck.

He stood, throwing his wrench into the red metal toolbox, and avoided meeting her eyes. "I'll come back later to fix the rest. It should work for now."

He fastened the clasps on the box with a firm snap and made to leave, but a tiny hand curled around his side and rested just above the zipper on his jeans.

His cock throbbed in his pants and the thrumming echoed in the blood coursing throughout his body.

The fissure in his control cracked wide open and he pushed his tools away, turning with lightning speed to face his wife. Her face softened and her lips parted. His resolve to avoid further emotional entanglement with Lila dissolved under the beauty of her face, flushed with passion.

He grabbed her around the waist, raising her feet off the floor until their lips met. He found acceptance and invitation without preamble in the contours of her warm mouth.

God, how long had it been? And why did he wait so long?

He crushed her against the wall, and her legs rose and curled around his hips.

She tasted like sherbet, tangy and sweet like summertime, familiar. He couldn't get enough. He wanted all of her. Right now.

Jake moved his hungry mouth over her chin and down her

neck. She cried out as he nipped the tender skin behind an ear, and the sound struck a chord within him. He growled low in his throat, the response ragged and raw like a man denied sustenance too long. He suckled on the smooth skin below her jaw and drank from the hollows of her collarbone.

His Lila. His wife. Forever and always.

Her hands dug deep into his hair, pulling him closer. He needed to feel her naked, have her skin warm against his chest. The comfort of familiarity and the joy of rediscovery flamed his desire to a roaring bonfire.

He leaned back, pulling the tail of her shirt up over her breasts. He caught her hands in one of his, holding her captive against the wall while he reveled in the sight of her. He'd memorized every curve, every hollow on her frame after they were first married, and he wanted to reacquaint himself intimately with each one again.

Beautiful breasts, framed by strappy tan lines, enticed him to lower his head and sample the ruby nipples. Her narrow waist flared to welcoming hips, which rocked against his erection.

"Jake…" Her voice interrupted his perusal.

"Let me look at you, Lila—it's been so long." He heard the need in his own voice and wondered if she heard it, too.

She quieted, shivering when his hand slid up her rib cage, cradling a breast, reacquainting himself with the feel. He grazed the nipple with the back of his knuckles, watching her sharp intake of breath push the mound harder against his hand.

He lowered his mouth and took the peak inside, rolling the bud back and forth against the heat of his tongue. The sensation filled his mind with longing, forcing the thoughts of repercussions and recriminations further away, behind a locked door. Those could be dealt with later, much later.

"God, Jake. Please…" She was always impatient, wanting the feel of him inside her, rocking her higher and higher. He bit the bud gently and Lila pushed forward, grinding against him.

"Don't stop," she said.

He wove a wet trail with his tongue to the other breast, showering the twin globe with the same lazy, excruciatingly slow treatment.

His pleasure came from her response, and with each successive moan, she pushed him closer to the edge, making it more difficult for him to contain his own need. But contain it he would, driving her gratification higher.

When he finally lifted his head, he could see her panting. Her chest rose and fell in rapid succession.

Jesus. They were dangerous together like this. He didn't think their sexual attraction could flare up again so fast and so hot, but he'd been wrong. He'd lied to himself all these years, thinking it couldn't be as good as he remembered.

And it wasn't. It was far better. He had to stop. Now.

He released her wrists and pulled the shirt hem back down around her waist.

He read the confusion and then the accusation in her eyes. *Why couldn't the moment last a little while longer?*

But they couldn't be together. He didn't know how many days he had. No one knew if he was truly "cured," not even the best specialists. Remission meant the cancer could come back at any time, and if it did, it would be worse the second time around.

No, he didn't have the luxury of time to love this woman the way she deserved to be loved. She needed to move on, forget about him. Find somebody else to grow old with, somebody healthy.

He pulled away, instantly regretting the loss of her body wrapped around his. He adjusted his jeans, trying to give his painful erection and full balls some breathing room. When he looked up into her face, he could see it coming. She tried to hold it in, but the turbulent emotion built behind the calm expression. Her lips trembled and her eyes shone with suppressed grief.

He hated himself more at that moment than at any other time in his life. And what he was about to say next turned his stomach.

"Thanks, Lila. But I don't have time for the distraction, though wonderful, I'm sure. I've got jobs to complete."

He backed up, avoiding his reflection in the mirror.

God, he was a hateful, cruel bastard.

His wife sat on the bathroom counter of her granny's house, resplendent in her arousal. And he was going to just walk away. Like a jackass.

She was a helluva lot better off without him.

Grabbing his toolbox and his heart off the floor, Jake retreated from the bathroom. And his wife. Leaving her as crushed and defeated as the day she rolled out of his life ten years ago.

He recalled that day with startling clarity.

The aluminum of the webbed lawn chair squeaked under Lila's butt as she shifted, lifting the backs of her thighs to catch the cooler breeze of twilight. Ordinarily she wouldn't be sweating so much, even in the early July Texas heat, but the hard set of Jake's jaw as he sat in the chair next to her made her sick with anxiety. The kind of anxiety that made a woman afraid and reluctant to face her own husband even though she knew the night wouldn't get any easier the longer it wore on.

And if she just had the guts to tell him she was leaving, get it out in the open and over with, she could banish the queasiness of regret and guilt and get on with the bleak and tarnished future of being divorced so young.

Maybe if she forced him. "You just gonna sit there?"

Jake's response was to lower his head a degree and stare at the St. Augustine grass of Granny's backyard.

Even in this, their final discussion, Lila had to be the one to push, to bring it to a painful close. "I'm leaving in the morning. Granny's taking me to the airport in Austin. I'm not taking anything 'cept my clothes, so you can have the stuff in the apartment."

The muscle in Jake's jaw jumped. Lila glanced away to the massive trunk of the pecan tree before she cried. She'd cried enough tears lately to fill a swimming pool.

"You can tell your parents why I'm going. I don't suspect they care to hear anything from me right now."

"You're wrong."

His quiet voice surprised her and she turned back, hoping to find something in his face that would tell her she was wanted. Needed. Loved. Except he wasn't looking at her, but at his calloused hands clasped tightly between his knees.

She loved those hands, strong and warm and capable. Always capable of holding her, loving her, reassuring her. Until six months ago.

Lila waited for him to explain. He didn't. She should be used to his withdrawal by now. His doctor said it was normal, that eventually, Jake would recover his old sense of self. But he hadn't. And with his abdication of life went his love for her.

"Wrong about your parents? I doubt it. They've never really liked me." And they sure the hell didn't think she was good enough for their only son now.

"Is that why they bought you the Mustang?"

The old anger burned like a fresh bee sting, bottling up arguments in her throat, but Lila held them back, for once keeping her tongue checked and her feelings to herself. Maybe if she'd done that from the start, she wouldn't be on the verge of hightailing it to Dallas to sponge off Granny's sister, Tilly. But she'd trusted her emotions, trusted Jake's, too, and it had earned her a one-way ticket out of Hannington.

"The Mustang is yours. I left the keys on the kitchen counter." She stood, rubbing the web marks on the backs of her legs, wishing that with a few vigorous swipes, her heart would be as untouched.

Lila looked at Jake hard, imprinting his familiar profile on her mind, all the while knowing she was stupid for allowing even the tiniest swell of hope. The knowledge didn't stop her from waiting, holding her breath, silently counting to ten and then twenty.

Nothing. Not a single word, or scrap of emotion she could cling to. Just icy distance.

"I'm selling the Mustang and moving home with my

parents. I'll send your half of the apartment deposit when I get it."

Exhausted beyond her years, Lila gave in. "Fine. You can get the information from Granny."

And then she turned her back on Jake Winter, her best friend, the boy she'd dated through high school, the man she married and cared for through his diagnosis with Hodgkin's disease, and now separated, all before the age of twenty.

Lesson Number Nine —

Men feel proudest when they find the right solution to a problem. Let your man not only offer solutions, but sometimes fix the problem with one of his suggestions.

Chapter Eleven

"Goddammit, Jake. You really want to do this?"

No. Although Howard Armstrong left him no choice. He couldn't stand around and let the arrogant bastard malign Lila. Too many people felt comfortable doing that and then orchestrating Jake's life while they were at it.

Personally, it pissed him off.

"It makes sense if you think about," he told Howard, who reclined in his high-back leather office chair. "She's willing to take the structure off the city's books and dump a load of cash into it. So let her. It'll be back on the tax rolls and you can collect the city's portion."

Howard sat with his fingers steepled on his lips, looking like the master of his domain. Unfortunately for the mayor, the extent of his authority was about as big as the town's annual Central Texas State Fair. A once-a -year event attracting a few thousand people.

Disappointment and a dose of resentment drew his broad

features down into a heavy frown. He didn't like losing his rec center to Lila. His wide, bushy brows almost met and provided an intimidating cover for his mud-colored eyes. Eyes trained on Lila.

There wasn't a damn thing Howard could do about the situation.

Lila had him beat.

"Surely raw land off the town square would cost the city less to develop for the recreation center," she offered.

She had the mayor's number, and Jake would have to make a point to watch her back. If any two people could make her life rough in the small town, the Armstrongs were it. Howard and Janie were formable and plain mean sometimes.

"Don't lecture me about real estate, little lady. I know my job. And part of it is helping to improve the quality of life for our citizens. That building has been a blight for too long and frankly, we'd be better off without it. But that's not going to happen now that you've come running in from the big city to save us from our naive and backcountry ways. Is it?"

He gave Lila a tight smile meant to put her in her place.

She straightened and leaned forward, resting a hand on the edge of Howard's antique oak desk. Jake could see the angry glint in her blue eyes.

"You don't like it because of what used to go on there. Admit it, Mr. Mayor. You think because a prostitute ran her business out of there, it doesn't deserve to be protected. To be respected and acknowledged."

Howard scowled, but didn't deny the accusation.

"As the great-great-granddaughter of that prostitute, I intend to preserve her home and her memory."

Howard stood abruptly, his face red with barely contained anger. His attempt to build and maintain a city of character flew in the face of Lila's efforts to save, and probably promote to great fanfare, the former whorehouse.

"I'm warnin' you two. That building better be more than just up to code. I'm not going to allow you to grandfather it in under any of the permits, Jake," he said, turning his glare on him. "You hear me? I want it safe and secure for our citizens."

Howard was such an asshole. That he questioned the quality of Jake's work made him madder. "Of course. I wouldn't have it any other way."

Jake motioned to Lila and they left the mayor's office.

They walked in silence through the lobby and out into bright sunshine.

They had a lot of silence lately. Since the bathroom.

"Jake, thank you so much. I—"

"Stop." They paused on the wide concrete landing outside city hall. "Let me make something clear. I'll do this project for you against my better judgment, and at the risk of really pissing Howard off. I realize I'm the only one in town who has the team to do the job. But I don't want to mislead you into thinking it means anything more than that." He stared into her sky-blue eyes, driving his point home. "It's a job. Not an opportunity for us to relive old times."

She flushed red. "You're not going to make me feel bad for what happened the other day, Jake. It's natural we still feel a connection, and there's nothing wrong with acting on it. We're both adults, and still married for Pete's sake."

Yeah, he heard her. And the man downstairs was paying close attention. He groaned inwardly at the thought of working side by side with her day after day. The stress of it would have him constantly taking cold showers and rearranging his junk.

He shook his head and tried for a subject change as he walked her to Rose's office to pick up the keys. "So this Prudence. She's really your great-grandmother?"

"Great-great-grandmother. And yes, she is. You should read her journal, Jake. It's amazing. She was extremely sharp and loving. Took care of the women she employed like they were family. It breaks my heart to think she might have been run out of town because people didn't like her. People like Mayor Armstrong."

"Wouldn't be the last time," he mumbled under his breath, thinking of Lila when she left Hannington for Dallas. She'd stuffed everything she owned in her old blue suitcase and disappeared into the sunset. Literally.

If he couldn't give Lila what she deserved, a full life with a husband and a family, maybe he could help her rebuild Miss Pru's. Regain what both women lost: a sense of love, belonging, and worthiness.

He could do that much.

Lila bounced the keys to the Goodwin store in her hand. Their weight felt good, reassuring. Like she'd put down roots, established herself once again. Although Jake's rejection the other day still cut deeply, she had to remember: baby steps. Crawling before walking. Walking before running.

She would do this. One painful step at a time. And right now, Miss Pru's was next.

She couldn't wait to get inside and get her hands filthy. Re-creating history from nothing more than rusty ceiling tiles and scarred wood gave her a fulfilling sense of accomplishment.

Never mind the soured project in Austin. Or the bad press coverage. Despite the owner's attempt to sue her for bringing the project in over budget and past deadline—his fault, not hers—the old hotel ranked up there as her favorite restoration.

She suspected Miss Pru's place would bump the old hotel back a spot. To number two. And she had Jake to thank for a large portion of her success today. Without him, she knew the mayor wouldn't have budged on his position. Miss Pru's might even now be reduced to a pile of rubble if Jake hadn't stepped in and championed her.

They were once again a team, and it felt right. The small success inspired her all the way down to her toes.

Marching purposely up to the front door, she fit the key in the lock. Although she got it in far quicker than Rose the other day, it wouldn't turn. She jiggled the entire assembly, trying to loosen the tumblers.

Nothing.

She pulled the key out and slid it back in, only more gently this time. Patience and a little TLC did the trick occasionally. She hoped.

It still wouldn't turn.

"Dammit."

The hairs on the back of her neck rose in sudden response to an invading body heat. Jake. He'd returned from the store across the street with bottled water.

"You never were mechanically inclined." His voice rumbled through her, tightening her insides in all the right places. She spun, pulling the key with her. A soft snap sounded.

Jake grinned and his eyes twinkled with humor at her expense. "Well, that presents a problem."

"How long have you been watching me struggle with this lock? You could've offered a hand. It would have been the gentlemanly thing to do."

"Yeah, but then I would've missed a good laugh. Don't get too many of those these days."

He was interested. Despite all his denials, he stood here, with her, just as she'd asked him. Sharing a joke. That had to count for something.

"Okay, funny guy, figure out how we're going to get this door open." She stepped to the side, allowing him access to the old beveled-glass door. From her mechanically challenged assessment, the lock looked hopeless.

His verdict, too. "We've got to get a new lock. You don't have one handy, do you?"

"Oh sure. I carry odds and ends like that in my trunk. You never know when you're going to break a key off in a nineteenth-century lock." She gave Jake a you-knew-better-than-to-ask-me-a-silly-question look. "No, I don't have one, do you?"

He looked off down the street and readjusted the cap on his dark head. His hair, damp and curly, clung close to his rounded scalp. "No."

"As the new lead on this renovation project, what do you suggest we do?"

He met her fixed stare, his green eyes shadowed in the shade of the veranda. "We go get one."

Lila nodded and strolled off the sidewalk to the passenger

door of his truck. Grabbing the handle, she swung herself up onto the bench seat, only to discover Jake hadn't moved.

"Well, let's go," she said, leaning out the open door, calling over the hood.

His hands rested on his hips, his brows pulled together in exasperation. "Now?"

"You got a better idea?"

Jake adjusted his hat once again and swore under his breath loud enough for her to hear. He dug the truck keys out of his pocket and strode to the driver's side and climbed in.

"I said I'd come take a look at the place today. I didn't say I was going to spend the afternoon running around, looking for a lock."

He never did do spontaneous very well. Too much of a planner. Always looking down the road toward the future. "Oh, don't be so short-tempered." She slapped him playfully on the shoulder. She meant the gesture in good fun, a means to keep him in a pleasant mood, but the feel of his muscles under her hand had her lingering, stroking with sensitive fingertips.

She ran her thumb against the hard ridge of muscle along his inner biceps. "If you're going to do the work, you might as well get used to the idea of taking extra special care with this old building. Its needs might be a little different than what you've been used to."

The diesel engine rumbled to life and Jake's eyes turned on her, drowning her in emotion.

Her needs were different these days, too. She needed him, wanted him. The good, the bad, and everything in between.

"What are we talking about here, Lila?"

"We're talking about seeing the project through to the

end. Uncovering the strengths and beauty behind the years of neglect and exile."

He captured her hand with his own. If he'd give her a sign, one tiny indication he still needed her, wanted her, she'd be the happiest woman in Bell County.

Without him, her story was incomplete.

But she wouldn't beg. Not yet.

He raised the palm of her hand to his lips. They were warm and soft against her skin. She closed her eyes.

"Sometimes it's better to have the memories than the real thing."

"Oh, I couldn't disagree more, Jake." She purposely misconstrued his meaning and steered the conversation into safer territory, staring out the window to Pru's place. "This old gal is going to be a beauty once we fix her up." She reclaimed her hand, pointing through the windshield. "Wait until you see what I have in mind."

Her mischievous tone won a smile. They were back on solid ground. "And what is that?"

"A day spa."

"A day spa? What the hell does that mean?" He backed out of the parking space and headed out of the square.

"You know, a day retreat. A place people can go to relax, be pampered, and get a massage."

He looked at her out of the corner of his eyes. "In Hannington?"

"What? You don't think people around here need to relax and get a massage?"

He shrugged his shoulders noncommittally. "I figured if folks around here wanted that sort of thing, they could go into

Austin or Fort Worth."

"They are both two hours away!" Lila leaned back against the headrest, contemplating Jake's desire to discourage her. He was doing a bang-up job so far, deflating her enthusiasm.

But not her determination.

The road stretched out before the truck with a dry wind rolling through the tall field grass along the side of the pavement. Lila adjusted a vent, targeting cool air toward her face.

She considered his position of devil's advocate. For every idea she had, he had a negative. For every step she'd taken forward in Hannington, he tried to push her back another two.

Although he helped her against Howard. And committed to taking on Miss Pru's.

"Why do you want me to leave Hannington?" She watched his profile and saw an almost imperceptible tightening about his lips.

He lifted his eyes off the road for an instant to meet hers. "A better question is why do you want to stay? This place can't provide the same opportunities as Dallas."

"This is my home." She knew that now. After ten years in the Big D, she realized she'd rather be with those she loved than with the money she made.

Home is where the heart is.

"It hasn't been for a long time." His hands grasped the steering wheel.

"So should I be banished from Hannington, never to return? Is that what you want, Jake? Do you want me to go away and never bother you again?"

She turned under her seat belt to study him. "If you can

honestly look me in the face and tell me you have no feelings for me anymore and wish me gone, I'll go. But don't hide behind the cancer. Don't push me away out of some skewed sense of honor, self-sacrifice, and responsibility. I'm all grown up now and I can make my own choices about who I love and where I choose to spend my nights."

The time had come. She'd crossed the line. If he said go, she'd go.

A loud boom filled the cab as he opened his mouth. The truck veered sharply off the road and Jake steered into the curve, guiding the vehicle to a more or less straight line. Lila grabbed the dash, hanging on as they slowed to a crawl.

"What happened?" She could barely hear herself over the blood roaring in her ears.

"Blowout."

The truck bumped an old timber fence post on the side of the country road and Jake unbuckled, turning toward her.

He pried her belt loose and grabbed her arms, running his hands up over her shoulders. "Are you all right?" His eyes were bright, concern crinkling the tan skin of his face.

"Fine. A little shaken, though." His hands skidded lower, feathering over her torso to her waist. He massaged the skin of her hip bones where the belt had cut.

"The belt didn't bruise?"

"No, I don't think so. But I might find differently in the morning."

He nodded and some of the concern left his face, but his posture remained tense, ready for action. Pushing open the door, he unfolded his legs from beneath the wheel and strode to the passenger side to investigate the tire.

Lila hopped out of the cab to see the damage for herself. The front passenger-side wheel hung in limp rubber ribbons. The smell of burning tread filled the air.

Fortunate for them they had the blowout on a desolate stretch of road. No oncoming traffic to put them in danger.

"You do have a spare, right?"

His gaze cut to hers. Obviously he didn't deem the question valid enough for a response.

Moving to the rear of the truck, he sank to his haunches and stared underneath the bed. "There's an L-shaped tool for the spare tire in the glove box. Would you get it?"

The glove box looked like a tornado had hit it. Papers dropped to the floorboard as she rummaged for the tool. A yellow sticky note on the top of an empty prescription bag caught her attention

Dr. Rogers, screening. 3:30 p.m.

This week! Jake had a cancer screening and he hadn't said a word. Before she could stop herself, old fears and anxieties flared up, making her heart thump painfully. Mostly because she was once again on the outside looking in.

What did she expect? For him to ask her to accompany him?

"Did you find it?" Jake's voice drifted from the tailgate.

Lila's hand swam quickly through the mess until it encountered the tire tool. Stuffing the papers back into the glove box, she hurried back to rear of the truck in time to see Jake stand.

"I found it." She held it up and he reached for it, only to disappear back beneath the tailgate.

She wanted to talk to him about the appointment, offer to

go with him. She knew without a doubt, if she brought it up, he'd shut down and she'd be right back out in the cold.

She should be used to it by now. But Gentrys were slow that way. They didn't take hints easily.

The spare tire gave a groan and began to lower from its underbelly nest.

"Well, hell."

Her gaze snapped from the tire to Jake's face and then back to the tire.

The spare was flat.

Lesson Number Ten —

For a woman, sex is both emotional and physical. For the woman to be gratified sexually, she needs the emotional fulfillment first. Understanding this requirement (and pursuing what she wants) helps her enjoy sex as much as the man.

Chapter Twelve

Lila didn't speak for several heartbeats as Jake sat there, his head hanging in his hands. When he looked up, it was directly into her face. "What are you, some kind of jinx on automobiles?"

"It could be worse, you know. We could be stranded on a deserted highway." She got a glare for the bad joke.

Surely someone would come by. They were in Texas, for God's sake, not the Outback. Though the lack of signal on her cell phone indicated it was, indeed, the Outback.

He was strangely quiet as he stood and brushed off the rear of his jeans.

"Don't tell me we're stranded out here."

He rolled the spare out and lifted it, throwing it into the empty bed. "Okay."

The tire clattered, resting flat against the corrugated metal of the truck bed. He strode to the driver's side and rolled the windows down before pulling the keys from the ignition and pocketing them.

"I'm heading back that direction," he said, pointing east, "where F.M. 1670 intersects. You going, or do you want to wait here?"

"Won't another car pass this way soon?"

"Not likely."

"Why?" She knew her questions were beginning to irritate him; she could see it in the firm set of his jaw.

"Lila, we're on pastureland out here. No one but Jim Stokey could happen by and he won't because he's in Dallas for his daughter's wedding."

She felt sufficiently castigated. "Oh."

"So let's get walking."

"Sure." She stepped up beside him and they headed off in the direction they'd come.

They walked in silence for fifteen minutes as she hurried to accommodate Jake's long stride. Her footwear was not only inappropriate for a five-mile hike, but hurt like hell on her feet. Ordinarily, she wore boots or tight lace-up shoes while on construction sites. She'd made an exception around Jake, however. Her shoe wardrobe now consisted of strappy sandals and heels.

Apparently toe cleavage attracted men. Or so the Bombshells had said.

"What's so funny?" Jake's brooding tone cut through the Bombshells' litany of surefire ways to attract a man.

"Oh, this whole situation, I guess. Here you are trying to avoid me like the plague and we go and get ourselves stranded together on a deserted piece of pasture. Kind of funny, don't you think?"

A grumble crossed the distance between them.

"Well, I find it funny. And I'm sure Otis would find the situation hilarious."

At the mention of the old foreman, Jake's head whipped in her direction. "Don't mention it to him. I'll never live it down." He shook his head in resignation. "Flat spare."

"What do I get in return for keeping the secret?"

His evergreen eyes cut back to her, caution guarding their depths. "What do you want? And be reasonable, Lila."

"The truth." It popped out before she could close her lips around the words.

At his immediate frown, she wished she could take the words back, eat them before she spilled them.

"You ask too much."

"You ask for nothing, Jake. Why shouldn't you deserve happiness as much as the next man?"

"Because I don't have any guarantees. I don't know if I'll ever be able to have children. Hell, I don't even know if I'm going to make it to my next birthday."

"That's such bullshit, Jake. You won't let yourself live because it would make you just like the rest of us. Vulnerable. Scared of failure. Fear of being an ordinary person, in ordinary circumstances, taking chances without any certainty as to the outcome. It's all a risk. Every day. Living is hard, commitment is hard, but making an attempt to do it right is the hardest part of all."

He glared at her. "Is that why you're here? To fix our marriage? Do it 'right'?"

His sarcasm stung, but she'd gone too far to back down now. "And what if I am?"

His look burned through her chest, laying a scorch across her heart. "I'd say you're out of luck."

Lila's hand rose of its own accord. It flew across the space between them and came into contact with his chest as he backed away.

She fell, tipped forward by the momentum of her angry fist. She hit the ground hard, her hands taking the brunt of the impact. Slightly dazed, her brain registered Jake's concern as background. Seconds passed as she regained her composure.

"Lila? Are you hurt?"

She couldn't look at him. Couldn't force herself to see the self-hatred in his eyes. She hugged the warm grass beneath her, closing her eyes. *Why?* Why did she have to love him so much? And why didn't he love himself just a little? Just enough to see he was worthy of all the things he denied.

His hands gripped her shoulders, rolling her onto her back. Lila refused to open her eyes. His hand snaked around her back, pulling her into his lap.

"Lila, open your eyes, dammit, and tell me you're okay." He shook, his voice gruff with emotion.

Squinting through one open eye, she took in the grief written across his handsome face. His strong lips were turned down and tension creased his forehead.

She wanted to smooth the worry and found her hand lifting to do so. He leaned into her hand, kissing the inside of her wrist, closing his eyes as she stroked his face.

Lila wrapped her hand around his neck, pulling him down to meet her lips. A spark electrified the air as their lips met and a tingle coursed down her spine, spreading fire in its wake.

The light pressure of his lips turned immediately intense, demanding. She submitted, opening like a rose in the morning sun.

His tongue drilled past her lips, past her teeth to the recesses of her mouth. He drank from her. He sucked her tongue, nipped the full center of her bottom lip, and licked the tender underside of her top.

She opened further, releasing all reservations of past mistakes and future doubts. She let herself glory in the sensations, forgetting the outside world, forgetting he didn't want her as his wife.

She sensed the control in his powerful body, through the tender circle of his arms and gentle caress of his hands. He traced the outline of her cheekbones with his fingers and glided down the column of her neck. His lips followed his hands, licking the pronounced hollow of her throat through the deep vee of her T-shirt.

"You taste like sherbet, Lila."

His comment sank in seconds later. "What? Sherbet?"

His hand drifted lower to her breast, kneading the flesh through her shirt, pulling at the nipple hidden beneath her bra.

"Hmmm. Sherbet."

She groaned into his mouth, encouraging his hand to find her shirttail and pull the fabric high, exposing her midriff.

"What flavor?" She loved to tease him almost as much as she relished the feel of his rough hands on her skin. His fingers found the clasp at the front of her bra and thumbed it open, freeing her breasts.

She felt the hot Texas sun caress a naked breast as he lifted her shirt higher still. The lavish attention of Jake's warm tongue took the sun's place, but the heat intensified, burning her, claiming her.

He sucked her nipple, testing. "Orange," he mumbled, his mouth wrapped around her breast.

The world spun away. It didn't matter that they were in the middle of a pasture on a deserted road. She would take him in the IGA given the chance.

His hand parted her legs and skimmed up a thigh and under her twill skirt to rest heavily on her silk panties. He cupped the slightly rounded mound, letting the weight and warmth drive her crazy.

When his fingers plucked the lace out of the way and brushed her center, she groaned, releasing a rush of air through her teeth.

Relentless, he teased her, stroking and staying just outside her warm, wet core. When his fingers finally dipped inside, Lila came apart in his hands.

"God, Jake...now!" She was ready, writhing with need. She moved a hand to the front of his jeans, caressing his concealed length from base to tip. He was rock hard. Even through the stiff fabric, she could outline the plum-shaped head of his erection.

She needed to feel him pulsing in the palm of her hand, trace the rigid outline of veins, taste the salt upon his skin. She wanted to feel her own power over his body, to know she had the ability to create the same fire within him that burned out of control inside her.

She sought his gaze in the bright sunlight. She found him watching her from behind shadowed lashes. His hat lay upon the grass at her side and his hair stood on end in several places, tousled from her roaming hands. A sensual smile played along the corners of his mouth and a mischievous look shone in his eyes, eyes that reflected the intensity of the overhead sky back to her.

Two fingers pushed inside her, filling her until she came off the ground, pushing against his hand. He lowered his head and recaptured her lips, imitating the dance of his hands electrifying her insides.

She worked at the front of his jeans, unraveling his belt and popping the button. The zipper slid down and he sprang up, straining against a pair of plaid boxers.

He disengaged his tongue enough to mumble across her lips, "I quit wearing briefs a while back."

Lila laughed outright, hugging him close.

She loved him. And she did the right thing by being here. In Hannington. This is where she belonged, in his arms.

He pulled back, lifting her until she straddled his lap, her skirt hiked high around her hips.

He grinned, licking the exposed nipple even with his mouth. "I like this position."

She threw her head back, laughing in agreement, offering herself to him. Her breast lay heavy in his warm hand, his thumb rubbing the peak to exquisite hardness.

She opened the front flap on his boxers and pulled him free. It was Jake's turn to groan. And he did, loud and low in his throat.

He shifted her weight with his hands and she felt the head of his erection nudging against the tight barrier of her panties. She leaned into him, pulling the silk to one side, and he pushed through, filling her in a swift drive.

"Ahhh." She sank low, taking all of him, filling herself with Jake until she couldn't distinguish between their bodies, their breaths. He grasped the back of her neck in a firm grip, pulling her lips to his.

He rocked her forward and back in successive motions, driving her crazy. She clung to him, shutting out everything but the feel of their bodies. When she thought she couldn't ride any higher, he slid a thumb between her folds and along her most sensitive skin until he found her clit.

"Jake!" She dropped her head back, the yell bursting from her lips. He held her tightly against his chest as he climaxed, too, his seed nestling deeply within the walls of her womb.

His head fell to her shoulder and the tension left his body all at once.

Coming back to reality, she noted her clothes were damp with steam and perspiration. And she loved it. She looked around the open pasture populated by mesquite trees and rough limestone rock.

She hadn't made love outdoors since they were nineteen. God, how glorious!

She pressed a hand against Jake's shoulder and leaned back, taking in the expression on his face, expecting the same rosy glow she felt within.

A cloud passed across his eyes and he fixed her with his penetrating stare. "Are you on the pill?"

The unexpected question hit her like an icy shot of water during a warm shower. "No. I haven't had the need for birth control lately."

"Goddammit." His hands fisted at his side on the ground, but Lila yearned for them to hold her.

He pulled himself together and reined in his temper. "I'm sorry. This was my fault."

"I had an orgasm, too. I'd like to think I was part of this afternoon delight." She said this with Jake still inside her.

"I'm not denying we're good in bed together. That would be a lie. But we can't afford to plan for a future." He'd said it figuratively, but there it was: he had an appointment for a cancer screening. "I'll drive you to Walgreens and buy you the morning-after pill."

She looked down their bodies to where they were intimately joined. They belonged together, like this, every day for the rest of their lives. She didn't care how long it meant, as long as they were together to share it.

And she didn't want the damn morning-after pill!

Her eyes shot back up, colliding with his wary stare. "Look at us, Jake." His gaze remained steady on her face. "Look at us!" Her voice tightened, thick with determination to make him understand, acknowledge they were right together.

His eyes lowered, trailing down her chest.

"We can't keep our hands off each other. It's like we're nineteen again. If this thing between us hasn't died in the ten years we've been apart, I don't think it ever will. Why throw it away?"

"I'm not worried about the health of our libidos, Lila." His lips thinned in self-disgust. "Knocking you up with a kid, although the chance is pretty remote with all of the drugs that have passed through my body, has me scared shitless. What if you do get pregnant and I'm not around anymore? What'll you do then?"

She recoiled at the vehemence of his words. At last, honesty.

"You don't know what tomorrow brings. It might bring life and life for many more days after that. It's a chance I'm willing to take. With you. It's called loving with your whole heart."

He moved his hands up her arms, and she leaned in for the expected embrace. But he set her back, disengaging their bodies. He stood, focusing on the horizon as adjusted his jeans.

His withdrawal left her feeling hollow, cold inside. She sat on the hard, warm earth, prickly grass tickling the underside of her thighs.

Could rejection be any more brutal than that? She wondered for a moment if Miss Pru had felt this way. Rejected. Over and over again.

She hated him in that moment. Hated him for his distance, his ability to withdraw and push her away like used goods. And she hated herself for wanting something so much. For wanting him. It was her teenage years all over again. Wanting to fit in, to win the approval of the town, Jake's parents. To have people see her as a worthy person and not just another Gentry girl.

The hurt swelled inside her, rushing up her throat to fill her mouth with mean words. But what good would they do? Mean words never helped. She bit them back and got to her knees, adjusting her skirt.

Jake walked a wide circle around her, like a wolf around a wounded mate. Watchful, but incapable of removing the pain.

With her bra and top back in place, she gained her feet and headed down the road, leaving Jake to his silence. She'd covered maybe twenty yards when she heard the tread of his boots behind her.

"Lila." His tone told her to be reasonable. She wasn't in the mood any longer to be reasonable. She wanted to knock him on his ass, make him hurt as much as she hurt. But it wouldn't accomplish a thing, except to drive him further away.

God. Wouldn't it feel good, though? For just a minute?

"Lila." He grabbed her arm and spun her around to face him. "Where are you going?"

"To civilization. We still have work to do. Miss Pru is waiting." And according to *her* sage advice, when one problem couldn't be fixed, a woman should turn attention to another. Eventually, the unsolvable would solve itself.

The deepening crease between Jake's dark brows told her he knew she hurt.

"So we're just going to go back to town like nothing happened out here?"

"If you can act like nothing happened, so can I." She turned and resumed her march to the road. But she couldn't act like nothing had happened. It had. Her hand snaked across her belly, rubbing the flat plane of her stomach.

What if they did make a baby? What would she do then?

Love it. Raise it. Be the best damn mother she could be. With or without Jacob Winter.

No use in worrying over an uncertain future. *Hell, it was her own advice; she might as well follow it.*

Lesson Number Eleven —

Love resides everywhere, in everything. If you open your heart to the land and people around you, chances are good love will find you.

Chapter Thirteen

Jake flipped the switch for the overhead light. His kitchen fell under the harsh glow of fluorescent bulbs. Not the most welcoming lighting for an early-morning visit to the refrigerator, but then his mood wasn't so pleasant, either.

He plucked the carton of orange juice off the glass shelf and pulled a chair out from under the breakfast table, the fridge door slamming behind him. The juice slid down the back of his throat, quenching his need for stronger spirits.

He'd given up heavy drinking years ago, but since Lila had come back to town, he found the pull of the bottle stronger, something in which to ease the turmoil.

And turmoil she created. His heart and his head were out of sync. His head pushed him one way, further away, all while his heart pulled him closer to her.

The notice for his appointment lay faceup on the table. Jake reread the words for the hundredth time. Yearly screening for cancer patients was rote, no big deal. But each time Jake had to lie on that long, icy steel table, he felt a degree of himself slip away. Never to be recovered.

He pushed the paper across the table, out of sight.

Rising out of the chair, he padded down the hall to his bedroom. Sleep would continue to evade him, so he might as well meet the day head-on. Plunging his body under the warm jets of the shower, he considered the previous day and how he'd been a completely selfish prick.

What the hell was wrong with him? Taking what she too easily gave up. He should have reined himself in, told Lila she deserved better. The woman had fought too long and too hard for her reputation and successful business to throw it away on coming back to Hannington and to him.

He hadn't said word one. Instead he dived inside her like they were having sex for the first time, barely slowing down to reflect on the consequences. Or, Jesus, to even take off their clothes.

He'd been too long without her company. Her support. Her compassion and courage. But damn, if she hadn't felt good in his arms, writhing under his fingers, igniting him with the touch of her delicate hands.

Lila had managed to keep her distance the remainder of the day, speaking to him only when necessary. After a passing truck had stopped an hour into their trek and given them a lift to the nearest gas station, she'd called Rose for a ride, leaving him for good.

He sure the hell couldn't blame her. He'd have left his dumb ass, too.

To make amends, he'd fetched the new store lock and installed it that night under the blaze of a shop light hung from a rusty signage hook under the store's canopy. He wanted her to know he took her seriously. The job, anyway. At least he could give her that.

Shutting his front door behind him, Jake stepped out into the predawn light. Stars twinkled overhead, wrapping him in familiar comfort. He could always count on the sky being the same, each and every day.

It used to be enough.

But not anymore.

"Lila Jean! It's Jake again!" Granny's voiced barreled into the kitchen where Lila washed fresh-picked tomatoes in the cast-iron sink.

"Tell him I've gone out, please." She shouted right back, not the least bit inclined to take his call. The humiliation of the other day washed over her anew, bringing heat to her face.

When would she learn?

"You get over here and take this call, girl. This is the third time the poor man's called today and I won't lie to him again!"

Stamping her foot, Lila twisted the tap off and marched into the den, drying her hands on a Florida souvenir dish towel as she went. Granny sat enthroned in her favorite recliner, an icy glass of tea at her elbow, the phone smothered between her hand and the side of the chair. When she saw Lila, she shoved the phone at her, her gaze threatening punishment if she didn't behave with the good manners taught her.

Sticking her tongue out, Lila grabbed the receiver and smacked it to her ear. "What?" her belligerent voice shouted across the line.

"Good afternoon to you, too."

Granny snatched the towel out of her hand and whipped it around, smacking Lila on the backside.

She danced out of Granny's reach as the matriarch waved a finger in warning.

"What do you want?" And why the hell did he sound in such a good mood?

"As your contractor, I'm reporting the progress thus far on the store."

Lila slouched on the brocade-covered ottoman. Crap, and she'd harbored hopes he'd called to apologize. "What progress?" She heard his warm chuckle across the line. She could picture his head thrown back, his sable-colored hair brushing the collar of his shirt.

"Oh, what a short memory you have. I fixed the lock on the door. Good as new."

He'd fixed the lock? After the other day, she'd figured he'd given up the job for good. She hadn't seen him around and truly, hadn't bothered to look. She'd needed time to lick her wounds and revise her plan.

"The next step is getting inside and assessing the damage. I need to know what you intend to salvage and what can be tossed as we break the place down."

"Oh."

"I have the rest of the afternoon free. Why don't we meet and go over a rough plan?"

Did she want to meet with him so soon after her disgrace? She caught Granny's frown out of the corner of her eye. Heck, she couldn't miss the downward curve of her rose-red lips.

"Hold on and let me check with Granny." She held the

phone out, covering the receiver and feigning an inquiry.

"What's going on between you two?" When Lila kept her silence, Granny sat forward in her chair, rocking the footrest downward. "Do I need to get in the middle of this like I used to? How about I call Jake's mother and find out what this is all about? I'm sure she would be interested."

"Ssshh!" she pleaded with her grandmother, almost laughing at the way the woman resorted to the tactics she'd used when she was a teenager.

"Don't tell me—"

Lila jerked the phone back to her ear, cutting Granny off before Jake could overhear her lecture. "Okay, I'll meet you there in twenty minutes."

She slammed the phone down and spun on her grandmother. "Don't you have a domino game with the Bombshells?"

"As a matter of fact, I do. If you're going into town, you can drop me off at Alta's." Disengaging herself from the chair, she flipped off Montel Williams and headed for the back of the house. "I'll be ready in five."

She saw the back of Granny's good hand as she sauntered down the hallway. Good grief, the woman could go head-to-head with the best of them and still come out a winner. Unlike her granddaughter, who still learned lessons the hard way, one painful experience at a time.

The garish glow of pink flamingos lining the driveway greeted them as they arrived at Alta's house. The birds perched on spindly legs sporadically throughout the front lawn, interspersed with painted wooden tulips and metallic-colored rocks. Whirligigs hung in pairs across the shaded porch, limp in the hot July sun.

Lila refrained from commenting on Alta's exterior decor, although the urge almost overwhelmed her. "What time should I pick you up?" she asked Granny, bumping the car into park behind the stationary RV.

"Earl said he'd drive me home. That way you and Jake can work things out." Granny released the seat belt and reached down for her purse.

"There's nothing personal Jake and I need to work out. We're discussing business."

Granny flipped the visor down to check her white curls in the mirror. "Uh-huh. Then why were your eyes all red and puffy the other night?"

Dang, if her grandmother didn't have eyes like a hawk.

"It's allergies. You know they bother me out here."

Granny flipped the visor back into place and shoved the car door open, giving Lila a stern, disapproving look. "You know you can go to hell for lying to your grandmother like that, don't you?"

Lila gaped. She watched her grandmother's back scoot across the seat and out the door. The woman could move, despite the cast.

"Don't wait up for me. It's a tournament tonight and I intend to win!"

The door slammed and Lila sat in the deafening silence. How was it possible that a little seventy-two-year-old woman could shock the hell out of her?

Because Gentry blood ran through her veins, that's how.

She recalled the story Granny had once told her about the way her parents had met in the town bank. Her father worked as a teller at the time before he went into the service, and her mother was a customer visiting the vault to deposit her coin collection. Smitten, Michael asked Sarah out on the spot. But she wouldn't agree. So he locked her in the vault until she said yes. And Lila was born eleven months later.

Shaking her head at Gentry grit, she pulled the Lexus away from the curb and headed to the town square and Jake. She wished she could lock him in a vault until he agreed to her demands, like she'd done in high school on a dare, but things weren't quite that easy.

She found his truck parked outside the store when she arrived, his face hidden beneath the brim of his hat as he slouched back in the seat, seemingly asleep.

Taking a deep breath, she squelched her nervousness. She wouldn't push him. Not again. The ball fell in his court now.

Tapping on the window, she brought him upright, his hat sliding smoothly back into place. He stepped out into the street beside her, his denim-clad legs unfolding with animal-like ease.

"I was beginning to think you'd changed you mind." His stare appraised her.

"No." She didn't owe him an explanation as to why Granny took fifteen minutes to spray her hair and find the right sandals.

He expected more, but she left him hanging. Looking up to Miss Pru's, she noticed the shiny new lock nestled against the worn wood of the door.

Rushing up the steps, Lila investigated the new fixture.

"This looks great. Where did you find it?" She stroked the hardware in appreciation. It was almost identical to the original.

"At the salvage yard in Temple." He pulled the key from his pocket and offered it to her. The key slid home and the door swung open at her light touch. Not what she'd expected.

"Did you fix the door as well?" Surprise colored her voice and she tried to deny the appreciative smile that touched her lips. Jake wouldn't weasel back into her good graces so easily.

Okay. He might.

"I figured I might as well get started, and this rusty mess seemed the logical place."

She found the light switch and stepped through the door, with Jake right behind her. It looked worse the second time in the flood of full daylight.

She sneaked a peek at his face beneath lowered lashes, wanting to catch his reaction to the interior. Would he see the potential she had? He wasn't surveying the mess, but looked directly at her.

Not the tender, toe-curling look she wanted, but a look born of incredulity. Her spine went rigid and her head shot up under his perusal. "What?"

His fingers drummed a staccato on his buckle and he shook his head in disappointment. "What were you thinking?"

She looked around at the store and then back at him. "About what?"

He kicked up dust as he moved around the store, his eyes never leaving her face. How he could maneuver without watching where he placed his feet, she didn't know.

"About what? About this place! It looks like a bomb went off in here!"

Lila's hackles came up all at once. This was her baby! "It's not so bad. I've seen worse."

"When?"

"Dallas. Numerous abandoned warehouses on the east side of town. We went in and made them viable storefronts. There are some major players lining those streets, thanks to us."

Jake grunted. His attention focused in on the ceiling overhead. "And you plan to turn this heap into a day spa?"

She bit her nail, doubt creeping into her mind. She didn't want anyone telling her it couldn't be done. She didn't want Jake rolling off reasons why she couldn't stay in Hannington.

It could. And she would.

"Well?" Jake strolled up alongside her, so close she could see the flecks of gold in the depths of his green eyes.

"A day spa," she affirmed.

"You really think the residents of Hannington are going to pay for that kind of pampering? In a former whorehouse?"

Her idea would work, dammit. She knew this business; he didn't!

"The tourism to this area would support a spa. I don't go into business without doing the preliminary research, Jacob. I'm not an amateur."

He stepped back, holding his hands up, palms out. The formal use of his name usually elicited such a response. "Whoa. Whatever you say, boss lady. I just do what I'm told."

Lila turned away, clenching her teeth together. "You have no idea how I wish that were fact and not fiction," she mumbled, straddling debris as she made her way to the staircase in the back corner.

"Knock knock!" An unfamiliar voice drifted to the back

of the store. Lila craned her neck around the staircase to see the source of the cheery feminine drawl. A plump woman in her midforties crossed over the threshold and into the store.

"Goodness! Will you look at this place?" Her ash-colored pageboy haircut swung as her head turned every which way, taking in the disaster.

"Afternoon, Carrie. What brings you by?" Jake greeted the cherub-like lady with an easygoing grin. Lila envied her.

"Afternoon yourself, Jake." She picked her way across the store to stand next to him. Lila stood partially hidden behind one of the candy cases, so the woman didn't spot her immediately.

"I heard someone finally bought this old place and I couldn't wait to come by and meet them. I've been hoping for years this day would come, and I couldn't stay away another second and not know who it was."

She stared at Jake with a sweet, appreciative Southern smile.

"Lila? I want you to meet someone." His voice drew the woman's attention to where Lila stood.

"Hello there!" the woman called merrily, waving her jeweled hand in Lila's direction.

Picking her way back across the store, she tried to ignore the way Jake's eyes followed her every move. She hoped she didn't have dirt on her face or something stupid like that. She checked to make sure her clothes were in order, no embarrassing peekaboos. And then she actually blushed. If he wasn't interested, why the hell did he stare so much?

"Hello, Carrie, I'm Lila Gentry." She extended her hand for the customary shake and was surprised at the woman's firm grip.

"Lila, it's so wonderful to meet you. I'm Carrie Goodwin. My father used to own this store."

"Oh, my. We've probably met then. I can't tell you how much time I used to spend in here as a kid."

Carrie smiled and at last, Lila saw the family resemble to Mr. Goodwin.

"I remember you," Carrie beamed. "You and Rose Garner used to come in together."

Lila nodded and looked around the first floor. "What can you tell me about this place? Did your father make a lot of changes to the structure? Do you have any old photos, or any old documentation?"

Carrie's hair swung back as she took in the damage to the tin ceiling. "Dad didn't do a lot. He made some changes to the ground floor here, but kept the big fixtures as you can see." She pointed to the original staircase and the bar. "The second floor is unchanged. He just used it for storage. From what he told me, the building sat empty for a number of years around the turn of the century. Dad bought it from the bank in the twenties and we've owned it ever since. Until now."

Lila thought about the second floor. Miss Pru's rooms. Unchanged. She couldn't wait to get up there and have a look.

"Do you know anything about a woman named Prudence MacIntosh who once owned the building? It would have been before the turn of the century. Someone sent me her diary and I'm trying to find out more about her."

Carrie's light brown eyes narrowed in thought. "Nope. Don't know anything about that. Dad did say, though, that the guys Howard hired to start salvaging the place found some stuff. Don't know what it was. You might ask Howard. He would know."

The mayor was the dead last person Lila wanted to question about Miss Pru.

"Now that I think about it, Dad said there was a photo album once of this place. Back when it was a boardinghouse. The album was part of the city's museum collection, but nobody knows what happened to it. It disappeared some years back."

Lila's heart sank. There might have been pictures of Pru in the album. "What a disappointment. Who runs that museum?"

"It's funded by the city, of course, but Janie Armstrong is the head of the board."

Jake stepped to the side, over a pile of rusty ceiling tins, making room for Lila next to him and Carrie. He watched her with what he prayed was a look of detachment and disinterest. But he boiled inside, full of base emotion.

How he made it here today, to stand next to her, smelling the clean fragrance of her shiny hair, was a testament to willpower. After the disaster of the other afternoon, he hoped she might decide to give up her ideas of restoring the building and return to Dallas.

But no, here she was. Standing strong and smiling, like the other day never happened. Her courage and spunk warmed his insides.

He could not, under any circumstances, fall in love with his wife. Again.

"Jake, Carrie says there is wonderful old plaster behind the paneling. Can we remove it and see?"

Lila was talking to him. He knew because he watched her

cherry-red lips move and all he could think about were those same lips parted in passion and screaming his name in climax.

Like she did when they were first wed. Like she did two days ago.

Jesus.

Clearing his throat, he met her eyes. They were heart-breakingly beautiful, wide and innocent. He could lose himself easily in those ocean-blue depths and sail forever, ignoring reality. Living through the fantasy.

She smiled at him, waiting.

Waiting for what?

"Jake, are you okay?"

A question. Lila asked him something about the paneling.

"You want to take the paneling down?"

Both women looked at him cautiously as he repeated the question, like they were dealing with a mental patient.

Get with the here and now, Jake. The here and now.

He crossed to the north-facing wall, letting them follow behind so he could get himself together. Lila had him turned upside down and it damn near felt like she'd banged his head on the concrete.

He had to maintain focus.

Knocking on the wall with a curled index finger, he listened. "We can peel the paneling off, but you never know what you'll find underneath. The brick could be crumbling and in bad shape, opening a new set of problems. There could be water damage, structural settlements, and other nightmares waiting behind here."

Lila's smile faded with each word.

The more he talked about the walls, the more he felt he

talked about their relationship. "Sometimes, it's better to leave what's underneath, buried. You never know what problems you'll find. It might not be worth the hassle."

"Is that your professional opinion?"

She had heard the meaning behind his words, all right. And she was mad. Her hands came up to rest on her hips and she stood with her legs spread, her tiny white sneakers planted firmly on the dirty hardwood floor.

Carrie made some well-timed excuse about checking her mailbox at the post office and hightailed it out of their path.

"Lila, in this business, if the risk is bigger than the payoff, you've got to reconsider. You've got to be careful—"

She waved a hand, cutting him off. "I hear you. But I don't care how much it costs. I want to see what's under there. If it's in bad shape, we'll fix it. If it needs to be rebuilt, we'll do that, too."

She fought like a pit bull. When she got something in her head, she wouldn't let it go.

When it came to them, how could he keep telling her no?

Lesson Number Twelve —

Silent words conveyed with the eyes are as powerful as those spoken.

Chapter Fourteen

Lila examined the staircase, wondering if it would hold their weight. "I want to see the upstairs," she told Jake, who stood on the other side of the ground floor, feigning interest in some old wiring.

She wanted to go up there and find Miss Pru's room. Maybe simply standing in the same place Pru had lived would enable her to soak up some of Pru's grit and gumption. Some of her wisdom when it came to men.

Because Lila needed help.

Although she had no idea which, if any, had been her great-great-grandmother's room. She imagined if she walked around, measured the vibe of the place, she might intuitively make a guess. Get a sense of the history that had occurred in the building.

She hoped she might get a sense of the love once residing in the place. Love between Pru and Luke Pierce.

She'd found a long entry in Pru's journal about the two

lovers that brought tears to her eyes.

> *Luke Pierce has invited me to work for him out on his ranch. Permanently. As in, move in and be his live-in girl.*
>
> *I do not understand it. He is rich. Lordy, the man has money. His house is a palace, at least what I would imagine as a palace. And he has servants and hired hands running all over the place doing whatever he asks.*
>
> *Everyone smiles and seems happy there. No starving serving girls or cowed washwomen. People come and go freely, speaking to Luke as though he is a friend.*
>
> *He seems to care for his employees, too. But he lives in that house all by himself. No wife, no children.*
>
> *I am not sure what to make of it, but the look in his eyes when I woke up beside him this morning sent me scrambling for my clothes.*
>
> *"What are you doing?" he asked from the bed. He was naked and rumpled in the sheets. The picture squeezed my heart. But I am easy. A pushover. A prostitute with a tender heart. Hard to believe there is even such a thing. I do not recommend it in my girls. They will not last long in this line of work with fragile emotions.*
>
> *The right people know how to work me over, and Luke was no exception this morning.*
>
> *I did not stop to answer his question as I thought it was rather obvious.*
>
> *The giant brass bed groaned under his weight as he shifted into a sitting position, the sheets falling down around his barrel waist. "Didn't we have a good time*

last night, Prudence? Why are you in such a hurry to leave?"

If I listened closely, I could hear the hurt in his voice. But I was not falling for it. I could not afford to get attached to this man. "Sure, we had a good time. And we can again whenever you want to visit me in town."

I had to keep the situation firmly in my control.

I managed to dress quickly, forgoing the stockings as I stuffed them into my purse. I wanted, needed, to get out of there before I committed to something the man would only later regret. And when he regretted it, I would then, too.

He came up behind me as I bent to slide closed the hooks on my boots. "Prudence. Stay. I'm asking—"

"No, Luke. You do not know what you are asking." Standing straight, I faced him. That was my first mistake.

Sweet Mary, the man was beautiful in the morning sunshine. Naked as the day he burst through his mother's womb, with all that wonderful hair framing his handsome face. I was lost.

I could read everything he was feeling in his eyes He was like a child in that respect, emotions exposed for those willing to look.

Drowning in his mesmerizing whiskey eyes, I felt drunk, off-balance, and I would have fallen back if Luke had not reached out and grabbed my shoulder.

I knew from the moment he walked into the Two Nellies that I was in trouble. And last night had confirmed it.

I could not look away from his gaze.

"*Didn't you like what happened between us in my bed?*"

I had to be strong and end this before I started believing it could work. He did not know what he was asking. For a prostitute, the madam of a whorehouse, to be his live-in lover?

No. I could not bear it. Not for the both of us.

"*Luke, honey.*" *I cupped his cheek in my hand, relishing the tickle of his mustache along my palm.* "*You do not need me living here. You need a companion. A wife.*"

"*I've had that already.*"

His statement caught me off guard. He must have read the surprise in my eyes.

"*She died five years ago.*"

I knew he had made his money out West from the railroad, but I never knew until now he had been married.

Moisture built up behind my lids, but I refused to shed tears. My heart was already breaking with the knowledge that I could not fix things for this kind bear of a man. I could not make things right.

Not the way he wanted. There was no fairy-tale life for cattle barons and prostitutes.

"*I am sorry for your loss. Truly I am. But what you are asking is not reasonable.*"

He grabbed me by the shoulders, crushing me to his chest. For a moment I was frightened, but when I felt he meant no further harm, I relaxed.

Surely he saw the sense in my argument.

"*Do you take rooms at the Nellies?*"

"What?" I pulled back, looking into his eyes. They were determined and almost detached from the tension in the room. He was figuring, working out the problem.

He could not buy me on something this important.

"Where do you live? Take customers?"

Where do I take men when they want more than a drink? "I run the upstairs rooms at Nellies. I have the large room facing the street."

He released me so quickly I had to catch myself on the bedside table.

"You can visit me there, Luke. Anytime." I needed to ease the tension and make an exit before I fell apart.

Unfortunately, I did not realize it was already too late.

Jake breathed deeply, inhaling the common smells of wood dust, plaster, and hot metal. Natural, relaxing odors. Normally. With Lila here, though, his muscles didn't have an opportunity to unclench and relax.

No, she had invaded his sanctuary. *The job site.* The one place he experienced some degree of peace.

"What are you thinking? That journal came from here?" he said, following her gaze to the second floor.

"Carrie said salvagers found some stuff and turned it over to Howard. If the book was found in here, I doubt seriously he's the one who sent it." Lila chewed her bottom lip, puzzled over the mystery. "With all the business of actually buying the building and then getting you on board, I haven't figured out who sent me the journal."

"Well, you can bet it wasn't Janie, either." Jake chuckled. "Threasa's the best of the bunch, but I don't know if she could take time away from her ranch to get caught up in this drama."

Lila's eyes went wide. "Threasa Thompson? That guy at the IGA, Randy, suggested I talk to her. Said she owned Luke Pierce's former ranch outside of town."

"She does. But I honestly don't think she's your mystery person. What would she have to gain by sending you Miss Pru's journal?"

"Luke and Prudence were lovers. I think they eventually married, although I don't have any proof yet."

He hated to burst her bubble. "I don't know anything about a Pierce. The Thompsons have owned that place for a while, back before the stock market crash of twenty-nine. That's how a lot of it got sold off. They needed the money to survive."

She shook her head, not willing to concede. "I don't know. But that's the second time her name has come up in connection with Miss Pru. I think I should go pay her a visit."

Jake grunted. She never did like being told what she could or could not do. The trait had served her well, judging by the accolades from the Dallas business community.

"You have to understand where Howard is coming from. As the county seat of a county that doesn't have a whole lot of industry, he has to do what he can to boost the perceived character. Old whorehouses within throwing distance of the First Baptist Church don't go a long way to that end."

Her eyes narrowed at his weak defense of Armstrong. "Character? He'd be better off trying to encourage businesses to open and offer incentives for tourism. And an 'old whorehouse,' as you say, would intrigue a lot of history buffs."

In the harsh glare of the portable lighting positioned around the ground floor, Jake noticed for the first time how tired Lila looked. It pissed him off that she'd endured nothing but obstacles since she came home. It pissed him off more that he'd helped to put those dark smudges under her eyes.

"You sure you want to do this?"

She threw him a look that sent her ponytail to bouncing. "What, go upstairs?"

She knew perfectly well what he meant.

This time though, it wasn't personal. It wasn't about him pushing her away. He truly worried if she was up for the challenge. More like beating her head against a limestone wall where Armstrong was concerned.

She pivoted to face him. The majority of the lights were behind her now, creating a halo around her head. "You don't think I can do this?"

He started to protest, but she cut him off.

"You don't think I know what I'm getting myself into?" Her cheeks went pink, a sure sign he was in for a dressing down. He deserved it.

"I'm getting tired of defending my decisions to you. Perhaps it *is* a mistake for us to work together."

No lecture. Just resignation.

Had he pushed her too far? "Are you okay?" he asked, ready to backtrack if she needed him.

She met his gaze briefly and then looked away. "Not that you'll believe me, but I'm fine." The message couldn't be clearer. She didn't want to talk about the sex they'd had the other day, although, Christ, he deserved to be bullwhipped for that.

Was he so green he couldn't keep it in his pants? Apparently around her, yes. And she didn't complain. That's how bad she wanted them to be together.

He felt sick.

Lila wanted to do this project, so he'd do it. Straight up. Time for him to get off her case and give her what she said she wanted. Professionalism and a good job.

"Here's the way it lines up, although you probably don't need me to tell you." She knew the drill as well as he did. "We'll get the safety issues on the ground floor addressed first: wiring, foundation, any asbestos remediation. Then get some men working on the exterior, examining the brick and mortar, see what needs to be repaired or replaced. Windows may be difficult, not much to salvage there. We can go with new or hire someone to craft replicas of the old weighted pulley ones."

She nodded as he paused after each point, her normally expressive face closed and blank.

"What about the roof? I don't want any more damage to the second story."

"Casler's crew will check it out. We need to determine how many layers of materials are up there, and how many need to come off."

He glanced at his watch. "If we have time today, I'll send him up there."

"I'd like to know if the roofline of the building next door has encroached and altered my roof at all."

The pharmacy immediately next door had built a crazy, heavily slanted A-frame roof swallowing two of the older structures below. It butted against Lila's roof and looked not just stupid, but detrimental to the integrity of the older structures.

"We'll take a look."

With the agenda out of the way, he should check the stability of the stairs like she asked, but she had the strangest look on her face.

"What's up?" he asked finally.

"I'm wondering if you're worried about your screening."

And just like that, the bottom fell out of his day. She turned the tables on him and he didn't even see it coming.

"Nope."

"I'm the one who's had all the therapy, and believe me when I tell you I'm pretty good at detecting denial."

"We are not having this discussion," he ground out, trying like hell not to clench his teeth.

"Why? Because it makes you vulnerable? Well, guess what, Jake, everyone is vulnerable. You're nothing special."

"I'll let you know what Casler finds out about the roof."

And then he walked away. It was that, or grab her and shake some sense into her head. But that always ended with his head being the one rattled.

Lesson Number Thirteen —

Sometimes you have to give your man distance and let him go. If he cares for you, loves you, he will come back stronger and more willing to stay the course.

Chapter Fifteen

Lila's world would never be the same. Not after coming home, not after truly seeing him in the flesh after so long, and not after being in his arms and experiencing how good they could still be together.

"Jake?" He'd come back in after stepping outside to make some calls.

He looked up, wary after their argument.

Why did she do this to herself? To them? She loved him, and despite his behavior, she thought he loved her, too. They just needed to get past the doubts, the second-guessing, and acknowledge the uncertain future. Together.

He met her halfway. "Yeah?"

"Do you think these stairs are safe?"

He slipped a pad and pen into his back pocket and headed for the staircase, steering a path well around her.

Stop it, Jake! she wanted to scream. *I'm not the enemy.* But she simply stood there with her mouth firmly shut and watched as he mounted the steps.

"Wait until I'm at the top and then you can follow me."

He made it to the top and pushed open the door. Light spilled into the darkened stairwell and Lila could see a hall running perpendicular to the stairs.

"You can come up. If it's too hot in here for you, it's going to get a helluva lot hotter up here. We can do this later if you want."

"No, I'm coming." Once in the hallway upstairs, Jake moved ahead of her, opening doors and checking out each room before he would let her wander in.

It was definitely hotter up here, but several of the windows were either broken or warped open, and a hot Central Texas breeze moved the dust around on the wooden floors as she peered in.

"Looks like the standard, run-down old brick two-story from the turn of the century. Nothing special."

She glanced from the window to find Jake examining the antiquated wiring in the hall. He pulled a tool from his belt and lifted the plate off a broken light fixture, totally engrossed in being Mr. Fix-It.

It did look like an inspector's worst nightmare, but she could see the potential in the solid structure with its wide-open rooms and tall ceilings.

And she needed this place. Needed it like nothing she'd ever done before. If she wanted to make a fresh start in Hannington, she needed a residence, a business, and a project.

Miss Pru's was all of that. And something else, too. Lila couldn't quite put her finger on it, but she needed to restore the old place to its former glory.

By doing so, she would restore the reputation of generations of Gentry women.

"It's going to be a bear of a renovation, and once we get into it, the cost could go through the roof. Literally." He dropped corroded bits of wiring on the floor and jammed his tool back into the case he carried on his belt.

He reached a hand out and brushed her cheek. "Lila, honey, I don't want to see you hurt again."

She leaned into the caress, not a lot, but enough to feel the rub of his calloused palm on her skin.

God. What she wouldn't do to crawl into his embrace and stay for eternity.

But then she pulled back, aware of the chemistry that at the moment seemed to be nothing but trouble between them. Sex, they were good at. Love, they were not.

"Jake, I'm a big girl now. Let me worry about what's good for me."

A rush of air swooped through the windows and rustled his hair, sending a lock spilling across his forehead. His eyes were a vibrant green in the diluted light.

Lila wanted to brush his soft hair back and cradle his face in her hands like she used to.

But maybe it was time to stop thinking of old times, and plan for the future.

"I'll make some calls and get some people down here." She pushed the anxiety down, so far down it made her feet feel like lead as she moved past Jake and headed for the stairs. "Don't worry about it. I'm sorry I bothered you with this."

"Why are you being so damn obstinate about this?"

She reached the top step and headed down. "Why do you care? I let you off the hook."

Yeah, off the hook was good. So why did his conscience keep yelling "backstabbing bastard" in his ear?

"Look, Lila, I said I'd do it and I will." Aw, hell. Shut up, idiot, before you promise her an early deadline. "And I'll have it done before Christmas."

She turned at the bottom of the staircase, her raised eyebrows letting him know in no uncertain terms she thought he smelled like a liar.

"Truly. I'll do it. But it's going to be expensive. If you're willing to lay out a few hundred grand, then I'll keep my mouth shut and do the work. I'd be stupid not to."

Her tight-lipped smile said she agreed.

If he knew her like he thought he did, then a big hot fudge sundae should put her in a better mood and say sorry better than anything. Well, almost better than anything.

"Come on." He led the way to the front door, refusing to listen to the voice that urged him to let her go and hire somebody else. "We're going to Miller's Drive-In for some ice cream.

"Your treat?" she said skeptically when he stopped to look back at her.

He tried to appear offended. "Of course. I invited you, didn't I?"

"Hmmm," she said as she breezed past him and out the door.

Jake parked in the weathered and pothole-ridden lot next to Miller's. The five-hundred-square-foot ice cream shop had the ignored, vintage shabby chic look that was so popular in small-town America. It had operated in Hannington since he turned seven and he, and every other kid in town, had spent every spare penny on ice cream, root beer, and cheap hamburgers.

"God, Old Man Miller's still running this place? He must be eighty by now," Lila said, squinting through the dusty windshield to the line of children and adults outside Miller's.

"He only works the holidays. Ernie, his son, has taken over and handles the business."

They left the air-conditioned cocoon of the truck to stand in line behind a woman with three small children, the youngest a hyperactive three-year-old who kept running through the tunnel of his mother's legs.

Jake began to have second thoughts about bringing Lila to Miller's when Otis pulled up in his wreck of a 1977 Dodge truck. Nearly all of the pea-green paint had been beaten off the thing by the summer sun, and now the vehicle resembled more a sick dog on its last leg than a truck.

"Hey, how y'all doin'?" Otis said as he emerged from the cab and ambled to their spot in line.

"Good, now that Jake has agreed to keep his comments and advice to himself and do the work I'm paying him for."

Otis blew out a heavy breath and looked at Jake. Maybe the old fart was on his side for once?

"Ah, now, Lila. You can't keep a man from speakin' his mind when he needs to," Otis chastised with a wink to her and a shift to his good leg.

"I can when he's the hired help."

Otis shrugged and gave Jake a sympathetic smile.

Nope, he stuck to Lila's side like they were related.

"What are you doing here?" she asked, shading her eyes as the sun reflected off Miller's front window. "I thought you'd been advised against eating sugar."

Otis had been borderline diabetic for a while, and the doc had told him recently to lay off the sweets and carbs and watch his diet.

"Ernie makes a special sugar-free smoothie for me. And I already cleared it with my doctor," he told her when she frowned.

"That reminds me, Jake. I ran into Rogers's wife and she said she's been trying to get you on the phone for the last two days. Something about a change in your appointment. Been moved to the teaching hospital in Temple."

Shit. And he thought they'd left behind this conversation at Miss Pru's. He looked over at Lila, who didn't say a word. She didn't have to. Her eyes were filled with compassion and empathy.

The mother in front of them finally stepped away with her now-quiet trio, all focused on eating their ice cream.

"Jake? Talk to me," she said finally. "Have they found something?"

"It's a routine visit. Nothing to worry about." He nodded to Ernie, who waited patiently while a fan blew over his head, moving the ends of his overgrown hair against his baseball jersey that proclaimed him "Coach."

He watched as Ernie leaned farther out of his window to hear the conversation.

"Sorry, Jake," Otis said, having the decency to appear contrite.

He had a feeling Otis wasn't truly sorry, but he would be later when he got him alone.

"Why are you going to Scott & White hospital? Sounds

more serious than a screening."

Jake felt eyes on his back. There were people behind them in line. Watching. Listening.

"Dammit, Lila. It's nothing. Now order your ice cream so Ernie can pull his body back inside to the air-conditioning."

She spun around, coming face-to-face with Miller's new manager.

"It is routine, you know. My sister goes in every year for a screening. Nothing to get upset about. And if you are, one of my hot fudge sundaes with extra hot fudge and nuts should cheer ya up."

Ernie disappeared back inside Miller's and the sound of tin container tops being overturned drifted out to their ears.

Lila turned back around, her mouth hanging open. "Why does Ernie know more about this than me?"

His patience was at an end, like this conversation. "Because he lives here. You don't."

She recoiled like he'd slapped her.

Otis shuffled his feet on the sidewalk.

Well, hell. And here he'd been trying to lift her from an already-foul mood.

"I don't really feel like ice cream right now. Otis, will you see she gets back to her car?"

Otis nodded.

"Jake—"

But he didn't stick around long enough for her to finish. He jumped inside his truck and slammed the door, keeping his gaze off the crowd staring at him.

Lesson Number Fourteen —

Explore your feelings. The better you know yourself, the better you can express yourself to your man. This will help you avoid saying words out of anger, which are the hardest words of all to take back.

Chapter Sixteen

Jake slammed into the trailer, throwing his utility belt on the shabby pile of cushions on legs that served as a couch. He'd had his trusty old job site trailer moved to Lila's building today and just in time, because he needed something out of the fridge.

"There better be a goddamn beer in here." He jerked the door open to find not just the two beers and leftover pizza he knew to be there, but a fridge stocked with more food than a cooler of its size deserved.

He took in the bottled juices and waters, the bags of fresh fruit, the cut vegetables and the sandwich meat. "What the hell…?"

Who had been in here? And why?

He had a suspicion.

He surveyed the trailer more patiently, looking for signs of an unwanted presence. Nope, the trailer was exactly as he'd left it this morning when he'd moved it, dingy but serviceable.

With the exception of the fridge full of his favorite snack foods.

He looked for the beer and found it in the inside door. At least she hadn't thrown it out. If she was going to invade his life and drop little surprises like this, she better have the decency to leave the beer.

Jake ripped the cap off and collapsed onto the couch. The rickety wood frame groaned under his weight, but held together. Barely.

He was about to down half the bottle when he noticed his running shoes lined up neatly near the wall next to the trailer door.

He didn't remember leaving his running shoes here. They should be at home, on the floor next to his shorts and T-shirt that needed to be washed. He had a system, and the shoes being here instead of there was not part of the system.

Had Lila gone in his house? He maintained a tradition of keeping people the hell out of his house. It was the one place where he could kick back and be whoever he wanted to be, in whatever mood he felt like. But somehow the thought didn't make him as angry as he knew it should have.

He probably felt forgiving with the prospect of so much food in his little dumpy trailer.

His looked for the familiar bloodstain on the toe of the left shoe, courtesy of a barbed-wire fence slapping him on the knee a couple of months ago. It wasn't there.

Setting the still full beer aside, he retrieved his sneakers and looked closer at the mesh fabric. They were spotless. Like new.

He flipped the shoes over, searching for the growing hole

in the soft tread that should be where his big toe pounded the pavement each morning.

No hole. In fact, the tread was fresh and unmarred.

His blood rushed in his ears.

Lila.

Lila had taken the time to stock his fridge and mend his favorite pair of running shoes. She had invaded his privacy, true, but she hadn't blustered in changing things around, cleaning up after him like a wife.

She'd gone for subtle things. Things that meant a lot to Jake, but that he never found the time to do for himself.

Shit. And he had been doing so good without her.

Hadn't he?

Lila examined the exterior brick of Miss Pru's house for signs of settling. Ordinarily, the weather-sensitive ground shifted building foundations in Texas so cracks—and sometimes severe movement—jeopardized the security of the structure.

Miss Pru's looked solid, with enough corner joints to allow for the expansion and retraction of the brick at various times of the year.

She wished her heart had the same capabilities.

"Tough ole gal," she said affectionately, patting the pitted surface of the sandstone-colored brick. Heat seeped into her palm, and for an instant Lila imagined she could feel the heart of the building beating faintly, like a slumbering giant.

"I'm not sure if you're referring to yourself or the building here." A familiar voice, full of amusement, caught her off guard, causing her to spin on the heels of her leather sneakers.

"Mark! What are you doing here? Why aren't you in Dallas?" She couldn't believe he stood there, on a dusty patch of alley sprouting with scraggly milkweed and cigarette butts, looking as fresh and cool as he typically did back in a swanky Dallas martini bar.

"Your progress reports were rather disappointing in their detail. I mean, I know all about your grandmother, but honey, what about this man? This Jake?" He waved an arm, the cuff of his exquisitely wrinkled linen shirt making slow circles in imitation of his grand gesture.

She threw a hurried glance around the alley, looking for signs of Jake's truck. She hadn't seen him since he left the ice cream stand hours ago. She'd done a bit of shopping for him and with Casler's help, had his running shoes repaired. A subtle *I'm sorry* without the mess of actually saying it.

John Casler may grow on her yet. They had one thing in common anyway: Jake.

But now, her unspoken wish had been fulfilled. A dear friend when she needed one the most.

The urge to leap into his arms and be comforted like a little girl raged in her heart. If one person, one friend, could make everything seem all right when it surely was not, Mark was that friend.

Lila sobered. He didn't come all the way out here to nowhere Hannington to check up on her. Did he?

She watched his worried glances, his appraising stare. He would, thank God. That's what friends were for.

She threw another look down the alley, but there wasn't any sign of the red-and-white Chevy or Jake.

Lila stepped into Mark, wrapping her arms around his torso. It felt so good to be held in a man's arms. Even if that man wasn't the least bit interested in her.

"Hey there, girl. Are you okay?" He hugged her and rocked her briefly, pushing her back so he could stare down into her eyes. "It's as I thought. There's more to this matter with Jake than you'd admit."

"Well, of course there's more. But I'm not going to tell you about it over the phone. Besides, you shouldn't be worrying about me—you should be taking care of my business while I'm away."

He wrapped his arm around her waist and propelled her out of the alley, toward the front of the store and into the shade. Lila fell in beside him easily enough, even though he stood a good six inches taller than her, with a longer stride to match.

"Your business is fine. Good, in fact, despite that asshole in Austin raising a ruckus. But you're not."

When they reached the front of the store, Lila sank down onto the freshly polished oak bench she'd placed out front earlier in the day. The heat had warmed the wood and it penetrated her cotton overalls as she sat.

Beads of sweat popped up on her brow, beneath the fringe of bang that had fallen loose of her ponytail. "Mark, I know you mean well, and I am so glad to see you, but everything is fine. I'm having a grand time with this old building, visiting my grandmother has been the best, and frankly, I couldn't be happier." She forced cheer into her voice, pushing back the emotion that threatened to spill whenever she lied.

She mustered up the courage to look over at his face as he

sat down next to her on the bench. She took in his profile: a smooth cheek, strong nose, and square jaw.

He looked off in the direction of the Curl 'n Swirl. Maybe this wouldn't be so hard after all. Lying to her best friend.

"You want to go grab some lemonade and I'll take you on a tour of Miss Pru's?"

When he didn't answer, Lila nudged him with an elbow. "Aren't you curious to see my new baby?" She hooked a thumb over her shoulder, pointing inside the dirty window.

Mark glared off into the distance, creases forming around his normally smiling eyes.

Lila followed his gaze, but all she saw were people hurrying in and out of the grocery store, their arms loaded with purses or sacks, or both. Everything as it should be.

Maybe Mark had never seen an IGA before. They definitely didn't have them in Dallas.

"Mark, you up for some lemonade and a tour?"

He tore his gaze away from whatever fascinated him and glanced quickly at her before resuming his watch. "Sure. I'll go get it. Why don't you head inside and I'll bring it over?"

He flew off the bench and tore down the steps, jogging across the street. Fortunately, there was little traffic, because Mark never stopped to look.

What the heck had gotten into him? First he showed up unannounced, demanded explanations, and then fled like the hounds of hell nipped at his heels.

Men. She couldn't understand them. Even when they were gay.

Jake threw his truck into park and leaned over the wheel, watching the polished man who had previously been hugging Lila walk his away.

He'd started down the alley minutes ago to meet her, a mixture of dread and anticipation warring in his gut, but when he spied her wrapped around another man, he had sat for a moment. He didn't know if he should be angry she could be proclaiming her love for him one minute, and the next, hopping in the arms of another.

But then he realized he should be happy. She'd found someone else. He didn't have to convince his wife life would be better without him anymore.

So he'd left the lovers to themselves and come over to the IGA because he had nothing else to do and time to kill before he trotted back across the street and acted none the wiser.

Just as he decided, yeah, he should feel relieved, he spotted the lucky man walking over to his truck. Lila sat on the bench in front of the store, staring in their direction.

"I take it you are Jake Winter," the man said, easing up to the door of Jake's truck with an easy grace he didn't normally see in other men. "Or some degenerate who likes to spy on unknowing women."

When Jake simply raised his eyebrows in calm response, the man smiled.

"The strong, silent type. You *must* be Jake."

Lila had been talking about him to this guy? "And you are?" he asked.

"Mark—the coworker and sometimes overnight guest."

Jake gritted his teeth. They'd broken the ice fast. "So you drove all the way to Hannington to stay overnight? It's going to be crowded over there at Lila's grandmother's."

He'd swear the other man's eyes sparkled.

"The more the merrier, I think, although I hear you like it nice and simple. Haven't you heard, my friend: one is the loneliest number?"

The conversation weirded Jake out. He didn't know whether to kick Mark's ass or brush his arm off the truck door and drive away laughing.

He slid a glance to Lila calmly sitting on the bench outside her building. This guy meant something to her. What, he didn't know. So he'd play nice and give Mark the message meant for Lila.

"I think, *Mark*, you might have the wrong idea about me. Lila and I are estranged. Meaning, we no longer live together, sleep together"—he'd pay for that lie somewhere down the road—"play house together, or anything proper married couples do. So if you're looking for my permission to chase Lila, consider it granted."

Mark leveled his cool amber eyes on Jake. He read a protectiveness there, speaking volumes of his relationship with her. Yeah, once upon a time, he, too, had wanted to protect her with his life. But when a man didn't have a life to offer, the point was sorta moot.

"You really this backcountry dumb?"

"What?" Jake croaked.

Mark narrowed his eyes as if inspecting an insect pinned in a display case. "I've always heard about redneck dumb, but growing up in Dallas, I didn't come across it often. Inner-city prejudice and narrow-minded, bigoted rich assholes, yeah, but I've never met an honest-to-God country dumb. I'm simply trying to determine if you're really this stupid, or pretending."

Jake pushed open the door of his truck, forcing Mark back three steps. He slammed the door behind him and looked down on Mark, who held his ground like a fierce, manicured show dog.

He couldn't kick Mark's ass; it wouldn't be a fair fight. But Christ, did this guy never give up? What more did he want Jake to say? He'd handed Lila over on a silver freakin' platter.

"We may be backcountry dumb out here in the sticks, Mark, but we can still recognize when a man is asking to have the shit beat out of him."

"The potential for a fight seems to be the only thing to rouse you. From the stories I've heard, you used to be roused in other ways."

Words clogged in his throat like cars during rush hour. "*What?*"

"Hard of hearing, too? So we've established you're blind, backcountry dumb, violent, and now, hard of hearing. So, okay, even though you are extremely easy on the eyes, I can see why Lila left you. Too many deficits."

He grabbed the front of Mark's neatly pressed shirt and dragged him close so they stared more or less eye to eye. "I think you'd better drive back to Dallas while you still have the use of your arms and legs. The scenery's not as pretty from the back of an ambulance."

"Oh, but Jake, darling, everything we want to see is right here. Now that Lila's back. Isn't that the point of this entire display?"

Jake heard her crossing the parking lot and turned to watch her running toward them, a look of complete horror on her face.

"What the hell is going on?" she yelled, skidding to a stop.

Jake released his shirt and Mark regained his composure instantly, grabbing Lila's forearm as she leaned into him for balance. A friendly gesture. A comfortable gesture. Intimate, dammit.

A pain, something like a knife thrust, slid into Jake's side and stayed, sending bursts of torture radiating up through his heart.

"Honey, we are talking man to man. And sometimes, men have to talk with their whole bodies."

Lila looked from Mark to Jake and then back to Mark.

"Well, are you done? Because there are things Jake needs to do on my building."

Had he just been a part of this very weird exchange?

Give up. It's easier, man.

With a slow exhale, Jake shook his head and left the pair standing in the parking lot of the IGA while he crossed the street.

Sometimes surrender made sense.

Lesson Number Fifteen —

Let him be a man. Honor him and cherish what makes him masculine. And take pride in your femininity. The results will be evident at night when the bedroom door closes.

Chapter Seventeen

Jake watched Casler kick up dust with his steel-toed boots as he crossed the construction site in the fading twilight. He thought he could be alone out here, away from the people and traffic, all the noise.

Jenna Hillcrest's place was ostentatious and overblown, but the site had a great view, one he could appreciate. Situated on a bluff, it overlooked a small valley full of old live oak trees standing tall among the encroaching cedar.

If he owned the place, Jake would come in and rip out the cedar and let the oaks have some breathing room.

The sun sank lower in the western sky and colors washed overhead, hot summer strokes of red, pink, and orange. He looked away from the beauty and at the beer can in his hand instead.

"Thought I'd find you here. Didn't know you'd have beer, though. Could've saved myself ten bucks." Casler raised his six-pack of beer and set it in the bed of the truck. He hitched a hip against the open tailgate and pulled an opener from his pocket, flipping the beer cap off his bottle of India Pale Ale and into the bed of Jake's truck.

He took a long swallow, something close to ecstasy crossing his darkened features. "So what's up? You don't normally drink, but when you decide to, you buy the shittiest beer in Texas? Are you punishing yourself or what?"

Jake tossed back the can, sucking the last of the liquid down his throat. He crumpled it and threw it over his head into the pile with the other one.

He gave Casler a level stare and pointedly ignored his question, tipping the lid off the cooler at his back and digging a can from the slushy ice.

"How'd it go with Lady Hillcrest the other day?"

Casler had pissed her off good and he knew it. It seemed everybody was on edge lately. Something in the water? Or was it Lila's return to town that had everything and everyone on its ear? Refusing to consider it a setback, he'd told Casler to go to Threasa's and start her job.

And he'd gone. Without a fight.

Interesting development.

"She couldn't be the one who put you in such a good mood, so it must be the wife."

"What do you know about it?" Jake asked, trying to decide if he should grab his cooler and go find an even more remote spot or if he should fess up to Casler he lost his head whenever it came to Lila.

"Ever since she came back, you've been on edge. Broody."

Jake couldn't believe he'd used the word to describe him. "Broody?"

"Yeah, man. It's obvious you want this chick, but something is holding you back. It's making you broody. I mean, shit, look at this sunset. Why are you out here by yourself when that's going on? It's romantic as hell." Casler tipped his beer at him before polishing off the last swallow.

He grinned, amused finally. "I'm not alone. You're here. And speaking of you're here, *why* are you here? Shouldn't you be at Threasa's?"

"I was there. Things were going good and then the shrew from hell showed up."

Jake shook his head. "Howard must be paying some kind of penance to stay married to that woman. Although, what the hell, he deserves her.

"And the job?" he pushed, knowing Casler wanted to avoid talking about Threasa.

"Fine. It's a much bigger job than probably even she recognized, but I'll head over there after I finish here each day. We've got until spring."

He knew it wouldn't take that long for Casler to finish the job. Maybe he wanted to stretch it out, stay out at Threasa's as long as he could?

Jake looked out, scanning the half-completed house on the pad. Although hot as hell, scraggly, and rock-strewn, he loved the landscape. Something about the wide-open vistas and raw connection to the earth held him there in Hannington, keeping him from moving on to bigger and more lucrative cities.

"So when are we all going to double-date?" Casler asked, laughing around the bottleneck in his mouth.

Jake sighed. "Never."

"Why the hell not?"

"Because we're not getting back together, and she's not staying in Hannington." If he said it enough, he'd convince himself.

"So you're getting divorced then?"

Jake rubbed his eyes. "Casler, don't you have someone else to torment?"

"Nope. You're my only friend." As much as Jake didn't think that fact rang true, he knew Casler felt it sometimes.

"Lila and I have been over for some time. It was a high school thing and we grew out of it."

"So why are you still married to her?"

The truth? "I don't know."

Casler fell silent finally, and Jake drank his beer, trying not to think about why he stayed married to Lila. Yeah, he'd sent her the papers, but when she didn't respond, he didn't press the issue. Simply let it rest. He didn't plan to ever marry again, and if she did, well, then she'd file.

Until then…

"Who's there?" John straightened from his slouch on the tailgate.

He followed Casler's look to the other side of the house pad. A tall, lithe woman stepped out of the shadows and into the last bit of light.

"It's Threasa Thompson. I'm sorry to bother you out here. Jake, your secretary told me you guys were still here and I wanted to come by and give John some good news."

Now, who would have guessed? Casler being pursued? "Sure. Come on over," Jake said with a wave. He hopped down from the tailgate, leaving an empty spot next to Casler.

He threw his empty can in the cooler and pushed it up to

nestle against the cab of his truck, where he secured it with bungee cords.

"Going somewhere?" Casler said.

"Yep. I gotta go. I promised my folks I'd be over for dinner and I'm late."

"I'm not invited?" he teased, but Jake heard the subtle request for an out, a reason not to linger alone with Threasa.

When would he get it? If Casler didn't seize the opportunity, she'd go elsewhere and he miss something good.

"Not this time. It's something of a summit meeting."

Casler snorted and eased his big body off the tailgate.

"We can move the party over to my truck. Come on, Threasa, and tell me the good news."

"It's not a big deal. If you need to be somewhere, I understand," she blurted.

"Didn't you just hear? I don't have anywhere I need to be. It's you and me. Now sit," he said, pointing at the empty space on his lowered tailgate.

Jake's hopped into his cab, watching Casler in his rearview mirror. Maybe he did get it. Maybe something of what Jake had said finally sank in.

Somebody needed to be happy, for Christ's sake.

Lesson Number Sixteen —

Surround yourself with family, or good friends. A good group of women can help you with problems your man cannot.

Chapter Eighteen

The doorbell rang as she hung up the phone. For an instant Lila thought it might be Jake. Hope blossomed on the tail of excitement, but then fear set in, and she prayed it wasn't Jake. Things were not progressing according to her plan at all. In fact, she considered it almost a complete failure.

"Who is it, Lila?" Granny shouted from the den over the melody of *The Ellen DeGeneres Show* intro.

"I don't know."

She looked through the diamond-shaped pane of glass on the front door and saw Margaret Winter standing outside.

Jake's mother! *Holy hell.* Could she be here to tell Lila to quit chasing after her son?

A pillar of the community, generous to a fault, and always full of good cheer, Margaret was a wonderful woman, but protective of her son in a way that always left Lila feeling slightly chilled, like she didn't measure up.

And damned if nothing had changed in the ten years Lila

had been gone from Hannington, because she felt like that self-conscious eighteen-year-old all over again.

"Well, who is it?" Ellen introduced her favorite new book in the book club, but Granny's voice drowned out the title.

"It's Mrs. Winter," Lila called back, trying not to shout. She didn't want to give the waiting Mrs. Winter the impression she'd gotten lazy or lost her manners in Dallas.

She opened the door and fixed a proper smile on her face to receive her mother-in-law.

"Hello, Margaret."

"Lila! It's so good to see you." Margaret's face lit up, and her eyes, very much like her son's, twinkled with emotion. Her enthusiasm did seem genuine. "When Jake told me you were in town, I had to come by to see you." She reached out, grabbed Lila's folded hands, and delivered a friendly squeeze.

"Would you like to come in? Granny and I are having some bread pudding." She stepped to the side, allowing room for Margaret to enter the foyer.

"That sounds wonderful. I'd love to."

Lila saw her mother-in-law to the dining room and placed her at the table, excusing herself to prepare the dessert for serving. Running to the den, she switched off the television and turned to Granny.

"Go in there and talk to Jake's mother while I get the bread pudding ready."

"We're eating that now? I thought you were saving it for the Bombshells' victory dinner." Granny stood, rearranging her purple-casted arm more comfortably across her chest.

"I'll make more."

Granny strolled into the dining room, allowing Lila to

breathe a sigh of relief.

Lila's hands shook as she scooped the still-warm pudding into dessert cups. Margaret's visit surely meant trouble.

Her mother-in-law had opposed her marriage to Jake on the grounds that they were too young and still had college ahead of them. Or as Lila had read between the lines: not good enough for her son. And then when Jake became ill, Mama had marched in, practically taking over their lives and Jake's care.

It had been a stressful experience.

With the bowls of bread pudding in hand, Lila paused inside the kitchen, listening to Margaret whisper covertly to Granny.

"This Jenna Hillcrest is becoming a pest. I know the woman has more money than God, but that's no reason to disregard common decency. Jake spends hours nearly every day placating her. I'm telling you, Barbara, she's trying to wheedle her way into his life to become the new Mrs. Jacob Winter. And she's barely divorced from her previous husband."

Lila nearly dropped the bowls. She collapsed back against the cabinet, cradling the bread pudding and listening. The news took the breath out of her like a sucker punch to the abdomen.

"What does he say?" Granny asked.

"To mind my own business. Of course, he says it sweetly," Margaret said.

Jake couldn't remarry when he still had a wife. Maybe this explained his disinterest and his completely callous attitude after sex. If another women held his heart, why would he want to entangle himself with his old ball and chain?

A tear slid down her cheek, followed by another. Lila so wanted to do it right this time, and everything couldn't be going more wrong.

"Lila, honey? Do you need any help?" Margaret called from the other room.

Swiping the back of her wrist across her eyes, Lila made her way into the dining room, plopping the bowls down on her grandmother's veneered bird's-eye maple table. She didn't look up to see their reactions, just planted herself in a chair and grabbed her own bowl.

The awkwardness hung heavy in the room. She could feel it crawling up her scalp. It was another awful feeling to add to her mountain of grief. Yet another event she had soured and turned wrong despite her very best intentions.

"Ah, I was telling your grandmother I think it's wonderful you're staying in Hannington. It will be nice to have you around again. In fact, I told Jake the very thing last night at dinner."

A streak of meanness gripped Lila. She wanted to hurt Jake's mother as much as she hurt her with the news of another woman. "I really don't know how long I'll be staying."

"Oh! I understood from Myra you bought the old store on the square. I'm sorry, I assumed that meant you were planning on staying. Jake said the work would take several months to finish and he seemed very interested in the project. Something about a bordello, and the mayor being quite upset."

She looked up for the first time, meeting Margaret's surprised gaze. "I can run the renovations and future business from Dallas. I don't need to be in Hannington to do it."

Why tell Margaret these lies? Lila didn't have any plans to leave. But she hurt. Hurt to hear that other women wanted Jake and maybe, he wanted them back.

She could see Granny's deepening frown from the corner of her eye. She would get a lecture about manners and the graciousness of hostesses when Margaret left; she could feel it in her bones.

"I hope you reconsider, dear. It would be wonderful for everyone—including Jake—to have you here. And we need someone with your talents and expertise. I mean, my goodness, a day spa. How wonderful!" Margaret's spoon played in the dessert, but she didn't take a bite.

Lila dropped her spoon against the bowl, the clank loud in her ears. "From what I understand, Jake's 'schedule' is so busy, he doesn't have any spare time for wives."

Margaret's mouth gaped. The look of shock on her mother-in-law's face should have made her feel better, but it didn't. It made Lila feel mean and small. She immediately wanted to take it back and apologize.

Granny rustled in her chair. "Margaret, you're going to have to forgive Lila. The doctor says she's suffering from a slight case of heatstroke. The medication is having an effect."

Granny turned her blue eyes on Lila. Anger brimmed beneath their smooth surface. "Why don't you go and lie down for a bit? Margaret and I can visit while you rest."

She'd been ordered from the room and with good reason. Granny's concocted story about heatstroke meant she'd get a lecture later. Her special way of excusing Lila's bad manners without humiliating everyone involved. Always had been.

Jake's mother bit her lip, on the verge of making a comment, but Lila's aggressively hostile behavior had made her hesitant.

"I'm sorry, Margie." She used her mother-in-law's family name, letting her know she'd screwed up. "It's difficult. Coming home. Things are the same, and yet, not the same. It's taking me a while to readjust."

Margaret slid her hand across the table and laid it on Lila's. "I know, sweetie. Let me tell you a little secret, though. I haven't seen Jake this motivated in ages. He blusters and pretends he doesn't care. He does. And he can't hide it from me. So don't give up."

Holy cow. She never expected this from Jake's mother. She practically pushed Lila to go after him. Maybe she'd judged Margie unfairly.

"Besides, I want to help with this day spa. Where can I apply for a job?"

If there is a lesson I have learned throughout my life, it must be this: do not torture yourself needlessly with what you cannot or should not have. I learned this the way a dog learns not to mess the floor.

Physically, one painful day at a time.

So why I find myself at the train station from time to time is a mystery. It is as if my feet develop a mind of their own and I walk, not in the direction of the station, but somewhere else, the stables or the general store.

But I end up there anyway. Standing on the wide oak platform under the shade of the veranda, with dust clinging to the tips of my black-heeled shoes, watching the train come in from some eastern city, the slow chug of the wheels spitting steam as it rolls to a stop.

Not many passengers depart. A few. Never more than a handful. Mostly people in rumpled traveling clothes looking dazed and unsure, as if they think they took the wrong train and surely this dusty two-bit cow town is not really where they meant to go.

Eventually, after talking to the ticket man behind the iron bars of the cashier's cage, they realize where they are and compose a more determined face, heading off in the direction of the waiting stagecoach. Sometimes, I see them later in the saloons around town and occasionally in the parlor of my own house.

I stay until the whistle blows and the people are gone. Until it is me and the noisy train, its black belly shoveled full of coal, belching plumes of white smoke over our heads.

The train makes its way out, heading north across the Red River and into the plains of Kansas.

Or so I am told. I always ask the ticket man where the train is going. As if I might one day buy a ticket and board the train.

I have never been to Kansas. And why should I? There are simply more towns like this one. More saloons, more hurdy-gurdy dance halls filled with young girls.

And always, more cowboys.

Hannington is just as good as any town.

I remind myself of this as I force my feet off the boardwalk and toward the cracked dirt street. Hannington is just as good as any town, better than some I have known.

Better than the filthy, overcrowded ramshackle tenement house I came from in crowded New York. Better than the poultry factory there, where I worked for two years, barely earning enough money to feed myself and pay rent. Better than the men I came to know on the docks of—

Enough. Refer to above lesson. Do NOT torture yourself with the past. You cannot change it, or relive it. You can only move forward and do your best not to repeat the same mistakes.

Life gives you second chances.

Take them and do better.

Jake ran. Past open fields and quietly grazing cattle toward where, he didn't know. It felt good, this burning in his lungs and his legs. He hadn't been able to sleep, so he'd decided what the hell, he'd get an early start on his run.

Except Casler had some kind of goddamn sixth sense, because the man waited outside for Jake, warming up.

He yawned, eyeing Casler, who looked fresh and awake. He could sleep for days, but when it came down to it, rest wouldn't come. Not in his cold, empty bed. It suddenly seemed more like a tomb than a bed.

He'd taken to sleeping anywhere he could snatch fifteen minutes of solitude. His truck in between jobs. His kitchen table as he went over blueprints.

Christ, it seemed he hadn't been able to sleep like a regular person since Lila'd come back into his life.

"Are we training for a marathon you forgot to tell me about?" Casler jogged beside him now, his words low and clipped under the strain of running.

"No."

"Then you want to tell me why the fuck you're trying to run my legs off? I'd like to use 'em later today if it's okay with you."

Jake kept his gaze on the road ahead. He could see the water tower in the distance, maybe two or three more miles. He could make it. And then he would stop.

But not before then.

"You can stop anytime, John."

He heard Casler's snort and felt him push forward before he blew Jake's doors off.

"Try to keep up, old man." The words drifted back to him.

He pushed himself harder. Faster. Maybe when he was exhausted enough, he would stop thinking of Lila.

Maybe.

But not likely.

Lesson Number Seventeen —

You may know what is best for you and your man, but he may not agree. Use persuasion and patience to make your claim. It will eventually pay off.

Chapter Nineteen

Lila left behind the brick streets of the town square for the open asphalt of the county highway. Her Lexus ate up the miles as she sped farther in the wide-open space of the county.

She'd called Reverie Construction for the last three days trying to get in touch with Jake, only to be told he was "out of the office." As to her question of "when the hell will he be back?" the response remained unwaveringly the same every time: "When the job's done."

Well, Lila had a job for him to do and she had had enough sitting around watching *Jeopardy!* with Granny, waiting for the damn phone to ring. So, with map in hand, she tracked down Jake like a wanted man gone into hiding.

He'd better not bolt when she found him, or she might do something crazy, like hog-tie the fool.

The drive to the construction site wound through a pasture of prickly mesquite trees and rocky granite outcroppings. Set back into the gently rolling hills, the landscape was harsh, but with a scrubby, endearing beauty that took Lila's breath away.

As she crested the last hill, the site came into view. Laid out on a sprawling concrete pad, the frame stood tall and open, ascending to a vaulted roof reminding her of a church nave.

"Beautiful" didn't do the house justice. "Awe-inspiring," maybe. Jake had outdone himself.

She could easily envision sitting on the front porch with the sun rising in the eastern sky, a hot cup of coffee warming her hands. Jake sitting next to her, his lanky frame sprawled in a wicker recliner, newspaper in hand.

Her heart constricted at the thought. Contentment. Yes. That's what she wanted. That's what had been missing from her life.

She pulled the car to a stop behind Jake's truck, scanning the site, looking for his familiar form.

Not finding him, she gave her face a once-over in the rear-view mirror and gathered her keys before she lost her nerve. She was about to enter Jake's domain without his permission and despite his rather obvious attempt to ignore her presence.

Glad she wore her running shoes, Lila sidestepped framing remnants, nails, five-gallon buckets, and other construction odds and ends as she climbed the low berm of dirt referred to as the spoil pile. She sensed the curious and appraising stares, but none of the men looked remotely familiar.

"No, man! You can't do it that way!"

Lila followed the sound of the scathing outburst. She knew the voice, and sure enough she spotted Otis at the far end of the house yanking PVC pipes out of the floor.

"If you set the height there, Ms. Hillcrest will be stooping to brush her pearly whites every morning. The woman's short, but she's not as short as a five-year-old."

She glided between the two-by-four frame supports to what must be the master bath, judging by the size of the layout and Otis's comment.

"Go cut some fresh pipe and do it right this time!" Otis sent the shamefaced young man on his way with a rough shake of his head. He spotted Lila in the doorway.

"I thought you might turn up sooner or later." Otis opened his wide arms and Lila ran into them. Otis had been one of her father's dearest friends during his tour overseas, a tour of duty from which he never returned.

Otis came home to Hannington, bearing her father's body. He stayed and tried to make up for her lack of a father, a father who had died at the hands of suicide bombers. He acted as a protector to the newly widowed Sarah and her young daughter, keeping the promise he'd made to her father, Michael.

Little did either of them know at the time, he would soon become her single stand-in parent. Six months after burying her husband, Sarah left town one afternoon and never returned again.

Leaving Hannington and Otis behind ten years ago had been the hardest thing Lila ever had to do, but he'd encouraged it, urging her to find her own way. And she had.

His bear hug squeezed the air from her lungs. She reveled in the comforting embrace. Otis had always made everything all right, chased away the fears of girlhood, and supported her as an entrepreneurial young woman.

He set her back, holding her at arm's length. He appraised her with a fatherly eye. "You're not eating enough of my cooking. Still too skinny. I want you back over at my kitchen table tonight girl, and I'm going to feed you chicken fried steak and mashed potatoes."

She laughed. Since she'd been back, Otis had stuffed her full of Southern comfort foods she'd been denying herself in Dallas. Nobody cooked like Otis.

It was good to be home.

"Can you go easy on the white country gravy? I want to eat it, not swim in it."

"With that kind of sass, I'll make you eat two slices of pecan pie, too." His eyes twinkled to match his grin.

She hugged him again and finally braved the question they both knew she would ask. "Is he around, Otis?"

A protective shadow crossed the older man's features. The pair went way back as well, with Otis teaching Jake everything he knew about the construction business. "He is, but I can't say he's in a mood to talk."

"He's in a bad mood? How about me? He tried to pummel my architect!"

Otis lifted his hat and scratched his bald head. "That must be the pansy-ass I'm hearing about." He held up a hand to hold off her outrage. "Not my words. Apparently Howard has had a run-in with your guy."

She didn't like his words, even if he was merely repeating the mayor. "He never mentioned an encounter. What happened?"

"Well, it seems Howard has uncovered a conspiracy. He's determined to knock down everyone associated with your little project in the hopes you'll tuck tail and head on back to Dallas."

"Crap. Why am I the last one to know about these things?" She kicked at the dust under her feet. "So what did Howard threaten him with?"

"Not so much threatened Mark, as let him in on the fact that he knows you've got a posse in town backing you."

Lila looked up in confusion. "What the hell does that mean? I've got a posse." Could he be referring to Pru's journal? And the silent benefactor who'd sent it, whom she now suspected to be Threasa Thompson?

Otis laughed. "To tell you the truth, little girl, I haven't spent a whole lot of time trying to figure it out. You know I never listen to half of what's said to me, and I follow even less of that."

She really had to get to the bottom of this secret admirer/benefactor—whatever and whoever this person was—right away. As soon as she got Jake back on track.

"I hear Mark's a snappy dresser. Smells good, too."

"What?" She leaned in, detecting another one of his teasing smiles at the corner of his mouth. "Mayor Armstrong did *not* say that."

"Your grandmother called me this morning," he elaborated.

Lord love a gossip. She should never have introduced Mark to her grandmother.

"Something going on there I should know about?" Otis's brown eyes crinkled with humor.

He thought she and Mark were involved?

Lila laughed out loud, feeling lighter. "Otis. Mark and I are not interested in each other that way. Trust me. We never will be."

Jake saw Lila the minute she pulled onto the site. His heart completed a painful three-sixty in his chest as he watched her long legs appear from underneath the car door, followed by her torso encased in a clinging white cotton tank.

She was a fragrant tropical breeze blowing through the desert. And he was a man in need of relief.

He watched her climb the steps to the pad, her light-colored trousers hugging the rounded shape of her bottom.

He felt an immediate response from below, a tightening of his balls inside his jeans, a pulsing he didn't need at the moment.

Turning his back on his wife, Jake studied the plans of the house under construction. The dimensions for the garage swam before his eyes as he listened to Otis greet Lila.

He couldn't make out their conversation, but the soft melody of her voice comforted him, reassured him in a way he hadn't felt in some time. She had the ability to do that, put him at ease with the simple sound of her voice. To Jake, Lila represented home. No matter where they were, what they were doing, as long as she was there, he was home.

He hadn't had a home in ten years, and he didn't want to start brooding over the fact now. He'd grown used to his bachelorhood and expected nothing more from life than heat and taxes. It was safer that way.

The hard gravel around the building site crunched underfoot as Lila walked toward him.

"Jake?" She forced a sunniness into her voice, which told him Otis had been talking too damn much. He just might fire the old cuss this afternoon, right after he gave him a piece of his mind.

"Yeah?" He stared intently at the blue layouts, but they could have been in Greek for all he got out of them.

"I'd like to talk to you about something important."

Ah, Christ, here it comes. "How long is it going to take? Because I've got a line of customers all with important business to discuss."

She huffed. A foot stomped the packed earth. "You could at least do me the courtesy of looking at me when I speak to you."

Jake made a display of throwing down his pen and turning. *Jesus, she took his breath away.* With her golden hair pushed back from her face in a loose ponytail and her warm skin void of makeup, she looked eighteen again.

He could smell her scent drifting on the hot wind.

"Let's have it."

She stared him down, her hands rising to rest on her hips. Jake caught a glimpse of the firm underside of her arms and the delicate curve dipping in the crook next to her breasts. He had a sudden urge to nuzzle his lips there, kissing a trail down her side to her hip.

"When are you going to be back at my site? I would like to move some walls on the second floor."

"My guys are there. Plus you have your architect, Matt."

She squinted her eyes at him. "His name is Mark."

"Whatever. Seems like you have enough expertise to make some simple decisions about moving walls. And I do have other clients."

Lila stepped closer, toe-to-toe, until she almost touched his chest. She looked up into his eyes and smiled. Jake went on alert. He knew that look. Lila had a plan.

She wouldn't convince him to come back to the job site just yet. He didn't want any more surprises like Mark or his retreaded running shoes, which, dammit, were as good as new. And crap, he forgot to grill Casler about that. Next time.

He could almost taste her breath on his lips. And speaking of lips, hers were sweet, soft, open, and right in front of him.

"Honey, I've been running with the big dogs now for quite a while. I know I have the expertise. Hell, if we were in Dallas, I'd be running the entire show. But these are your guys and I would prefer if they got their directions from you. Call me old-fashioned."

He grunted and her smile grew wider, feeding off his challenge.

"You don't believe me?" Her tone mocked his disbelief.

He cast a glance down to the gap in the front of her tank top. He could see the swell of her breasts as they disappeared beneath white cotton. Did he see pink nipples or was that wishful thinking?

"Sweetheart, if you dress like this, I'm sure that's why you're as successful as you are." Her color rose a notch as his words drove home, but she didn't back down. She wouldn't until he said enough painful words to drive her away.

Why did he have to say hurtful things? He wanted to take it back. Apologize.

"You're right about that. Works on men all the time, as I'm finding out."

A rush of anger sang through his veins. The thought of other men appraising his wife's breasts as he did now made him want to punch someone. Someone like that ass Mark.

"You'd better watch out, Lila, someone is liable to take

you up on an offer you can't fulfill."

She smiled and he admired her strong white teeth. "Oh, plenty have accepted my offer, and I have yet to meet a man I couldn't handle."

She stepped back and took the sun with her. He fell into shadow without her next to him. He wanted the sun to return.

"I expect you back on the site tomorrow morning."

He would do it. In fact, had already been planning to. And he'd make sure no other man, Mark or anyone else, stood this close to his wife, breathing in the scent of her skin, eyeballing her sexy figure, thinking dirty thoughts about taking her on her granny's bathroom countertop.

"I'll drop by tomorrow when I have time."

"Fine." She glanced at her watch, retreating while she spoke. "And Mark will be there, so I would appreciate you using some of the manners your mother supposedly taught you."

Jake ignored the urge to follow her and demand she tell him about Mark. Were they seeing each other? Had they slept together?

"I can drop by around ten."

"Wonderful." Lila turned, providing him with a scenic view of her curvy backside. He wanted to sidle up to her warmth and wear her like a second skin.

She waved a hand over her head in farewell.

Who'd just won here? He scanned the site to find Otis watching him. He looked away, pretending to be absorbed in checking the plumbing for water, but Jake saw his smile.

Lila felt smug with herself and her surroundings. She'd brought Jake around to her way of thinking and it wasn't as painful as she first imagined. He could be reasonable upon occasion, with a little incentive. She ignored the niggling feeling of guilt in the back of her mind.

She couldn't be faulted if Jake and others thought she and Mark were more than friends. Did it put her in the wrong to use the misconception to her benefit?

A metallic-colored SUV climbed the drive to the construction site ahead of Lila. She watched as the driver parked the diesel-powered monster directly behind her Lexus, blocking her between a construction trailer and the rumbling Suburban.

A woman slid from behind the wheel, all legs and breasts, topped off by a shiny mane of curling blond hair. Her open high-heel sandals were completely inappropriate for a construction site. As a matter of fact, her entire presence was inappropriate for a construction site.

She breezed toward Lila, her perfect, rounded, pert, non-jiggly breasts standing at attention beneath the thin silk of her black camisole. They didn't move, which told Lila a lot. The hips, however, were swinging like an old barn door.

"Hi there." Her white teeth shone like a freshly painted white picket fence. Lila looked away, down toward a narrow waist evident by the form fit of the camisole.

Lila hated her immediately. She was perfect. Medically perfect.

"Hello."

Miss Perfect Breasts didn't seem to notice her stony expression.

"Is Jacob here?"

Oh, Jacob, was it? How very upscale. Probably the wife of an oil executive out to oversee the construction. She gave the woman's left hand a cursory scan.

No rock.

A chill raced down her spine. Lila wanted to know her business with Jacob, but refrained from asking. She didn't come out here prepared to do battle. Hell, she wore a ponytail and not a trace of makeup. How could she compete with the queen of pert?

Maybe it was better she didn't know. She picked an imaginary piece of lint off her cropped linen pants and caught a glimpse of Pert's lacquered silver toenails framed by toe rings. *Ugh!*

"He's around the corner." She pointed to the other side of the trailer.

"Thanks, hon." Pert clattered off in the direction she indicated, unaffected by the visual daggers she threw at her sculpted back.

Lila had to look. She couldn't resist, couldn't stop her eyes from dropping to the chiffon-clad rear walking toward Jake.

Slapping a hand over her eyes, she peeked again. Yep, firm, round, and...pert.

Lila's feet moved on their own; she simply obliged and let the rest of her body follow. She wouldn't spy exactly, just... um...make sure Jake hadn't disappeared.

Skirting the other side of the trailer closest to the tree line, Jake came into view, leaning over his paperwork.

"Jacob! Hard at work I see." *She* came into view, too, standing back from Jake so he could have a nice long look if he wanted.

Lila's heart nearly jumped out of her chest when Jake turned, giving the woman the once-over. He was a married man, for Pete's sake. Married to her!

Backtracking to her car, Lila slid into the driver's seat. The burning leather on her bottom barely registered as she considered Jake and Ms. Fake Boobs. More there than a professional relationship? Could this be Jenna, the woman Margie had told Granny about?

Putting the car in reverse, she hit the gas pedal and grunted as the seat belt locked her into the seat.

What the hell...? The SUV! She'd backed into the woman's SUV.

Holy hell! Would nothing go her way?

Lesson Number Eighteen —

Angry women do not make good wives. They make lonely women. Take it from me, a person who has asked many, many men why they visit my rooms rather than stay at home with their families. Letting anger, resentment, frustration, and unhappiness build inside you only drives your man away. Communicating with him cannot be worse than having him here with me, can it?

Chapter Twenty

I visited the jailhouse today. The place is horrible. It is so tiny and crowded, reeking of old alcohol and tired, sweaty men. I should be used to the smell by now, but I demand my customers come to me after they have had their bath; whether it be their weekly, monthly, or yearly matters little to me, as long as they have had it.

A young man, barely more than a boy, met me at the jailhouse door, his hair neatly combed and oiled in the front. When he turned to escort me to the cells, I noticed the back of his head was snarled from bed.

It is strange how the mind works. When I am in an unpleasant place like the jail, my mind wanders, searching for distractions, something to keep me from thinking about what I am doing. Hence, the young man today. Like a mother, I wanted to smooth his tangled hair and demand he wash his hands, freshen his clothes.

But when I stepped through the door leading to the

cells, I focused my attention on the girls inside.

"Ladies." Most knew the routine. They had been here before, as had I.

They lined up as close to the bars as they could get, a weary lot of women in various states of dress.

There were eight in all, three of whom I did not know.

I looked over my shoulder to the fidgeting youth in the entry. "Charges?" I asked.

He scampered back through to the office, which really only consisted of a rickety table with a kerosene lamp and an accompanying chair.

"Miss Prudence, we knew you'd come, ma'am." I looked at the girl on my left, her hands waving at me through the bars. Determining age is difficult among this class of prostitutes, but I placed her younger than twenty.

I have learned to read the eyes in this regard. They are the best indicator of a woman's age. The hope in her brown eyes told me life had not beaten her down. Yet.

"I told these others help would come, soon enough."

I nodded and walked down the line, examining the girls, judging what could be done, if anything.

"Two disorderly conducts, three public drunkenness, one theft, and two aggravated assaults." Mr. Tangled and Dirty stood close behind me, the corridor along the cell crowding us together.

He had a kind smile, an innocent smile. I wondered if he knew who I was and what I did to earn a living. But then he was too young to be tainted by the vice from my end of town. "Thank you, Mr...?" I did not know his name, but he had the look of the old sheriff. A son or nephew, perhaps?

"Billy Smith, ma'am." As I suspected. Well, he would learn soon enough.

"Well, Mr. Smith, I believe forty dollars will set these women free. Do you agree?" I gave him an encouraging, reassuring smile intended to set any fears he might have aside, so I might depart the jailhouse immediately.

My reticule was open and I was ready to hand over the fines when he realized I meant to pay.

"Ah, I'm not in charge here, ma'am. I'll need to check with the new sheriff before I release these ladies to your charge. If you can—"

The door at the front of the jailhouse flew open, jarring the entire structure. "Prudence!"

Luke. Hell.

"Where are you, woman?"

He raged into the corridor outside the holding cell with all the energy of a caged animal, his eyes wild and searching. When his gaze fell upon me standing outside the cell next to Mr. Smith, who, poor boy, was cowering behind me, Luke stopped short, confused.

He towered over the two of us, sucking the air out of the very room. For an instant, I viewed him as the other people in Hannington must view him. The big, scary man with the long hair who refused to carry a sidearm. A man of his size only needed fists to make his point.

"Mr. Pierce, there is no need for all the excitement." I did not want him to place us together in an intimate relationship. It would lead to talk. And more talk was

not what Luke Pierce needed.

The man was considered something of an eccentric as it was.

"But the washerwoman at the Two Nellies told me you were in jail!"

Oh dear. "I am sure she did. But what she meant to say was I am visiting the jail. Not being held."

Luke looked from me, to Mr. Smith, to the women behind the dingy cell bars. Bless the man, I saw his face flush when he comprehended the situation.

He tried to cover his actions with a good degree of bluster. He cleared his throat and stuffed his fists into his trouser pockets, speaking for the benefit of the nine other sets of ears in the room. "Of course."

Several seconds passed before Mr. Smith found his tongue. "Ma'am." He fell back a step, closer to the cell, but farther from Luke's reach. "You and the gentleman better come back when the sheriff is in to discuss your business. I can't let the prisoners go without his consent. He's got different rules, this new sheriff."

Lord save me from weak men. "And when, Mr. Smith, will the sheriff return?"

"How much?" Luke rode over the boy's answer, once again in control.

I could smell the uncertainty rolling off the young man. Sweat beaded his upper lip.

I peeked at the ladies who up until this time had been minding their behavior. They, too, had obviously caught the odor of fear in the room, for a few had stepped back from the bars with pinched mouths.

"*How much, boy? What are the fines?*"

Leave it to Luke to cut to the bottom dollar. But this was a delicate situation, and I did not want Luke to anger the new sheriff, drawing attention to the deal I had always had with the old sheriff. Whenever single women of questionable reputation were picked up and charged, we had an understanding that I would pay the fines and take the girls home.

If I could convince them to truly return to their homes, or pursue another line of work, all the better. If not, well, they went back to their dance hall, or saloon, or crib, and would end up back in jail soon enough.

So the pattern went. Until Luke appeared.

"Mr. Pierce, how kind of you to inquire on these girls' behalf. I assure you the sheriff has assessed reasonable fines and they will be released soon enough." Not that I believed a word of this, but I wanted the sheriff to know I was not willing to compromise our deal.

"Thank you, Mr. Smith. I will return shortly to discuss the matter with the sheriff."

I nodded at Luke, who stood with his fists clenched at his sides, clearly unhappy with my refusal to let him handle the matter.

"Mr. Pierce, good day." I squared my shoulders and attempted as much dignity as I could muster, marching out the door without even a glance for the girls in the cell. They knew the routine.

"Ms. MacIntosh." The words were barely discernable as they ground out from between his teeth, his head tipping in acknowledgment.

The sun shone impossibly high in the midday sky as I stepped outside and headed south, down to the Acre. I had not gotten very far when Luke caught up with me, his strides eating up the soft pine planks of the boardwalk.

"Prudence! What the hell was that all about? Why were you acting like you didn't know me?"

I would still act like I did not know him. We were in the middle of town, people coming and going all around us. The boy back inside may have been too young to know about me, but certainly everyone on the street identified me clear enough.

The audacity of my natural hair color, red, and the fairness of my Northern Irish complexion set me apart from the rest of the community as surely as if I had run naked down the middle of street.

I talked as I walked, refusing to stop. "Mr. Pierce. I think it would be better for your sake if we kept our correspondence restricted to—"

My feet nearly left the ground as I was whipped around so fast, my feathered hat slipped to one side. "Prudence, I don't give a tinker's damn what these people think of me!"

Luke was angry and justifiably so. It was hell being penned in by the dictates of society. I did not make the rules and I sure the hell did not like them, but I was forced to abide by them just the same. "I care!" I whispered fiercely. "My job is hard enough as it is. I don't want to bring more misery than is already due." His whiskey eyes bore into me, the hurt evident on his expressive face.

"But what about you, Pru? Who's going to take

*care of you? See to your needs? Comfort you when
you need it?"*

*This sweet, blessed man. His words tore through my
heart, bringing me joy at the same moment it brought
me exquisite pain.*

*Who indeed would comfort me when I needed it
most? Up until this moment of my life, there had been
no one.*

Jake tensed at the sound of Jenna's sugary voice. *What did
she want now?* It had only been a matter of days since she'd
picked a fight with Casler. Did she come back now to irritate
the hell out of Jake?

Looking up from the worktable, he took her in all at once.
Christ, the woman dressed like she was on the runway for Victoria's Secret. Like any other man, he could appreciate beauty,
but his tastes ran to the more naturally acquired kind...the kind
bestowed by God and good breeding, not the scalpel.

Jenna left him vaguely uncomfortable, like he'd sneaked
into a peep show.

"Come out to check on the skylights?" He forced himself
to be pleasant. She'd paid him to do a job, after all.

"Oh. Sure." She seemed surprise by the suggestion. "I've
been trying to get a hold of you all week, Jacob. You haven't
returned any of my calls."

True. He avoided all women at the moment, his wife in
particular.

"Houses don't get built by dreaming about 'em, Jenna.

I've been here most of the week." *Hiding out.*

She gazed at him through the lashes of her giant doe eyes, her lined lips pursing into a pretty pout. "I was hoping to ask you for an escort to the Cattleman's Ball in Fort Worth next month, if it doesn't conflict with your doctor's appointment. If you want to go, I need time to pick a dress."

Jake barely heard her. Out of the corner of his eye, he spotted Lila peeking out from behind the construction trailer. *What the hell was she doing…?*

And then it hit him. Lila was spying on him with Jenna. She was jealous.

He leaned in closer to Jenna, cutting her off in mid-sentence, something about a custom dress from Los Angeles. He got a nose full of her overpowering perfume and it recoiled the skin along certain delicate areas of his anatomy.

"When did you say it was?"

"Next month, the seventeenth—"

A swaying branch near the trailer recaptured his attention. Lila had gone.

"Sorry. Can't make it. Conflict."

Either he'd done his work well and warded off two women, or he'd just signed his own death warrant. Lila had never taken well to jealousy when they were married.

"Are you sure? I think we'd have fun." Jenna closed the eight inches separating their bodies, planting a wet kiss on his lips.

He experienced the exciting tingle of awareness the opposite sex evoked, but compared to his desire for Lila, it paled. No, it withered.

Fortunately, it ended as quickly as it began.

"Sorry. I can't get out of it."

"Well. Your loss then, because my dress will be stunning!" She turned, picking her way across the site back to her truck.

Shaking his head, Jake returned his attention to his blueprints. Maybe now with all the women gone, he could get some work done.

The image of Lila standing proudly before him in her damp tank top drifted through his mind. Compared to Jenna, she was hotter than a Texas summer.

A feminine scream raised the hairs on the back of his neck. He threw down his pencil and raced in the direction of the hollering and sputtering. As he rounded the corner, he skidded to a halt.

The rear end of Lila's Lexus hung off the black iron ramming plate of Jenna's Suburban. Obviously, the two vehicles were stuck together tight, because Lila grabbed a crowbar out of her trunk and went to work on the Suburban.

She didn't look up once, not even as Jenna continued to scream, holding her hands to her head.

"Are you crazy? What're you doing to my baby?"

"Your baby tried to eat my car."

Jenna made a grab for the crowbar, but Lila shouldered her back, knocking her against the hood.

He didn't know what to do first: help Lila get her car unhooked, or protect Jenna from Lila.

"Jake, do something! This woman's crazy. She's tearing up my car."

A loud wrenching of metal on metal filled the air. The grill on the SUV gave way at one end, setting Jenna off into another round of hysterical squeals.

"Stop it! Stop it! I'm calling the cops! Do you hear me? I'm calling the police." Jenna teetered on her high heels around to the driver's side and retrieved her cell phone.

Her long manicured nails prevented her from dialing 9-1-1 the first two attempts, but on the third she gave a shout of triumph and placed the phone to her ear.

Jake didn't bother interfering. Her call wouldn't make it off the site. With all the flint and limestone hills around, cell phones didn't have much success unless you went to higher ground. One of the reasons he liked it out here. No phones.

He moseyed over to Lila, checking her progress. Her bumper rested on the towing reels of the Suburban. With only one corner of the grill free, she still had a lot of work ahead of her.

"What happened?"

Her back arched with tension. His ploy with Jenna had hit home. Looking up from her bumper, Lila glared at him, red-faced with exertion. *Or was it pain?*

"That ridiculous woman wedged me in. I couldn't get out."

As if that were all the explanation she needed for tearing up another vehicle.

From behind the Suburban, a squeal rang out and Jake saw Jenna race up the drive in search of a more cell phone–friendly locale.

"Can I help?"

She straightened, the crowbar between them. Her chest rose and fell with her rapid breaths. Perspiration darkened the cotton of her tank, outlining her hardened nipples.

Jesus. He needed help. He wanted to drive his wife away, and here he was, harder than a log within two minutes.

Her blue eyes glowed with anger, but she stayed strangely calm. Way too calm.

"Yes, Jacob, you can help me by showing up on time tomorrow."

He didn't flinch. Outwardly. She'd just seen him practically crawl all over another woman and make a date. Or at least that's what he had intended her to see. And all she had to say was show up on time? Okay, he'd bite.

"No problem. But first, can I help you with this?" After a huge breath, she handed the weapon over.

Stepping away from the kissing cars, he dipped his head in the open side driver's door of the Suburban. He flipped a switch under the wheel and the tow bar lowered, disengaging the Lexus with a soft lurch.

Lila watched the entire process without a word. A dawning comprehension flitted across her features. The tiniest smile curled the corners of her lips.

"Well, dammit all. Wouldn't you know?"

"See? All it requires is a little patience. You don't need a crowbar to do the job."

"I'm all about patience, Jake." Her sad eyes choked him up. "Sometimes you do need a crowbar to make your point."

He didn't have words to express his feelings. He stood at the edge of a deep gully, contemplating whether or not to jump. He could go back or forward, but he could never stay the same again.

The future yawned before him, dark and uncertain. The past ribboned behind him, the mistakes glowing with vivid markers.

"Miss Pert wouldn't have left the keys in the ignition by

any chance, would she?"

The moment ended, but the sensation stayed with him.

Jake checked the ignition. Sure enough, they dangled loosely with a "too sexy" key chain identifying the owner.

"Yep."

Lila already headed back to her car. "Would you mind backing this monster up so I can get the hell out of here before she comes back?"

He stood on the running boards, looking over the top of the open door. "What about your insurance? Jenna is gonna need that."

Lila pointed her middle finger at the Suburban's windshield. Her insurance information was scrawled across a loose piece of stationary, secured under the wiper.

He grabbed it and set it in the passenger seat, waiting for the diesel engine to warm before he brought it to life. In the rearview mirror he could see Jenna pacing up the drive, her lips moving with anger, the cell phone gripped in her hand.

Calming her down and convincing her not to press charges against Lila would take some work.

An irritated honk focused his attention straight ahead. Lila turned in her seat, her thumb commanding him to push back.

"Okay, okay. Keep your britches on, woman," he mumbled to himself.

When the Suburban eased back, the wheels of the Lexus cut sharply and the car U-turned, heading up the drive to the rural road.

She didn't turn, didn't even glance his way, as the wheels crunched gravel, leaving a wake of dust in her path.

Yeah, he'd pissed her off. But it was what he'd wanted, right?

Lesson Number Nineteen —

Children and chores can intrude on a couple's nightly rituals. As much as it may pain you and the children, demand time alone to be with your man. He will be so grateful and so will you.

Chapter Twenty-One

Lila guided Granny through the spotless double glass doors of the Hannington Dairy Queen. The smell of ice cream and waffle cones greeted her as soon as they crossed the threshold.

She needed a large M&M's Blizzard in the worst way, especially after the devastating revelation yesterday. The size of her rear be damned!

Jake couldn't—wouldn't—share his personal pain with her, but he would with a woman like perky Jenna? The slight had cut Lila deeply, and even today, her hands shook when she thought of it.

"My goodness, Barbara! Will you look at that cast?" Mary Beth waved frantically from behind the counter. "I was wondering when you'd be up and about. I was telling Delbert the other night I couldn't imagine you cooped up in the house for very long."

Granny knew the impact her reappearance would have in town, so she'd made Lila iron her best summer jumper.

Her arched brows were penciled in with Lila's help and her characteristic Rogue Sensation lipstick skillfully applied. She looked her best for the event. And Lila would go to the trouble every day of the week if it made Granny this happy.

At least she could count this part of her return to Hannington as a success.

"Heck no, I got too many responsibilities to lie around watching *Ellen*."

Mary Beth busied herself making Granny's customary cup of coffee.

"I don't see the gals yet." Granny scanned the dining area.

"We are a little early." Forty-five minutes to be exact, but she kept the comment to herself.

"Well, let's grab a table." Granny picked her way through the dining area to the far back table, stopping to say hello to familiar faces along the way.

Lila set her bags down in an empty chair and watched covertly as her grandmother settled herself into the chair across the table.

Mary Beth arrived with the coffee and slid into one of the empty seats, her brawny arms lying flat against the brown Formica. Her eyes fixed on Lila.

"So what did you do to make Mayor Armstrong so mad? Everyone has been talking about you two. Of course, I don't listen to gossip, it's so rude. I want to know somethin', I go directly to the source."

The chance to set the record straight. "I don't know exactly—"

Granny cut her off. "She bought the old Goodwin store. Made Howard madder'n a hornet. What could he do? Stop the sale of property at the city's expense? No! The ornery old cuss meant to tear that thing down, even after we told him of its historic importance."

Lila sat back in her seat, content to let someone else do the talking. People listened to Barbara Gentry.

Mary Beth's eyes lit up like a child with a new toy. "Really? I'd heard something about that. Mayor Armstrong put up a fight?"

"Armstrong's not a businessman. He's a politician, and the sooner he learns the difference, the better off Hannington will be," Granny told Mary Beth.

"Why's he so dead set against the idea, anyway? What's his problem?" Mary Beth frowned, throwing her weight into Lila and Granny's side of the ring.

A flash of green outside the window caught Lila's attention. An old beat-up farm truck pulled into a space. She watched it, thinking of Otis's truck. People around here were loyal consumers of American automobiles, no doubt about it.

"There's Threasa Thompson, now. We can get her take on this whole business." Mary Beth nodded the brim of her DQ visor to the parking lot outside.

Lila sat up straight and looked closer at the woman sliding out of the green truck. "That's Threasa?" she asked.

"Uh-huh," Mary Beth said as three sets of eyes followed Threasa's approach to the side door. "You probably don't remember her from school. She was a few years older than you.. Quiet gal. 'Course around Janie, anyone seems quiet."

She leaned conspiratorially closer and Lila received an idea of just how gray the top of Mary Beth's head truly was.

"Word is—and I haven't confirmed it yet—that John

Casler is seeing Threasa. At least he's been going out to her ranch a lot. Doing work." Mary Beth winked.

Casler. Small world, Lila thought. She and the big guy had a quiet truce after the IGA incident. He even went as far as helping her snag Jake's running shoes so she could have them repaired.

Threasa breezed in the side door, all grace and willowy beauty even in jeans and beat-up cowboy boots.

Lila seized the opportunity. "I want to talk to her. I'll be right back."

She slipped out of the booth and headed for the front counter. Her heart pounded in her chest. Confrontation always made her stomach knot, but if Threasa had sent Miss Pru's journal, Lila wanted to know. And more importantly, why.

"Excuse me," she said, drawing Threasa's attention from the overhead menu. "I'm Lila Gentry. I wondered if you have a minute?"

Threasa looked at her and smiled, acting not the least bit surprised Lila approached her for a private meeting. "Sure. Let me order a coffee and I'll join you at a table."

Lila took a table on the opposite side of the restaurant, away from Mary Beth and Granny. If Threasa had less than stellar motives, she wanted the opportunity to hear about them first, without an audience. Then she could decide how to deal with the woman.

Lila watched as she approached, noting when Threasa surveyed the small dining room and sized up the rumor potential.

Yeah, not the best of clandestine spots, but it'd have to do.

"Tell me about Luke Pierce."

Threasa's level hazel gaze stayed strong. *Nope, not blown away at all._*

"You got the journal, then?"

"Uh-huh. After reading the inside cover, it's no mystery I'm related to Prudence MacIntosh, but how did you end up with it? And why send it to me?" Lila flattened her hands on the tabletop to keep them from fidgeting. They did that too much these days.

"Maybe some background will make things a little more clear." Threasa took off her cowboy hat and set it next to her on the seat. Running a hand through her light blond hair, she sighed before beginning.

"I've been doing some research myself lately, checking into my family past. My ranch used to be part of a much, much larger spread back in the 1880s, owned by Luke Pierce."

Lila nodded. This much she knew.

Threasa cleared her throat. "He eventually moved back to his home in Kansas City and sold the ranch to the Thompsons, the ranch managers. By then, the days of the cattle drivers were over. People couldn't drive the cattle across the open range like they used to. So railroads took over."

"Oh," Lila said on a long exhale, understanding dawning at last.

Threasa laughed, a low and rich sound catching Lila off guard.

"Story's not over yet. The Thompsons ran the place into the ground, burned out most of the grazing land, and sold it off piece by piece. What I have left is nothing compared to the size of the ranch under Pierce. Anyway, by the time I arrived on the scene, it was done for. My parents wanted to sell, but couldn't find anyone to take it over. So I did when I became of age.

"Now, growing up, I knew three things: I'd take over the ranch when I got old enough, I stuck out from folks around here, and I'm adopted."

Threasa paused to take a drink of coffee and Lila stared at her, confused. She knew from the way she delivered the last bit about being adopted that it was important, but how it figured into the big picture, she didn't understand.

"When my birth mother was pregnant with me, she came down from Kansas City to investigate her family history, namely the Pierce ranch. I don't know anything about her circumstances, or what drove her to come down here really, but once she arrived, she never left. She died giving birth to me, and the Thompsons took me in and adopted me after a bit."

Lila closed her gaping mouth. She glanced over at Granny, who watched her closely from across the Dairy Queen. And then she looked back into Threasa's light eyes. "Are you saying what I think you're saying?"

"If you think I'm saying we're related, then you're right. That's what I'm telling you. Luke had three children: Lila, Emma, and Alice. Emma is my great-great-grandmother."

Stunned, Lila leaned back against the sloped back of the booth. Life continued to surprise her. Just when she thought she had a handle on it, a curveball came out of nowhere.

A cousin. She had a cousin, probably several times removed or something, but a cousin right here in Hannington.

Still, one thing didn't add up.

"Why didn't you just call me, or come see me when I got back into town? Why all the secrecy?"

Threasa smiled tightly. "You know who my brother-in-law is, right?"

"Howard."

"I think he means well in his effort to make Hannington a place of great character. A place people feel proud and secure calling home. That's his reasoning for pushing so hard to get rid of any trace of the old days. Prostitutes and corrupt city officials don't do much for the reputation. So I couldn't very well tell him I wanted to resurrect the grand ole days. Oh, and could I please have Prudence's journal he took out of her place?

"So. I stole it. And sent it to you."

"Does he know?" Lila imagined the reign of fire he'd bring down on her head if he knew she had it.

"No. But he will eventually. I owe it to him to tell him. But first, I wanted you to win." Her cousin smiled for the first time since they sat down and Lila knew from the warmth in her eyes, she'd made a new friend and an ally.

Lesson Number Twenty —

Offer him praise when he does something nice. Perhaps he sharpened your knives or fixed the hole in the outhouse that let in too much cold air. Or maybe you like the way he kisses you before bedtime. Whatever it is, tell him in words and then follow it up in action.

Chapter Twenty-Two

"Jake, sit down. Please," Dr. Rogers said.

Jake feigned interest in the rack of car magazines and *National Geographics* in one of the doc's impersonal patient examination rooms.

Why doctors thought patients would read issue after issue of polar bear mating rituals and Papua New Guinea cultural practices while they waited for the results of life-changing tests, Jake didn't know. He couldn't.

Hell, it took every bit of patience he had not to burst from the room and head for his truck.

He dropped into the chair opposite the doctor, his knees spread wide and his hands folded between. "Let's get on with it, Doc."

"Of course. Cutting right to it, the results of your tests concern me." He held his hand up, forestalling Jake's barrage of questions.

"They concern me only in that I don't think they're telling

us the whole story this time. I'm recommending more tests."

Jake rubbed a hand over his eyes. He suddenly felt very old and very tired. "What's the problem?"

"There are some abnormal blood cell counts the usual screens aren't accounting for. I want to know what's causing the increase, and we'll need another test for that."

He tried to read the doc's expression. Rogers was good. All he could see was patience and, hell, *concern*.

What a weak word. Concern. Not strong enough to mean, holy shit, trouble ahead! More like yellow-level alert. A person could easily overlook yellow alert until it escalated to red.

"Okay." He drew the word out, really not wanting to ask the next question, but knowing just the same he couldn't avoid it. "What and when?"

"I hate to do this to you, Jake, but scheduling is crazy right now so we'll have to set it up for Wednesday."

Two days. The doc wanted him to wait two days to see if the cancer was back. Was Rogers insane? "Nothing sooner, huh?"

Rogers shook his head. "That's as soon as we can do it. And Jake, this is more for my benefit than yours. The screen results came back well within the normal limits, but there was a variation. And I want to know what's going on. So, it's me making this call."

Jake stood with a quick exhale. Nothing more to say then.

"I'll be back on Wednesday."

Rogers smiled. Jake didn't.

He beat the doctor to the door and let himself out into the drab hallway. He paid his bill and pushed through the double glass doors into the parking lot.

The smell of hot asphalt assailed his senses. The roar of a nearby diesel sounded in the background, drowning out the wrens nestled in the trees around the perimeter of the parking area.

Everything seemed so normal.

Right. Except would he be alive next summer to hear the same sounds? Smell the same fragrances? A test at the Cancer Center on Wednesday would tell.

Jake pulled up in front of Lila's building and threw his truck into park. He stared through the windshield, wondering where the last hour had gone. He didn't remember the drive back from Temple.

Finally, he noticed the new glass in the storefront windows. Bright and open, it took about fifty years off the old place, making it appear fresh and new even though the facade dated back to 1870.

If only he could feel as good with a little TLC.

"Back again, darling?"

Jake gripped the steering wheel, but kept his gaze focused straight ahead.

Mark.

Where the hell had he come from? And why hadn't Jake heard him approach?

'Cause your head is back in Temple, idiot.

Jake turned to Mark. Even in the heat, the man looked cool as a cucumber. Whatever the hell that meant.

"That's what I'm paid for," Jake said, swinging his truck door open, forcing Mark back a few feet.

"And here I thought it was your charming smile."

Jake stared at him.

"You were supposed to be here at ten a.m. to take delivery of some materials. Luckily I was here and signed for it."

"Where's Casler?"

Mark laughed. "Just because I signed for some materials doesn't mean I'm your secretary. How should I know where that big, bad Native American is?"

Jake frowned. Casler should have been here to cover him while he was away. Something important must have come up.

"What were you doing here this morning?"

Mark stopped examining his nails—wait, had Mark just been examining his nails? Jake shook his head, refusing to spend more time trying to figure the guy out.

"I *am* part of Lila's team," he said like Jake suffered from a mental deficiency. "And I am an architect."

"Well, why don't you tell her then that this project is going to eat her lunch?"

"Because it's not," he said mockingly. "It's beautiful, full of potential and unfulfilled glamour. Look at the details, Jake. Even you have to admit the place has charm."

He didn't have to admit anything. He just did the job.

He headed inside and tried to close the door on Mark, but the man was like a dog that wouldn't heel. All excited with loads of energy.

"What can I do for you, Mark?" Jake paused inside the door, surveying the preliminary demolition work on the staircase. He had an expert millworker coming in today to custom-make the balusters, newels, and handrails needed to restore the staircase to its original state. Lila wanted it to be a focal point for the downstairs.

"I need to know if you plan on taking Lila to this benefit

next week, or if I'm going to have to be the man with the bigger balls and do it?"

"I'm going to pretend you didn't just talk to me about your balls, Mark."

"Regardless, I still need your answer."

Jake met sharp and assessing questions with a look that would have made lesser men quake in their boots.

Mark laughed. "Bullies don't have much effect on me. Sorry."

"Where is Lila, anyway?" If the man was going to be in the way, he could at least be useful.

"Busy," Mark said, as he took out a tape measure and began to measure the front window.

"Something we have in common," Jake mumbled under his breath.

"So do you have something to wear to this shindig or do you need to borrow a tux?"

He refused to answer and they were in silence for all of fifteen seconds.

"Ah, Jake, sweetie, you've got company. Some librarian type in white orthopedic sneakers?"

Could it be the cherry on top of his completely crappy day? Jake turned from the staircase to see Janie Armstrong coming through the door.

"Thought I'd drop by and take a look at what you've fought so hard for, Jake." Janie put a hand to her nose, sniffing madly as a plume of dust disturbed by the guys working the staircase rose up around their feet.

He took another deep breath and counted. He'd been doing that a lot since Rogers had issued another round of tests.

"Lila is putting this building back on the tax rolls like she promised. It will be a fully functional commercial establishment by the end of the year."

"As a day spa, I hear?" Her lips clenched together, forming a pruney oval.

"You'd have to talk to Lila, but that's what I understand."

"This could have been a perfect recreational facility for teenagers, Jake. I'm so disappointed that you couldn't see that."

Could nothing be simple today? Maybe he should split and take a run. Call Casler and go have a beer.

Mark cleared his throat near the window. Janie whipped her head around and stared openly at him.

"Janie Armstrong, Mark...?" He didn't even know the guy's last name.

"Mark Shrine," he said, extending his hand.

Janie smiled, although it didn't reach her cold eyes. "Nice to meet you.

"So where is the lady of the hour? Off plotting her next purchase in Hannington?" She barely concealed her scorn.

"You know, for a woman your age, you really shouldn't frown so hard. It will eventually leave wrinkles you can't get rid of."

Janie's mouth dropped open. Score one for Mark.

"Besides, you're not that old. Even though you obviously want people to believe you are."

"Who the hell are you?" She came back, angrier than Jake had seen her in a long while.

"The next best thing to hit Hannington since Lila."

She looked at Jake. He shrugged his shoulders, glad Mark's

doggedness had a new target. "He's the architect."

"Well, good luck getting code approval on this wreck." And with that, she sailed out the door. The silence after her departure was deafening.

Mark looked at Jake. "Was that a threat?"

"You can bet on it."

"Oh, she is so *not* having the last word." Mark tossed his tape measure in a bucket and followed her out the front door.

Jake rubbed his head, trying to release a mountain of tension that wouldn't budge.

At least he'd be able to get some work done now.

Watching a lover sleep is the most comforting feeling. And I felt comforted this evening, watching Luke sleep in my bed, his big, wide feet dangling off the end of the mattress. I covered him as best I could, but there is nothing to be done with a man who defies all propriety by being well over six feet tall.

The feeling of joy lasted for all of two minutes before reality came bursting in like an uninvited drunk, as it inevitably does. I looked around my room, my own little sanctuary from the rest of the world, and spied his money clip on the dresser. It was bulging with bills.

What other man would leave his money plainly visible for the taking in a whorehouse?

A man with too much. A trusting man. A good man.

Luke Pierce.

My heart broke with the sudden cruelty of the

situation. Here was a kind and loving man offering me the world, if I would come and be his live-in lover. I could have everything my heart desired.

Food, clothing, a house, horses, money. Everything.

But I would still be a whore.

I would still be paid for my services.

I would not be a wife. A mother. A partner.

And there it was. I could no longer deny it. I was falling in love with Luke Pierce, the eccentric cattleman with a heart bigger than his ranch and kindness enough for the entire town.

But he did not love me. He did not want me as his wife. He did not want me, Miss Prudence, the madam of a boardinghouse, to be the mother of his children.

Did he?

He had not asked me to marry him. He asked me to live with him at his ranch.

Living under the same roof would almost be a bigger sin than prostitution.

And why should he want to ruin his reputation by marrying me? I would not do so, if I were in his shoes.

God bless the man, he did not live by the societal rules the rest of us did. Luke Pierce had his own code. That much I was quickly coming to learn on my own. If he wanted a live-in lover, by goodness, he would have one.

Just not me.

I cared for him too much.

So as I covered his bare shoulders with my shawl, I knew what had to be done. I knew what I had to do to protect Luke from himself.

Leave. End our affair.

He would not understand at first. But years from now when he was married to his wife, he would thank me for setting him straight.

It had to be done.

But would my heart survive the separation?

Lesson Number Twenty-One —

Take advantage of time you have alone with your man. Maybe it is only a few minutes in the barn, or a whole night in bed. Make it count with lots of touching, kissing, and sweet words.

Chapter Twenty-Three

Word came in from the LP Ranch today. Luke made it to market and sold his herd. Got a good price, too, from what one of the hands told.

Now I know, at last. Where he went and for what reason. Although I told my dear Luke it was over between us, I never expected him to vanish. It was a sad occasion, the day I realized I was hurting him more than helping. Yes, I could ease the physical stresses of his body, but I could never give him the peace of mind he craved like a thirsty man searching for water.

Luke needs a companion, a helpmate. A wife. A partner. After I turned down his offer to live with him, he continued to visit me here in my rooms, but I think we both knew it would end soon. I could see him slipping further and further away from his own life, sleeping here, taking his meals here. He came to know everyone at the Two Nellies by name, bestowing *courtesies like my girls were ordinary women on the street. He was insinuating himself into my life, since I had refused to do so in his.*

He may not have noticed the hostile stares from people about town, but I did. And I could hear the questions mumbled behind my back.

"She's draining him dry. He won't have a penny when Pru's done with him. What's she have over him, anyway?"

My heart felt like a brick of ice this last month, waiting for news of his whereabouts and health.

It has been difficult lately in the Acre since I told the mayor I would not help him corrupt the new sheriff. The decision has brought me grief on two fronts, from both the mayor and the sheriff, the latter intent on cleaning up this end of town. After the mayor's last vicious threat, I worried for Luke. His association with me would bring him nothing but shame and ruin. But I never should have doubted. Luke is too good and strong to be tainted by small men.

If only I can hang on until the mayor learns bullying a woman like me gets him nothing, if not barred from every establishment in the Acre. I decreed he is no longer welcome in my rooms or the Two Nellies. Not if he continues to threaten people so he can collect protection money.

Who will stand up for the poor, the sick, and the vagrant?

Nobody. Except me. A short, skinny, unschooled whore. If I don't take a stand now, I might as well turn over and run. I have encountered his kind before.

When will people learn that no good comes from men like the mayor? They cannot be paid enough money, or kowtowed to enough. They are landlords, fat off the labor of their tenants.

"The courage of the Irish." I hear it whispered in the hall and in the kitchen when no one knows I am around. Irish, indeed! We are a tough lot to be sure. It will take much more than threats and bad words to put me off my cause once I have taken to it.

I just pray the people who have courageously chosen to rally around me hold. If not for their own sake, then for the good of the town.

And Luke, my darling, my heart. I say a blessing for you every night. That one day, your mind finds peace and your heart love.

Lila put the journal down as the doorbell chime sounded outside her bedroom door. Granny had gone out with the Bombshells again, deciding upon next season's uniform. Something about choosing pink pinstriping this time around in an effort to be subtler. Lila didn't think subtle could be achieved with the Bombshells, not with all that white/silver/blue hair and vibrant pink lipstick they favored.

The bell rang again. "I'm coming!" Jeez, some people were so impatient.

She opened the front door and a slim, middle-aged woman stood on the other side of the glass storm door.

"Can I help you?" Lila said after several seconds of waiting for the stranger to state her business.

"I'm looking for Barbara Gentry." The woman's voice croaked, throaty and low. Lila guessed she'd been a heavy smoker at one point in her life.

"She's out. Would you like to leave a message?"

The woman stared at her, hard, and it unnerved Lila. Did she know her? From before, growing up in Hannington? She looked at the stranger a second time, taking in the faded blond hair, still healthy and shiny, worn loose around her shoulders in a simple but elegant cut. She equaled Lila's height, if not a bit taller, with longer legs. Or it could have been a trick of the eye with her breezy butter-colored linen pantsuit.

Her features were even and delicate, but deep wrinkles, heavier than a woman her age should have, surrounded her eyes and mouth.

The woman's makeup highlighted her warm brown eyes and her cupid mouth. A small crescent scar marred her lip line, a familiar image triggering a flood of memories.

Jesus H. Roosevelt Christ. This woman could not be Sarah Gentry. Could she?

The woman noted Lila's shock and reached for the handle on the storm door. "Perhaps we could talk until Barbara returns?"

Lila beat her to the handle and locked it from her side. The other woman jerked her hand back at the sound of the lock clicking into place.

"Who are you?" Lila demanded, sweat breaking out on her brow.

"I didn't mean to upset you. I apologize. I'll return when Barbara is available."

She started to turn, heading for the steps.

"Stop right there! Who are you?" Lila knew panic rang

in her voice. She could hear the shrill ring of anger, despair, terror, hurt, expectation, hope, and grief bounce back off the glass and into her face.

"Please," the woman began.

"Cut the crap, lady, and just tell me who you are."

But she knew. She knew from the way those damn brown eyes pleaded with her to understand. "You're Sarah. My mother."

Sarah nodded.

Lila fell back, knocking the hallway console table sideways and sending Granny's collection of knickknack hummingbirds to the carpet.

"You're Lila, right?" Sarah said from the other side of the glass, the fingertips of her right hand resting gently on the door.

Lila couldn't speak. She shook her head.

"You are. I can see your father's nose and chin and my forehead and mouth."

Lila picked herself up and stood ramrod straight. She didn't know what to do. Let Sarah in along with the waves of grief pushing against the walls of her heart or slam the door and call Jake, sobbing out her fears and doubts?

What would Jake do? He'd run from the emotions, the commitment. Just as he ran from Lila. Unwilling to let anyone, even himself, have a second chance.

Lila took the few steps to the door and unlocked it, letting Sarah inside. They stood staring at each other. Neither one obviously knowing what to say.

"I was hoping to ease into this, talk to Barbara before I went looking for you."

"Well, that's screwed. You got me."

Sarah swallowed and looked down to the mess of the

hummingbirds. She bent and picked them up, setting them one by one back onto the half-moon-shaped entry table.

"Barbara always loved birds. Does she still keep feeders out for these little devils?"

Sarah's hair swung forward, leaving the back of her neck bare. Lila noticed an old scar, although still pink, running across her spine.

That sudden vulnerability deflated the bulk of her anger. She backed up and squatted down to Sarah's level, restoring the last bird back to the table.

"Come in and I'll get some coffee started."

Sarah nodded and Lila turned, not waiting to see if she followed, but knowing now there wasn't any going back.

She pulled the coffee down from a shelf and scooped the grounds into the coffeemaker. Sarah didn't say a word, but she could feel the other woman waiting patiently. A calm emanated from her, surprising Lila.

How could her mother be so calm about coming home after pulling a disappearing act for twenty-five years?

The weight of the time made Lila shake her head. Twenty-five years. She hadn't seen her mother since she turned five years old. Lila remembered it like it was yesterday.

It had been a warm September day and she'd woken early to dress for kindergarten, unable to sleep from the excitement. She'd only started a week earlier, but had already found friends and couldn't wait to get back to school.

Sarah had helped her get dressed, pack her lunch, and brush

her hair. At the time, she remembered thinking how much her mom loved her. Sarah had spent the morning showering her with attention, letting her have two glasses of chocolate milk instead of one, putting pink bows in her ponytail, and letting her wear her special Sunday church shoes to school.

Lila had felt so happy and so very loved. But then Sarah didn't show up after school. She'd waited and waited on the playground, but Sarah never came. So a teacher had called Barbara at her bank job.

Granny came right over, scooping Lila up in a big hug. They got some ice cream at Miller's on the way home and she forgot all about her mother's disappearance until they pulled up into the driveway.

Granny had tried to act normal, but she could tell something had gone terribly wrong. She found her grandmother sitting in her mother's room on the bare bed, looking into the empty closet.

Sarah had cleared out, taking everything with her and leaving the room as clean as if she'd been a guest and not Granny's daughter-in-law.

At the time, Lila didn't really understand Sarah wasn't ever coming back. But as the years passed, it became painfully clear her mother had abandoned her for a different life.

A life that involved a vivid scar on the back of her neck.

Lila looked up from the brewing coffee to Sarah. "So where have you been for twenty-five years?"

"California."

No hesitation, no remorse, no apology. No, "Hey, kid, sorry I ran out on you when you were five, but you know, life sucks sometimes and you gotta run."

"So you just had a whole different life out there?"

Sarah's measured stare started to piss her off again. How could the woman be so calm?

"Not a good one, or one that I'm proud of, but the last five years have been better and I've been gathering the strength to come back."

Lila turned away with two polka-dotted mugs, filling them with coffee. She set a steamy cup in front of Sarah before she met her eyes again.

"Why come back now?"

"Because"—and here, Sarah's throaty voice faltered for the first time—"I have responsibilities and a family. And I wanted to see you."

She almost spit the coffee in her mouth back into the cup. "You have responsibilities? Are you kidding me? I'm thirty. I don't need a mother. I have Granny, thank you very much."

Granny, who had been everything to Lila. And still was.

"I know. And you're a very beautiful thirty. I tried to picture you, what you'd look like, but nothing I dreamed of even came close." Sarah lowered her eyes with a wistful smile and took a drink, leaning a hip against the counter. "What I mean to say is I owe you and Barbara so much, and I would like the opportunity to get to know you two again. If not to be a mother and a daughter, to be a friend. If that's possible."

She couldn't believe this conversation. A mother who wanted to be her friend. It was too surreal.

"Frankly, Sarah, I'm unsure. There's a lot about you I don't know. What am I saying? I don't know the first thing about you. I don't even know why you left."

The recrimination didn't faze Sarah. She remained cool

and collected, but then Lila noticed her white-knuckle grip on the edge of the countertop.

"Yes. I realize that. I'm hoping you will allow me to explain myself—not to justify or excuse what I did—" she talked right over Lila's protest. "—But I know you need to know. And I need to tell you, as part of my own therapy on the road to healing."

"So this is about your need to heal? To move on? I don't think I can help you there." She set her mug on the counter and brushed past Sarah out of the kitchen and through the back sliding glass door to the chain-link-fenced backyard.

Maybe Sarah would get the hint and leave. Come back when Granny was here and she wasn't. But then Granny would have to deal with the pain and right now, more pain was the dead last thing she wanted for her grandmother.

So when Sarah followed her out back and sat in the patio chair across from her, Lila didn't react.

"I have been in therapy for quite some time Lila, figuring out who I am, the repercussions of choices I've made, and how to make wiser decisions from here on out."

Therapy, she could relate to.

"I'm finally putting my life back together. After twenty-five years, I know who I am and what I want and I'm not afraid to go after it."

"So what was the problem when I was five? Did you just decide being a mom was crap, and moved on?" She knew her words were ugly, but she couldn't stop them. Maybe it would be better to take her frustrations out on some innocent lawn furniture.

"I understand your anger, Lila. And it's valid. One hundred percent."

But. Always a but.

She waited for Sarah to continue, to apologize, beg forgiveness, do something besides sit there looking at her with sympathetic eyes.

Sarah looked away finally, at the crepe myrtle trees in beautiful full bloom. The chiffon-like dark pink flowers shaded the patio table and added a tranquility Lila usually appreciated.

"After your father didn't come back from the Middle East, I tried to keep it together. For both our sakes. I knew I had the most important job in the world, raising you, but it was hard. So very hard without your father, and I eventually lost the battle to hang on to myself. I got lost, too, in a way. I didn't know who I was anymore or what I was doing. I had to leave to go and find me before I, too, went missing in action."

Lila wanted to say, "But you were my mom. The most important person in the world."

Sarah zeroed in on Lila, no longer watching the wind blowing through the blossom-heavy trees. "What I discovered was that I was right here all along. Everything I wanted. Everything I needed was right here. I wasn't lost. I was blind. And Lord help me, it took almost twenty years to figure that out."

Silent tears escaped at the corners of Sarah's eyes and for the first time, Lila saw a chink in her composure as her mother fumbled in her pocket for a tissue.

She didn't want to cry. Dammit. She didn't want to show this woman any emotion other than anger, but Lila couldn't stop the tears that slid down her cheeks. She couldn't stop the well of emotion bubbling up from her chest and escaping past her lips.

Suddenly Sarah was there, her arms wrapped around Lila, her soft linen blouse pressed against her cheek. Nonsense words stumbled past her lips and into Lila's hair. A lot of "I'm sorry" and "I hope you can forgive me someday" made their way into Lila's foggy brain.

She cried for the mother she'd never known and the mountains of pain Sarah had obviously suffered; for herself who'd almost repeated her mother's mistakes by leaving Hannington and Jake, but just scraped by realizing ten years sooner where her heart truly lived.

And crap, she cried because she realized she shared more qualities with Sarah than she'd ever imagined.

As Lila regained control and dried her tears, Sarah's arms fell away and they were back to sitting across from each other at the table.

"So why now? Why did you decide this moment was right to come back?" She had no idea what she expected, but what Sarah said next shocked the shoes right off her feet.

"I read a small Associated Press piece a few weeks ago, you know, one of the around-the-U.S. color pieces that is short, but interesting. In it, the reporter talked about a small Texas town and one woman's fight to restore a piece of Old West history. A former brothel on the Chisholm Trail.

"Beside the story was a small black-and-white photo of you standing outside Prudence's old place. And I thought if you're going to reopen Miss Pru's, you'd probably want to do it right."

Sarah lifted her worn leather satchel off the concrete next to her chair and removed an old leather-bound book. She passed it to Lila.

"Open it. I think these may help with the interior restoration."

Lila accepted the book and lifted the cover. It creaked softly in protest. There on the first page rested a black-and-white photograph of a lovely young woman, standing confidently, her gloved hand resting atop the back of a chair. Her features were even and beautiful, her smile wide and genuine, almost infectious, Lila decided. Her hair disappeared in a loose coiffure under a smart hat with a jaunty feather.

She wore a high-collared white blouse with a great deal of lace at the throat, which cascaded down to a trim waist, outlined to perfection under a jeweled shell belt.

A snappy two-piece suit consisted of a short jacket with large lapels, to show off the lace of course, and a heavy A-line skirt brushed the floor, matching the hat. A beautiful embroidered ribbon pattern scrolled up the sides of the skirt from the hem.

The plate under the Victorian-styled image: Prudence MacIntosh.

Immediately she thought of the journal and Carrie's story about the missing photo album from the city's museum. She glanced up at Sarah. "Where did you find this?"

"I stole it from someone a very long time ago."

"Howard and Janie Armstrong?"

Sarah struggled to find the words. "Ah, well, how did you know?"

Something clicked in her mind and at last it all made sense to Lila. "Howard knows you stole the original photo album and he wanted to punish you by refusing to give me Miss Pru's journal."

"It seems Prudence left more than a photo album behind. She also left a diary hidden away inside the building. Howard recovered it and would have destroyed it as revenge against you, I guess, but someone intervened and made sure I got it instead.

"What did you do to Howard to make him dislike our family so much?" she asked Sarah, eager to know at last what made the man so unpleasant.

Sarah took a deep breath and let it go. "I refused to date him."

Lila waited for more revelations, but Sarah didn't have any. "That's it? You wouldn't go out with the guy?"

"He thought because our family didn't have the money or standing his did, that I would fall into his arms. I didn't. By that time, I was already in love with your father."

A spurned boyfriend. It all made sense now. She wondered briefly if Threasa knew this part of the story.

Lila flipped quickly through the book, excited by the number of photos inside. Dozens of interior shots of Miss Pru's! Although her great-great-grandmother was not in all the images, it was a gift beyond measure. She could return Miss Pru's to its original grandeur.

"I don't know what to say," she told Sarah.

"The response, Lila, is thank you."

Lila whipped her head around to see Granny coming in the side gate from the driveway. How long had she been there, listening to her and Sarah?

Long enough, she decided, when she saw the guarded look in her granny's eyes.

Nobody said anything for several seconds, and then Sarah stood to face her mother-in-law. They stared at each other, two feet between them, but Lila figured it could have been miles. Neither moved.

"I'm going to go inside. Let you two talk." She got up and scooped Miss Pru's album under her arm. As she closed the sliding glass door behind her, she saw Granny take a seat at the table with Sarah following suit.

Lesson Number Twenty-Two —

Take your time. Cherish the day, your children, and the sex you have with your man. All of those can be taken away in a heartbeat, maybe never to return. Savor them. You will find greater satisfaction if you do.

Chapter Twenty-Four

How many hours in a day? For Jake, it seemed more than the average twenty-four. Monday, the day of his appointment with Dr. Rogers, had come and gone, but Tuesday hung on and on and on.

He feared Wednesday.

"Yo, Jake. We gonna work or what?"

Jake lowered the bit of molding he measured for the ceiling and gave Casler a glare. The man had been an ass all morning and his mood didn't seem to be improving as the day wore on. Not that Jake could blame him. His mood sucked, too.

"I am working, *Takoda.*" He put a heavy emphasis on his nickname, letting Casler know in a friendly way to lay off.

Casler gave him the finger and returned to working on the electrical requirements for all the damn lights Lila wanted on the ground floor. The room would be brighter than an August day in Texas if she flipped the switch on all the lights down here.

"Oh, my."

Jake closed his eyes, praying for ten good minutes in the day when he could get some work done. Lately, his ability to do his job had gone to hell.

He swiveled on the ladder to see Lila standing in the middle of the room, almost under Casler's feet. Casler gave him a look that said, "get your woman out from under me," but he saw the smile he flashed her when he thought Jake wasn't looking.

He never had gotten to the bottom of their truce. In the end he figured as long as they weren't fighting on the job site, he could live with Casler helping her out behind his back.

"I couldn't stay away. I'm as excited about this project as I was on my very first restoration." Her smile kicked the voltage in the room up another one hundred watts. Jake felt singed by its warmth.

"It's on schedule. The staircase will be finished today and we can proceed upstairs once code okays it."

She clapped her hands and her pure joy forced a smile he couldn't hold back.

"Nobody's ever clapped for work I've done. This is a first."

Her eyes met Jake's. "Well, I'm glad I was your first."

His gaze went to her breasts and lower, remembering in vivid detail the day his truck had a flat.

The smile slipped off her face at the innuendo. Embarrassed, she glanced up at Casler, who busied himself with the wiring.

Jake saw his back shake with suppressed laughter.

"I, ah, meant the applause," she said.

Jake crossed to her, stepping over rolled-up drop cloths and cans of stain to be used later on the hardwood restoration.

"I know what you meant. Come up here and I'll show you the moldings and wainscoting we've started."

He guided Lila by her elbow to the front of the store, giving them some distance from everyone else. He tried to ignore the sweet smell of her hair and pointed out what had been accomplished and what remained to be done.

She stared at the walls, a grin the size of Palo Duro Canyon on her lips.

"Something bothering you?" he asked.

She looked into his eyes, confusion bringing her brows together. "Bothering me? What do you—"

His smile cut her sentence short.

"Stop messing with me. I'm in a good mood today and I don't want anyone to ruin it."

"I can see that. You win the lottery?"

"I wish," she fired. "No. I'm just high on life. It's full of surprises and wonder. You never know what's around the corner."

Yeah, full of surprises, at least that much rang true.

But he didn't want to rain on her parade, so he kept a ridiculous smile on his stupid face.

He didn't fool her. "You hear me, Jacob Winter? You never know what the next day will bring. That's all part of living honestly. Accepting the uncertainty."

Jake bent to examine the wainscoting, leaving Lila to talk to air. He didn't want to burst her bubble, but his life was a living hell of uncertainty right about now.

She bent down beside him, laying a hand on his knee. Her touch burned through his jeans. "I know you went to see Dr. Rogers. How'd it go?"

He did not want to have this discussion now. "The wainscoting remnants we found behind the paneling gave us a great model to patch the parts too damaged, or just gone. It was expensive, though. At a height of seven feet around the entire ground floor, it cost you a pretty penny."

"Jake, I know you don't want to talk about it. Whatever is between us doesn't matter. I'm your friend. Always have been and always will be."

"Thanks," he said curtly, standing and forcing Lila to drop her hand.

She followed suit and they stood quietly, examining the wall.

"It's beautiful. I've got photos now to compare it to and I can choose the color for the inset panels to hopefully come close to the original."

Jake nodded like he knew what photos she referred to.

"Sarah Gentry came home."

Her words didn't register right away. Sarah Gentry? Where had he heard?

"Your mother?" he said, incredulous.

She nodded her head.

"So, she wasn't dead."

"Jake!" Her voice cut the silence.

He shrugged. "Sorry. I assumed since she never came home, she probably died. Why would she stay away so long?"

"It's a long story. But after I saw how much it meant to Granny to have her back, it made it all okay."

"She just strolled up to the front door and said, 'Hi, I'm home'?" He couldn't believe it. And that Lila didn't freak out about it. No panic. No sweating or hand-wringing.

She *had* changed.

She laughed now. "Actually, that's very close to what really happened."

Jake led the way out the door to the bench on the sidewalk. "Keep talking. I'm listening." He went to the cab of his truck and removed a thermos of lemonade his mother had dropped by earlier.

"She's been in California most of the time and from what I can gather—she hasn't told me the whole story yet—she's lived a really tough life."

He blew dust out of two plastic cups and poured them each a tall amount of the still-cold drink.

"She eventually got her act together, went to school, and became a therapist. She has her own practice and everything."

He took a swallow of his lemonade and watched her face. A calm acceptance radiated from her eyes and the set of her shoulders. This was the new Lila, the woman he didn't know much about. "So is she here to stay?"

"I don't know. But it doesn't matter. I don't think we could shake her now if we tried."

Jake looked away, at the traffic passing through the town square. Nothing but the model of cars had changed in the scenery over the last thirty years. Lila had come home, but she wasn't standing still. Her life moved forward. Jake's didn't.

"It's only confirmed what I've come to realize this last year, Jake. It's never too late."

He'd see about that tomorrow.

"If you're glad, then I'm glad for you and Barbara. You let me know though if things get a little out of hand over there. I can come and pick you two ladies up and take you to dinner.

Or whatever."

He stood and tossed his cup into one of the city-supplied garbage cans standing sentry outside Lila's building. He needed to get back inside and back to work, away from his wife's quiet determination.

One thing at a time. And right now, tomorrow's doctor visit loomed like a summer storm on the horizon.

Lila climbed in the passenger seat of Sarah's green Honda Accord, noticing a faint trace of vanilla. The early-morning heat filtered through the tinted windshield in a dreamy haze and the smell of the cream leather seats and the homey scent made her heart lurch with unexpected happiness.

Back home in Hannington. With family.

"All set?" Sarah asked, closing the driver's door and starting the ignition. She was just as put together today as she had been the day she stepped onto Granny's front porch searching for the family she'd left behind.

Sarah's hair swung softly against the shoulders of her short-sleeve denim shirt. Judging by the perfect and stylish fall of her mother's mid-length hair, Lila knew she'd paid a pretty penny for the cut. But in L.A., didn't everyone pay a premium?

"Yep."

Sarah backed out of Granny's driveway and headed for Main Street, her brown eyes on the road ahead. Lila could tell by the high set of her shoulders that she was tense. "It's been some time since I visited Michael's grave. Please correct me if I take a wrong turn."

"Oh, right," Lila said. Sometimes she wished she could forget the way to Greenwood Memorial. Too many people from her life, too many relatives she never got to know, were buried there. Her father. Her grandfather, dead of a heart attack before Lila was born, and a host of great-uncles, some killed in World War II, others after, laid to rest inside the hedged boundaries of the green fields.

When Sarah called her this morning, the last thing Lila expected was for her to ask for company when she visited her father's grave. It made sense, though. Today was her dad's birthday. If he had survived his tour in the Middle East, he'd be fifty-five.

The drive took ten minutes, mostly because of the traffic lights on Main. Sarah parked in the paved lot outside the white two-story colonial structure that served as both chapel and business office. Lila hung back a few paces watching Sarah as she stepped to the line dividing the sidewalk from the dark, tar-covered asphalt and stopped, her feet pointing in the direction that would take her to Michael's marker.

She caught her breath, watching her mother's silent struggle, and for a moment felt unsure what to do. Should she intervene, lead Sarah into the headstone-marked field, or wait?

Sarah made the decision for her and crossed over onto the sidewalk, walking rapidly through the quiet Spanish oak–lined cemetery.

"Your father and I had a special tradition for his birthday," she began, her voice husky. "It was never about one day out of the year—we always made a week out of it. I would give him small presents leading up to his actual birthday and finally, on that day, we would celebrate. Breakfast in bed, a leisurely nap in the afternoon, and dinner out."

"What types of gifts?" she asked Sarah.

"Oh, um, personal, ah, well, I did all of his favorite things. And showered him with attention."

Did Sarah actually blush? What would make her blush? *Oh.* Lila let the matter drop. She didn't need to really know anything else about her parents' sex life.

Sarah smiled and slid a glance Lila's way. "When he was deployed overseas, I would write letters every day, so he could open them each day preceding his birthday."

Lila knew the story. Michael Gentry, a Marine, spent two birthdays overseas. The final one came in 1990, months before his death during Desert Storm. Lila had just turned five and hadn't seen her father in two years.

She couldn't remember what he looked like other than the photos Granny kept on the walls. She just had an impression of a big man with rough hands who held her close at night before tucking her into bed.

Sarah patted the side of the shoebox under her arm. "I have twenty-five years worth of birthday letters in this box. One hundred seventy-five letters to be exact."

Lila's heart clenched involuntarily and tears stung the backs of her eyes. Her mother had been writing to him all these years?

"There is so much I should have done, Lila. I've wasted so much time. Days and years I can never recover. Gone. Like Michael."

Her mother reached across the inches and laid a hesitant arm across Lila's shoulders. Her touch was light, but sure. Up ahead, she made out her father's marker, a horizontal monument with an engraved image of a book detailing Michael's dates of birth and death in bold black letters.

They left the sidewalk and picked their way between headstones with Lila leading the way. She didn't know how to respond to Sarah with her stories and motherly pats on the back. She wanted to leave her grief and resentment behind and could feel the distance between the two of them lessening every day.

"Tell me about Jake."

Sarah's question couldn't have surprised her more if she said she'd won the Mega Millions lottery.

"Barbara told me a little bit. The two of you married out of high school?"

She didn't intend to, but she found herself telling Sarah everything. His illness, their separation, her subsequent therapy, and her decision to come home and patch things up with Jake.

"I know you're scared." Sarah's eyes were intelligent and empathetic. *She understood.* "Worried that it might be too late. How do you convince someone to take another chance when so much time has passed?"

"Well, crap. Sounds familiar, doesn't it?" Lila shook her head, sighing. Yes, she and Sarah had a lot in common.

"So tell me, Dr. Gentry, what's your game plan? I think I might need to compare notes with you."

Lesson Number Twenty-Three —

Do not get wrapped up in expectations. They can sabotage a marriage.

Chapter Twenty-Five

Lila settled in the hammock swinging gently between two pecan trees in her granny's backyard. The shade blocked the brunt of the late summer sun's intensity. She opened Prudence's journal.

> Most of my customers from outside the Acre have stopped visiting. At first, I only noticed fewer visits and callers coming later in the night. Then, those infrequent visits trickled down to the regulars here inside the boundaries of the Acre. And now, with the pressure on from the mayor and the sheriff who have allied against sin, even the Acre regulars don't have the money to spend with my girls. Which means I don't have money.
>
> Thank goodness I have saved for such an occurrence, but my savings is small. While it will keep me and mine in food for some time, it will not last forever.
>
> Out on the street, I see evidence of the city's new push to make me leave town. Police patrols in the Acre

are more frequent and they are arresting or fining people regularly. It is intimidation, is what it is. Trying to make me and all the other unwanted (but valuable taxpayers) down on this end of town submit to a new set of rules.

And what does the mayor want? Protection money. I have never paid it and I will not start. I pay my taxes and fines when assessed and contribute greatly to the charitable missions in the city. More so I daresay than the rich.

I am glad that Luke is not here to witness this struggle. He would end it in a minute. But then where would he be? Disfavored by the rich and elected alike in this city.

No, this is a battle I and the folks in Hell's Half Acre have to fight. We may not win, but we will fight it with just as much dignity as America's forefathers did when fighting British taxation and oppression.

Jake felt like hell. He couldn't get his mind to shut off. He'd already gone for a run, by himself since he couldn't find Casler. And had three out of a six-pack of beer to dull the litany of never-ending thoughts in his head on the impending test tomorrow. The alcohol only intensified his mood, which pissed him off more.

And to top it off, the night couldn't be more beautiful. The temperature had finally relented and a light wind blew down from the north, cooling off things to a very acceptable eighty-two degrees.

He sat on his back porch and listened to the night. Coyotes in the distance howled and a nearby mockingbird sang. He grunted in amusement. Only unmated mockingbirds sang at night.

"Life's a bitch, sometimes, hey, pal?" he said softly to the bird.

The bird quieted as a car pulled into Jake's drive. He walked to the end of the porch and looked around the corner of his house. Lila's cream-colored Lexus sat next to his pickup.

He stood straight and downed his beer. Rubbed his eyes and then his head.

"I'm around back," he called to her after her heard her ring the bell twice.

The screen door banged closed, and then he heard her feet crunching through gravel as she made her way to the side of the house. She was silhouetted by moonlight as she came through the open back gate, stopping below him at the set of three stairs.

"I wanted to come by and check on you. I know we sort of tabled our discussion earlier, but I ran into John Casler at the gas station and he said you were, ah, in a bad mood or something."

Maybe he'd rethink this truce between Lila and Casler.

Turncoat.

"I'm fine. Just trying to unwind, you know?"

"Oh." She had a hand on the rail but seemed hesitant to come up on the porch.

Jake sighed. "Since you're here, you want a beer, soda, or something?"

"A beer would be nice."

He made his way into the house and grabbed a pair of

cold ones from the fridge. Lila sat in one of the two empty chairs when he stepped back out onto the porch, her legs tightly crossed at the knee and her hands folded in her lap.

She took the beer he offered.

"Thanks for doing such great work on Prudence's place, Jake. It looks wonderful. And it means a lot to me, despite the fact, you know, that you didn't want to do it."

She took a small sip of her beer. And then a bigger drink. He watched her lips wrap around the top of the bottle, suck, and then relax as the liquid rolled back and down her throat.

His mouth went dry. He took a drink. "Sure."

He took another, bigger, longer drink.

She stood and set her beer on the floor. "I have to do this, Jake. I just have to." Her tone was a little bit desperate and a little bit lost girl.

Before he could ask what she needed to do, he found out. Her arms were around his neck and she pulled his head down, pressing a hard kiss to his mouth.

For about one quarter of a millionth of a second, he contemplated the consequences of kissing his wife, and then he thought, in typical Casler tradition, "Fuck it."

He grabbed her T-shirt and kissed her right back.

Jesus, she smelled good. Fresh and ripe.

She reeled back. "If you want me to go, I will. I won't understand it, or like it, but I'll go if you want. I just had to kiss you. You know, confirm you're here. Alive."

Yeah, he knew. Understood.

But she wasn't going anywhere. He nipped at her throat and felt her shiver and lean into him. "Shut up, Lila."

"Right."

She dropped her keys next to her beer with a resounding clang and then a jingle as they settled. The sound echoed and was picked up and imitated by the mockingbird.

Jake grabbed her hips and guided her backward toward the door, all the while making love to her mouth. He didn't know who was hungrier; sweat had broken out on his brow, but she felt hot, too.

Her small groans spilled into his mouth, muffled by his tongue in hers. The sound had his erection taut and heavy. Ready.

They made it inside and he stood back, watching her take her clothes off. As her shirt flew back and her bra landed over the threshold between the kitchen and the porch, he stretched out a hand and skimmed his fingers over a breast and down her belly.

The groan was out loud now. Goddamn. The sound of her made him pant. She kicked her pants off and hooked her thumbs into the tiny elastic hugging her hips. It was gone in less than two seconds.

She had a beautiful body. Lithe. Tight. Her breasts were round and heavy with upturned nipples. Her waist tiny, but flaring out to curvy hips. His eyes flew to the soft brown hair between her legs.

"I don't expect anything by this. It's a release I think we both need," she said, forcing his gaze back to her face.

He couldn't convince her to stop talking with words, so he put his tongue back into her mouth. He forced her back until he felt the couch bump the back of her knees. He laid her out and then fell in beside her, pulling her until she was on top and he could feel every delicious inch of her silky flesh.

He kissed her all over. Didn't miss a spot in the fifteen-minute homage that was part base need and part worship. How had he done without this for ten long years?

He dipped his head between her legs again and rested his cheek against her inner thigh, slowly licking his way between her folds. She arched off the cushions the same moment she grabbed his head.

He held her down, taking up residence between her thighs until her cries told him she was seconds from coming.

"God! *Please*. Hurry. No. *Wait*. Oh, come on!"

Her confusing commands had him laughing for the first time in days. The sex became more about the two of them than it did about release.

Lila lifted her head from the couch pillow, throwing him a look. "This isn't funny, Jacob Winter. I need you. *Now*."

She grabbed his arms, pulling him up until his chest met hers. He bypassed any more words or soft kisses and instead shoved her legs apart and drove himself home, sinking down until he was completely buried inside her.

Lila released a sound somewhere between a heavy grunt and long sigh. "Ahhhh. God. Yes."

She raised her legs, twining them around his back, forcing him deeper still. Which was fine by him. He wanted to be so deep inside her, he lost track of everything but the pleasure.

The muscles in his shoulders and neck strained as Lila arched her back again, rocking into him with a force to equal his thrusts. He felt his orgasm closing in and he wanted to bring Lila with him. He reached down between them and drew a hard pink nipple between his teeth with just enough pain that it drove her straight over the brink.

"Jake!" she screamed before he felt her tight sheath begin to shudder around him. He thrust deeper, sending the couch lurching forward on its round wooden feet, directly into the side table. The lamp rocked forward and with his final surge, it fell off the table and onto the floor, shattering.

And then he, too, slipped over the edge.

He gripped Lila hard, like a drowning man does a life preserver, holding on until he came back to reality and his breathing slowed.

"Your lamp" was the first thing she said after his earth-shattering performance.

"What?"

"The lamp on the end table. I think we broke it."

And then she started to laugh, and so did he.

Yeah. The sex had rocked his world and apparently his living room. Jake looked at the floor. They'd moved the couch at least a foot. "I don't know how I'll explain those gouges in the floor to a buyer if I ever decide to sell."

Lila laughed again and Jake was struck anew by how much he had missed her in *and out* of his bed.

He smiled, feeling himself stir inside her, grow hard. He was ready to move the couch another foot. Maybe even break the other lamp on the opposite end table.

Lila slid her shoulders beneath her warm peony-scented bathwater and closed her eyes, holding back the heavy burden of long forestalled resignation. Jake may have sent her into a screaming orgasm tonight—correction, last night, it was now the wee hours of the morning—but he didn't ask her to stay over. Yeah, so she'd said sex wouldn't mean anything more than an orgasm, but she lied. Hello! She was trying to win him back.

But nothing, *nothing,* worked.

Sighing, she laid a warm washcloth over her eyes.

No plans equaled no commitment. Jake Winter 101. She knew the drill by heart. She shouldn't be hurt. This shouldn't feel like her heart breaking, because she knew from the beginning it would be difficult.

She just didn't realize it might be impossible.

Throwing the washcloth off in disgust, she grabbed Prudence's journal from the bath-side stool.

Crap. And she thought her life was hard. Her great-great-grandmother had had the entire town against her at one time.

These last weeks have shown me the absolute and final truth of a lesson I learned long ago. The only person you can change is yourself.

My business is long dead, the customers gone. Several of the girls have returned to families or headed out to find their own peace, either in town or farther west. This is not their war. It is my war. Against corruption, against greed and indecent men who would rather rule single-handedly as opposed to governing democratically.

But in the end, the girls paid the price alongside me. The boredom and the isolation got to many after a while and fighting broke out. Small squabbles became insurmountable and so many left, preferring to risk adventure. *It is good, I suppose. My money is nearly spent and the only thing I have to show for it is my resolution.*

When the funds are wiped out, I will be forced to sell the house if I want to eat. Or, more likely, I will go down with my ship, like a sea captain. Who wants to buy a bordello in this town? The mayor? I would rather starve.

And so I might.

Lesson Number Twenty-Four —

Surprise him with fresh bed linens. He will appreciate the smell and feel of clean bedsheets and thank you for your hard work.

Chapter Twenty-Six

"Jake, I'm happy to report there is no recurrent cancer. You're clear."

Dr. Rogers gave him the good news as they sat facing each other on a matching pair of rolling doctor's stools in the examination room. At first he didn't react. The news had to filter in, past the doubts, past the resignation. And then, he knew.

He was okay. He was free.

Something broke inside him and a wash of cleansing emotion surged through his body, like river water through a weakened dam. Jake knew he'd never be the same again. The years of preparing for a tragedy that never came had taken a toll. He'd lost Lila. He'd lost his joy in life.

But he could start again.

"That news was a long time in coming, Doc."

"I know. And I really am sorry to put you through the scare, but those initial blood cell numbers were worrisome. I wanted to be sure."

"Yeah."

Jake stood, letting the doc know the powwow was over. He pushed his stool back under the counter and faced Rogers.

"So, I guess I'll see you in a year."

"Sounds good."

Jake turned to leave.

"Jake, try to let go of some of the stress. Your mental state can have a great deal of effect on your physical state."

He frowned at the doc.

"As your physician, I'm prescribing a little more fun and a little less worry. All right?"

Gratitude swelled his heart. For the doc. For his own future. He even considered breaking more furniture with Lila. Maybe a bed this time? He smiled and funny enough, it was genuine. "Sure. You're the doctor."

Jake headed past the nurses at the reception desk. Their conversation drifted out to him as he hit the door.

"A supercell's forming from Fort Worth all the way up here. Weatherman on channel eight said this could be another big one, like back in ninety-seven."

"Gosh, remember how many tornadoes came out of that thing…?"

Jake headed back to Hannington. He kept replaying the doc's good news in his head. *No cancer.* And then he replayed his night with Lila.

The two of them had really torn the place up. His living room was worse than a demolition site, but he didn't feel the least bit bad about it. In fact, he felt optimistic.

If she could take all his bullshit over the last months and weeks and still come back for more, maybe they did have something that couldn't be killed. And he'd tried. Given it his best shot. He'd lived his life denying any weakness, in fear everyone would see just how scared he truly was. He avoided judgment. He avoided accountability.

But Lila was still in Hannington. Still talking to him. Or not talking, depending on their state of undress.

He smiled. How would he go about a reconciliation? Walk up to her and say, "Hey, I don't have cancer, so can we make up and have more sex?"

No. That wouldn't go over well. Even though he had a lot of years of makeup sex to account for.

Okay. How about, "I realized that I never stopped loving you and want to start over"?

Not bad. Might work.

Jake cracked the window on his truck and let in the hot Hill Country air. It smelled of rain. Flipping on his radio, he tuned into the local AM station and waited for a weather report.

Rain would shut down a couple of his job sites. Not that he would mind; it would give him plenty of time to track Lila down and talk to her about his long overdue revelation.

"—weather is pushing up from the Gulf of Mexico and with it comes severe thunderstorms, possibly flash floods, and tornadoes. Tarrant County is under a tornado watch until nine p.m., along with several other counties, including—"

Jake turned the volume down. He needed to call his crews and have them stow the vulnerable supplies and prepare for a gully washer.

But first...

He dialed the number he'd never really forgotten.

"Barbara, how's the arm?"

"Fine. And don't try to sweet-talk me, you devil. Where have you been? And why haven't you been over for dinner?"

He laughed. Thank God some things never changed.

"Working for your granddaughter. Or hasn't she told you about all the changes she's demanding on her place downtown?"

"Oh, I know all about it. Who do you think orchestrated the whole thing? But what I want to know right now, Jacob Winter, is why you aren't taking Lila to the big party tonight in Fort Worth?"

Huh? "What party?"

"That big cattleman's thingy-whoo. Something about charities. I assumed you were going since Lila was biting at the bit to promote her day spa."

Jake rolled up the windows, cutting out the background noise. "She never mentioned she wanted to go."

"Well, seems you're outta the loop, then, as Lila likes to say. But don't feel bad"—her voice lost its reproachful tone—"you're welcome to come on for dinner, if you want. I'm making meat loaf with mashed potatoes and gravy. But Lila's not here. She's headed to Fort Worth this afternoon and is staying the night from what I understand. Mark came and got her and they went together."

She'd gone with Mark. That stung. He didn't know why it should. *Because he was a dipshit. And years of numbing his pain had had the consequence of also numbing his joy. Jake didn't recognize joy until it sat square on his face and wiggled.*

And Lila with her big, loving eyes and tender heart was his joy. He saw it now.

"No, thank you, Barbara. I'll take a rain check for a future date. But if you talk to Lila, please tell her to be careful. There's a big storm blowing in and a tornado watch for Tarrant County. You know how these storms can be."

Dangerous. And unpredictable. And that's why he had to check in with Otis and the other foreman to make sure everything got secured for the night.

"Lord! That F5 tornado out in Jarrell a few years back sucked the street pavement right off the ground. Left nothing but barren dirt fields for acres and acres. I had some friends out there. Some retirees. They lost everything 'cept the clothes on their backs. Hope we don't get one of those."

No. Not one of the killer tornadoes. Not in Hannington. But then the citizens of Jarrell probably said the same thing right before the spinning monster chewed through the town, killing twenty-seven people.

"I'll check in with you later. And Barbara, you know what to do if the storm gets risky, right?"

A snort sounded loud and indignant in his ear. "Hell, yes. Sarah and I will hop in the storm cellar."

He ended the call and dropped his cell phone onto the empty bench seat beside him.

He didn't know what to worry over first. Putting on a tux or getting down on his knees to beg Lila to take him back.

Lila sipped her cocktail and stared out the wall of filtered glass windows. A storm approached from the east, throwing downtown Fort Worth into a premature twilight.

Rolls of dark and swollen clouds shadowed the city, dumping buckets of rain on people rushing from work to the dry haven of their cars.

Miserable weather for a party, which suited her fine, because her mood matched.

No word from Jake. It had been fifteen hours since she'd shared the world's greatest sex with the man and he hadn't bothered to call. Or drop by.

No more acting like a teenager. She wouldn't wait another minute by her phone in the hope Jacob Winter would call. No, Lila Gentry had had enough.

Weeks of chasing the man, trying to convince him they could make another go at their marriage, had brought her nothing but heartbreak. And Lila was tired, so very tired of heartbreak. She needed to let go.

Through the thick glass she heard the muffled echo of thunder. Reaching out, she laid her hand on the window and felt the reverberations from the sound. She sniffed loudly and took a deep drink from her Manhattan.

"Crying into your drink is so cliché. How about we laugh instead? At those stupid bastards who lost their case against you?"

Lila tipped her head to the side and stared at Mark. If he weren't gay, she'd consider falling for him. He was attentive, intelligent, funny, handsome, and built. The top five things women wanted in men.

"That is cause for celebration. Though if I stay in this business, it won't be the last suit I face." She sniffed. "And I'm not crying. I think there's a leak in the ceiling and some rain splashed into my drink."

"Really?"

She stuck her tongue out at him. Reason number six why Mark made the perfect guy: he could also pull her out of a bad mood and make her laugh.

"Aren't you supposed to be touting your new day spa? Look at all these women. Potential customers."

Lila looked around the party. The crowd in the ballroom represented her ideal customers. Upper-class, educated couples with disposable income and a desire for finer things. Customers like this didn't just want a place to go and relax, they thought they deserved it. Which would be the cornerstone of her marketing campaign. If she ever got around to telling anyone about Miss Pru's.

Mark was right. She should be mingling and talking—it was the entire reason for attending—but her heart wasn't in it. Not today.

"Maybe later, after the dinner." She grimaced at such a lame excuse and Mark saw right through it, too. But he let it go. She hadn't told him about her night with Jake. He'd graduated from an Ivy League school; he could figure it out without all the graphic details.

"Looks like we just beat the storm." He nodded to the wind whipping the trees in the park below.

"Yeah, it's a little bit scary being so high up, surrounded by glass in a storm like this," she said, chills rippling over her arms. *Where'd her jacket go?*

"Well, if we're stuck up here for a while, at least there's plenty of booze and fine food. Too bad there's not a television. We could watch reruns of *Friends*."

Lila laughed. Leave it to Mark to see the good in any

situation. "Actually, I did see a TV in the kitchen earlier. The staff was watching the weather."

Mark got a mischievous twinkle in his eye. "You did, did you?"

She tipped her chin in the direction of the kitchen.

Mark left without a word and she trailed along behind him.

Jake tried Lila's cell phone again. He got her voicemail. Again. He pounded the steering wheel with his fist.

"Lila, it's Jake. Call me back immediately. I'm worried about you in this weather. If you haven't already, get someplace safe. Three tornados have touched down on the outskirts of the city. More are expected."

He jammed his finger on the end button and gripped the phone in his hand, praying for it to ring.

"Shit." He threw the phone across the bench seat. He felt powerless. Helpless. He should be with her now. Not sitting here on Interstate 35, minutes from downtown, watching the beginnings of debris sail across the highway and into the trees.

He was more scared for Lila's safety at this moment than any time over the last ten years waiting for cancer to kill him.

Traffic lined up in front of him as far as he could see. The highway had become a parking lot. Apparently, everyone had the same idea: get home before the weather gets any worse. Except Jake wasn't trying to get home.

"Goddammit!" He pounded the dashboard this time, a resounding crack in the molded plastic rewarding his angry fear.

Visions of her covered in glass and debris ran like a bad eight-millimeter film in his head. If a tornado landed in the middle of the downtown area, it could leave a wide path of destruction. He thought of the supercell in Oklahoma City back in 1999. It spawned numerous funnels, some categorized as F5s. Nearly 40 people were killed with nearly seven hundred injured.

And Lila was out there, in the middle of a forming cell.

Lila and Mark slipped into the kitchen, making their way between the stainless steel counters lined by busy waitstaff to the television set against the back wall. A couple of chairs sat haphazardly around the color TV, but they remained standing, caught off guard by the news report on the screen.

"—tornado has touched down in downtown Fort Worth near Seventh and Henderson Streets, heading east into the heart of downtown. Citizens are advised to take immediate cover, and stay away from windows and outside doors. Get into a basement or an inside stairwell if possible. Underneath a heavy desk or table. For those people caught on the highway, get to an overpass or some form of cover immediately. Do not try to outrun the tornado.

"I repeat, a tornado has touched down in downtown Fort Worth, heading east —"

Lila looked back over her shoulder to the people in the kitchen. Some had heard the report and appeared stunned, their food trays hovering. Others, who hadn't heard, went about their job blissfully unaware.

She looked at Mark. "If a tornado has touched down, why haven't the sirens sounded?"

He opened his mouth, but just then they heard the muted shrill of the sirens outside. They both hurried to the kitchen door along with the staff, swinging it open to find the majority of the partygoers gawking out the window. Every person in the restaurant had a front-row view of the storm only blocks away, courtesy of the four walls of floor-to-ceiling windows.

Lila's heart fell into her feet. The sun had started to set, but the tornado spun to their west, backlit by strong light. A dark, angry knot of clouds hovered low in the sky with a thick tail plunging down to the meet the city's skyline.

Everybody watched in slow motion as the funnel advanced on a building and sparks from electrical lines flew into the sky, illuminating the swirling mass of debris.

"That's gotta be the Dollar America Building," she heard someone murmur. "It's not far away, just on the other side of the river." The crowd watched in silence as a large explosion of light lit the underbelly of the tornado and then disappeared inside the growing mass.

A shout from behind the crowd near the heavy oak doors of the thirty-fifth floor restaurant made heads turn. "Everyone, into the stairwell. Now!" The manager stood holding a door open, waving his arm for everyone to move.

One thousand people in formal wear started scrambling, hurrying away from the windows and into the hallway that led to the elevators and stairs. Dull thuds echoed around the room as debris began to hit the glass.

Lila gaped over her shoulder as the tornado grew larger, creeping closer. More debris—oh God, was that a car?—

swirled around the edges of the swollen funnel; larger, more dangerous-looking projectiles flying perilously close to the windows of the Financial One Building where she and Mark made their way inch by inch into the outside corridor.

Mark wrapped his arm around her back, hugging her to him and pushing them forward with the crowd. She thought of Jake and what he might be doing. Sitting safe and sound in his house, she hoped. Not out in this.

Jake couldn't go any farther. Locked in traffic beneath the overpass, he had to wait out the storm with the hundreds of other cars parked on the road.

While the conditions outside his window were growing more dangerous by the minute, the consuming fear in his heart ate away at him until he couldn't sit a second longer. Jake threw open the door on the truck and dashed into the rain.

He could see the top of the Financial One Building as he ran, but no sign of the tornado advancing on the other side of downtown. Although from the ragged pieces of glass and other debris raining down around him, he knew the tornado was not far away.

He saw mini-blinds, chairs, and big, lethal pieces of glass scattering the sidewalks. One enormous triangular piece of glass drove into the soft ground of the open grassy area directly ahead, tremoring with the impact.

Only one place big glass like that could come from: the office buildings. Like the Financial One Building where Lila sat unprotected on the thirty-fifth floor.

Jake dodged a sailing trash can.

Less than five blocks stood between him and Lila, but hail had started up again. Large softball-sized hail.

One of those to the head would kill him. If flying debris didn't.

Come on, Lila. Be smart. Stay safe. Get to the stairs or inside the ladies' room. Get away from the windows, he thought.

He chanted it over and over, hoping if he said it enough, she'd somehow get the message and protect herself since he couldn't do it.

Life really had shitty timing sometimes. Had it only been today the doc had pronounced him cancer-free? That Jake would live another year, probably many more? And his first thought had been about Lila. How hard he'd been pushing her away, only to discover he wanted her here in Hannington and with him.

If cancer hadn't killed him, neither would a tornado.

Jake ran faster.

She could see the open doorway to the stairwell. Although one hundred people stood between her and the safest spot on the thirty-fifth floor, Lila figured she and Mark were out of harm's way.

That is, until all the windows on the west side of the building blew and shrapnel flew through the restaurant and out into the corridor. It was too late to try to shut the double oak doors. Besides, people were still blocking the entrance, trapped like cattle being led to some kind of designer slaughter.

She plunged to the floor next to Mark at the same time someone shouted, "Get down!"

A man on her left fell into her as a hurtling piece of glass whizzed by, scraping his face. He looked dazed and in pain, but not critical. And then the blood began to flow.

"Are you okay?" she yelled over the screams in the hall. Mark took his elbow and helped him to sit upright. His wife, several steps ahead, turned back and saw him on the floor.

"Walter!" She dropped to her knees and crawled around several people to reach him.

Lila ripped a large swath of cloth from the bottom of her dress and held it to the cut, which bled like a compromised dam.

"Put pressure on it," she told him as his wife arrived at his side. He nodded and took over, his wife's hand supporting his.

Lila huddled next to Mark, reviewing the scene around them. They couldn't make it to the stairwell. Too many people were in the way, most on the floor in various positions.

She peeked over his shoulder to witness the blinds and curtains blowing out through open windows, table settings disappearing off tables, hell, entire tables disappearing along with chairs on the far west side.

She could hear the rumbling of the tornado now, like a very large and heavy train coming down the track. The debris that had been previously sucked out the window came crashing back in through the north side, sending glass and objects spinning into the restaurant.

Mark grabbed the back of her head and forced it down to the floor. "Don't look up. Cover your neck with your hands," he shouted in her ear.

She covered the nape of her neck with her hands, thinking that a fragile barrier separated her from certain paralysis if a shard of glass sliced through her hands and into her neck.

And then she thought of Jake again and what his life and death battles must have been like all these years. To always have an ax hanging over his head, waiting for it to fall.

That wasn't the way to live. In fear. Life should be celebrated, no matter how long or short. For Jake, he'd made sure there were as few people as possible to grieve over him after he was gone. But Lila had always thought he had it wrong, and now she knew for sure.

If she died, here, tonight, she'd have very few regrets—outside of losing Jake. She'd lived a good life, done her best. So if it was her time, she went with a light heart.

She didn't think he could say the same. So she had to stay alive. Convince him to open up and live again. Share himself with the people who loved him. And to celebrate life.

Celebrate it with her.

Lesson Number Twenty-Five —

Use making love as an opportunity to affirm your devotion.

Chapter Twenty-Seven

A block from his destination, the police arrived. Jake ignored them, his eyes fixed on the thirty-five-story glass building dead ahead. A marvel of cutting-edge design when it was built in 1970, the building had sustained the worst kind of beating from Mother Nature.

Shattered glass crunched under his heels as he jumped the curb and headed for the entrance. The cops discussing the near miss of the tornado yelled at him, but he ignored them and wove his way through debris, keeping a wary eye overhead.

He slid in through the front door and raced for the set of stairs that would take him to the mezzanine and the bank of elevators. He refused to think of Lila lying injured. Or worse.

Shit. The elevators were off-limits. They could be damaged. He'd take the stairs all the way to the top. Looking around, he found the stairwell and charged through the door, taking the steps two at a time, counting the seconds that delayed him reaching Lila's side.

When he reached the third floor he heard people above him.

"Are you folks all right?" he asked, searching the knot of shaken people for his wife's familiar face.

"Is it over?" a young man in a black business suit asked him.

"Nearly. Glass is still falling. The wind is vicious, but it appears the tornado missed us. The police are right outside."

He heard a woman sob as he pushed past and climbed higher.

On the twentieth floor he encountered a throng of people. He stopped to let several people by, again searching for Lila.

"Were you folks at the party on the thirty-fifth floor?" he asked a middle-aged woman in a gold gown.

"Yes," she said, her warm brown eyes tearing up.

"Do you know Lila Gentry? Is she okay?"

The woman shook her head and moved on.

Jake swallowed his terror and searched over the heads of the people moving down the stairs, praying to see the accustomed bounce of his wife's blond curls.

She wasn't there.

Fuck. He climbed higher still, sweat breaking out on his forehead and his heart pounding.

Come on, Lila, where are you?

And then he saw her. Up a flight and just coming through the fire door into the stairwell.

"Lila!" Jake nearly collapsed to his knees, his relief was so great. She'd never looked more beautiful. He would never again take the sight of her for granted.

Mark saw him before Lila did. He smiled brightly and

nodded, stepping back to let Lila go ahead. Jake raced the last set of stairs until he stood directly below them, people flowing around him.

His heart pounded in his ears. His hands shook with suppressed emotion. He found his vocal cords wouldn't work, even though his mouth opened to emit the words: "You're safe!"

She saw his boots first and her eyes flew the rest of the way to his face. "Jake! What are you doing here?"

Her hands came up and he noticed the blood for the first time. It covered her hands and arms and a large portion of the front of her dress.

"God, Lila, you're hurt." A hot moisture burned the backs of his eyes as he found his voice at last.

"No, no. The man next to me was hit, cut his head." Tears slid down her cheeks. She reached for him and he was there, wrapping his arms around her waist, lifting her up into his embrace. Blazing a trail of kisses from her forehead to her lips.

This is where she should be. Always and forever. In his arms. Safe. Secure. Home.

He knew that now.

"I'm a dumbass," he said, staring into her shocked eyes.

"Pardon?" She blinked, confused.

"I'm a dumbass for not following you to Dallas ten years ago. For refusing to own my fear and recognize I needed you more than I needed my damn pride. I'm as imperfect as they come, darlin'. But after running through a tornado this evening, I realized that's not even the scariest thing I faced today."

"The prodigal son has returned at long last." Mark gave Jake a healthy slap on the back and moved down the stairwell several steps.

Jake caught an exchange of glances between him and a flamboyantly attired young man with an overly styled Mohawk. And in that moment, it all made sense to Jake. Mark's behavior. His extravagant use of trendy grammar, and his impeccable sense of style.

The man was gay. Damn. He was a Texas-sized dumbass this day. Jake owed Mark a huge apology and a thank-you for caring for his wife so well.

"I can't live without you. And I realized that no matter my future, cancer or no cancer, my life is mine to make something of. No more hiding. I'm out. And I'm proud."

"About time," Mark yelled.

Jake laughed at the humor of the statement, his and Mark's.

Lila shook her head, and stared into his eyes. He recognized the love shining there. "How did you get here?"

He thought back over the last several hours, the struggle to reach her. "It doesn't matter. I'm here now, Lila Winter, and I'm never letting you go to another party in Fort Worth without me."

The tears came faster, but with a smile this time.

"You called me Lila Winter."

He returned her smile and added a hot tearstained kiss on her lips. "I did. And I'm hoping that this time when I give you my name, you'll keep it."

The second tender kiss tasted warm, sweet, and full of so much life. Thank God. He wouldn't blow this second chance. This do-over.

"Are you asking me to marry you? Again?" She laughed.

"I am. And in front of all these people."

She lifted her head, looking at the people standing on the stairs with them. An impromptu cheer went up and she blushed a very becoming shade of pink.

"Well, then. I accept."

Today is a new beginning. Not a fresh start or a clean slate as the evangelicals might tell, but a chance to fulfill my potential as a woman. And to consider the day began like all the recent other days! Hopeless and grim. Despite the dawn of a new sun.

Today, Luke Pierce came home. What a homecoming it was, too. He blew into the Acre after an absence of several months, shotguns loaded and holstered on his big stallion, challenging any and all who stood between him and the Two Nellies.

Challenging all who would keep him from me.

I didn't discover until much later that Luke's charge down into the Acre followed a heated meeting with the sheriff. Luke was of course the winner in the debate — or so I consider him to be. But I get ahead of myself...

Upon hearing the clatter down on the boardwalk from my window above, I made my way downstairs to find Luke prying the boards off my front door. The sheriff had installed them as a preventative against the wages of sin, warning off would-be customers from the Two Nellies. Thankfully, all it did was keep looters from making off with the remaining whiskey.

I met Luke at the door, and without a word, he

grabbed me and tossed me over a shoulder and swept me from the house.

"Luke! What's eating you! Put me down," I shouted against his strong back.

"Prudence," he growled and patted my bottom with a firm palm. "Now is not the time to argue with me, woman. I mean to change this situation, and removing you from this place is the first step."

"You will do no such thing, Luke Pierce! This is my fight and I intend to win or die trying." I knew I would never best Luke in a physical fight, but I put one up nonetheless. The dead last thing I wanted was Luke punished for my sins.

"It's set and done, Pru. You're finished in the Acre and the sheriff has agreed to let all charges drop if you vacate. So that's what we're doin', darlin'. Vacatin' pronto."

"But my house!" The customers and the girls were long gone and the property was the sole possession remaining.

Luke dropped me across the front of his saddle and climbed up behind me. "After we're married, I'll deed it back to you free and clear. You can do what you want with it then, on the condition you never live in the Acre or run a saloon down here again."

In that moment I questioned everything. What I was fighting for, who I was fighting against, and what the future held.

And my dears, I had the final epiphany!

Love had arrived on a stallion with double-barrel

shotguns and I would be twelve kinds of fool to shoo it away. So I did what any Irishwoman with good sense would do.

I kissed Luke on the mouth and smiled up into his warm whiskey-colored eyes.

"Take me home, sir!"

Epilogue

The open house for Miss Pru's doubled as a reaffirmation of the wedding vows Lila had taken with Jake ten years ago.

At least that's how she intended it, but some little old ladies had a different notion.

"Good grief, Lila Jean. Stop fussing. We only invited a few extra people. No big deal. We got more food and there's plenty to drink. Have a good time."

Granny patted her cheek and smiled, her blue eyes shining with happiness. Truthfully, Lila loved the attention. She'd been surprised when one of Granny's Bombshells appeared in the doorway earlier announcing more chairs were needed, thirty more to be exact.

But then the realization sank in. The people of Hannington liked her. They'd come to wish her well.

Now it was Sarah's turn. "You look beautiful. Let me see the whole picture."

Lila dropped her mother's hand and twirled a slow circle

to show off her knee-length cream-colored dress. The off-the-shoulder neckline with cap sleeves showcased Granny's pearls, while the wide taffeta bow made her waist appear tiny.

Lila loved it. And the fact Sarah had worn it when she married Michael made it all the more special.

"Thanks for letting me wear your dress," she told her mother.

Don't cry. Don't cry.

Sarah clutched a tissue in her hand, lifting it to her eyes. "Oh, you're very welcome." She turned and smiled at Barbara. "And thank you for saving it all these years so I could see my daughter married in it."

"Oh, goodness. Both of you stop crying. You'll ruin my mascara."

Lila laughed and pulled the women into a hug. She closed her eyes, making a memory to carry with her all the days of her life.

Lila opened her eyes to the sunshine streaming in the bay windows. She knew the room had once belonged to Prudence. She never found the proof, but she knew in her gut—her great-great-grandmother had once lived in that room.

"Is Threasa here?" she asked Granny.

"Yep. Front row. Next to that strong, silent hunk."

"The Armstrongs?"

"Janie, but not Howard."

Lila sighed. She and Threasa had eventually confessed to Howard about the journal. He had promptly thrown them both out of his office. Threasa said it had more to do with Janie's leaving him than the restoration of Miss Pru's, but to try to make amends, Lila invited him to the open house.

"You didn't really expect him to show, did you?" Granny asked.

"No, I guess not. Thought I'd give it a try, though."

Sarah captured her hand, folding it between both of hers. "This is your day. Focus on you and Jake, who, by the way, is waiting patiently downstairs for your arrival."

Lila followed Granny and Sarah out of the room and paused in the hall before shutting the door. She turned back to the sunlit space overlooking the town square and whispered, "Thank you. Your wisdom made all the difference. I'm home. Happy. And I'm never leaving again."

Acknowledgments

A cosmic-sized thank-you is due to the endless, unwavering support of Candace Havens. Without her dedication, this book would not have been published. Ever. She is the truest, most wonderful friend a woman could ask for. I am blessed.

Also by Shannon Leigh

FORBIDDEN KISS

Rom Montgomery seeks the unobtainable: forgiveness. He wanders across continents and through time searching for salvation and the means to right an ancient wrong. To gain the respect and position she's desired in the academic world, Jule Casale hopes to discover the unknown artist behind a masterpiece of Renaissance art. When Jule comes knocking on Rom's door, it's the closest he's ever come to finally finding redemption. The closer he draws to correcting his past mistakes, the more his secrets threaten to destroy the woman who might hold the key to his future.

TYCOON REUNION

Sparks fly when a project brings a heartbreaker back to town and into the path of the woman he left behind. He's determined to win her over in the boardroom ... and the bedroom!

Looking for more strong heroines and to-die-for heroes?
Try these Entangled Select novels...

READY TO WED

by Cindi Madsen

Wedding planner Dakota Halifax loves to be in love. But when her fiancé jilts her, she can't figure out how the heartbroken celebrate others' true love. Until she reconnects with her childhood best friend, the surprisingly sexy and all-grown-up casino bouncer Brendan West. Maybe she can fall back in love with being in love. But then her ex reappears, begging for another chance, and suddenly Dakota questions if she'll ever understand love. Can someone once-burned and twice-shy ever find her way down the aisle again?

WINNING LOVE

by Abby Niles

Cage fighting helps Mac "The Snake" Hannon manage his demons, but it doesn't take away his pain. Gayle Andrews chases tornadoes, determined to save others from experiencing loss like she has. Her new neighbor, Mac, intrigues her, but his tragedy means he can't deal with Gayle courting disaster at every turn. When a raging tornado puts Gayle's life in danger, Mac's head tells him to walk away, but his heart pulls him into the eye of the storm. But will it be too late for Gayle and Mac to have their happily ever after?

A DUKE'S WICKED KISS

by Kathleen Bittner Roth

The Duke of Ravenswood, secret head of the British Foreign Service, has no time for relationships. Miss Suri Thurston knows the pain of abandonment. When Suri appears in Delhi, the Duke's resolve is tested as he finds his heart forever bound to her by the one haunting kiss they shared once upon a time. With Suri's vengeful Indian family looking for her death, and insurgents intent on mutiny tearing their world apart, can their love rise above the scandal of the marriage they both desperately want?

DYED AND GONE

by Beth Yarnall

When Dhane, a dynamic celebrity hairstylist, is found dead, Azalea March suspects foul play. Her friend Vivian confesses to the murder and is arrested, but Azalea knows there's no way she could have done it. Vivian's protecting someone. But who? Now Azalea and Alex, the sexy detective from her past, must comb through clues more twisted than a spiral perm. But the truth is stranger than anything found on the Las Vegas Strip, and proving Vivian's innocence turns out to be more difficult than transforming a brunette into a blonde.

A SHOT OF RED

by Tracy March

When biotech company heiress Mia Moncure learns her ex-boyfriend, the company's PR Director, has died in a suspicious accident in Switzerland, Mia suspects murder. Determined to reveal a killer, she turns to sexy Gio Lorenzo, Communications Director for her mother, a high-ranking senator—and the recent one-night stand Mia has been desperate to escape. While negotiating their rocky relationship, they race to uncover a deadly scheme that could ruin her family's reputation. But millions of people are being vaccinated, and there's more than her family's legacy at stake.

TANGLED HEARTS

by Heather McCollum

Highland warrior Ewan Brody always wanted a sweet, uncomplicated woman by his side, but he can't fight his attraction to the beautiful enchantress who's stumbled into his life. He quickly learns, though, that Pandora Wyatt is not only a witch, but also a pirate and possibly a traitor's daughter—and though she's tricked him into playing her husband at King Henry's court, he's falling hard. As they discover dark secrets leading to the real traitor of the Tudor court, Ewan and Pandora must uncover the truth before they lose more than just their hearts.

HONOR RECLAIMED

by Tonya Burrows

An interview with a runaway Afghani child bride leads photojournalist Phoebe Leighton to an arms deal involving a powerful bomb. Forming an unlikely alliance with a team of military and government delinquents called HORNET, she meets Seth, a former Marine sniper with PTSD, who ignites passions within her she thought long dead. Racing against the clock, Seth, Phoebe, and the rest of HORNET struggle to stop the bomb before it reaches its final destination: The United States.

MALICIOUS MISCHIEF

by Marianne Harden

Career chameleon, Rylie Keyes, must keep her current job. If not, the tax assessor will evict her ailing grandfather and auction off their ancestral home. When a senior she shuttles for a Bellevue, Washington retirement home winds up dead in her minibus, her goal to keep her job hits a road bump. Forced to dust off the PI training, Rylie must align with a circus-bike-wheeling Samoan to solve the murder, while juggling the attentions of two very hot police officers.